"There is a sense of propriety that must be followed…"

Henry raised his eyebrows. "When did you arrive at Moreland Lake, then?"

"Just this morning," Catherine responded. "Had you asked that question first, you would have spared yourself the trouble of the other two."

He laughed. "Well, now that we have had proper introductions and proper conversation as good etiquette demands, we can abandon the need for practicality!" he exclaimed, to which Catherine bit her lower lip, trying to suppress a smile. "Ah, I see what you are thinking!"

"You've only just met me. How could you possibly know what I'm thinking?" She laughed.

"Let's see now." He studied her intently. "You are thinking that I'm an odd man."

"I do not think that at all."

But in truth, she had been thinking that he was unlike any man she had met before. And that was not necessarily a bad thing.

She found Henry Tilman to be a breath of fresh air, light in conversation and a bit witty.

There was nothing threatening about him, however, and she felt an immediate yearning to know him better…a fact that made her feel warm and tingly.

Sarah Price comes from a long line of devout Mennonites. She strives to write authentic and accurate stories that reflect over forty years of firsthand experiences with Amish communities. Ms. Price has advanced degrees in communication (MA), marketing (MBA) and education (PhD). Previously, she was a full-time college professor. Since being diagnosed with breast cancer in 2013, Ms. Price writes full-time from her home in Florida.

NEWBURY ACRES

Sarah Price

Recycling programs
for this product may
not exist in your area.

ISBN-13: 978-1-335-45494-2

Newbury Acres

HARLEQUIN®
™ www.Harlequin.com

Printed in U.S.A.

Author Note

The locations mentioned in this book are fictitious, as are the characters. All attempts to maintain accuracy in describing the different communities are based on the author's personal experience with the Amish (1978 to present).

Chapter One

"*Mamm*! Someone's pulling in the driveway!" Catherine called out from the side yard as she hung the damp laundry on the clothes line. The sun was shining, and with the warm summer breeze, the day's laundry would be dry in no time. Which was fortunate because she had gotten a late start on the washing that morning.

Her mother must have peered through the open kitchen window by the sink. "Oh, help! That looks like Duane and Wilma Anderson's horse and buggy."

Catherine glanced over her shoulder, her dark brown eyes trying to see her mother, Ruth, through the window. "Were you expecting them, now?" she asked as the sound of the buggy's wheels on the gravel grew louder.

"*Nee*, not today. I sure hope that everything's fine with her mother yet!"

Quickly, Catherine pinned the remaining clothes. After wiping her hands on her plain cobalt blue dress, she picked up the empty woven basket by its one unbroken handle. Her bare feet hurried across the grass and up the porch stairs that led into the house. Once inside, she set the basket on the floor near the washing machine in the corner of the mudroom. Through the open doorway into the kitchen, she could see her mother hurrying to wipe down the counter and table. She had made pancakes for breakfast, and the younger children had made a sticky mess with the syrup. And the last thing that Ruth Miller wanted was for anyone to stop by and see her kitchen anything less than perfectly neat and orderly.

"Knock, knock!" a voice called through the mud room's screen door.

"*Kum* in, Wilma!" Ruth called out.

Wilma opened the door and peered inside, a big smile on her face and a strand of her almost perfectly gray hair flying loose from under her stiff white head covering. At fifty years of age, she was a stout woman, which was surprising since she had no children. However, Wilma often was a fixture in Ruth's kitchen, especially during canning season. Without any children of her own, she often claimed that she wanted to adopt Catherine, a kind joke that always made Ruth reply that, as much as she wanted to oblige, she actually couldn't do without Catherine. She would, however, happily offer her next oldest daughter, Sarah, for adoption, an inside joke because Sarah was a tomboy and preferred working in the fields to any kind of housework.

Regardless of being favored by her mother's friend, Catherine did enjoy Wilma's company. She was always pleasant and kind, eager to listen to stories about the children, and never one to shy away from helping out with the spring cleaning. There would be few, if any, people in their church district who would ever say anything uncharitable about Wilma Anderson. "I didn't catch you at a bad time, did I? Duane just went out to the barn to see if he could talk to Martin."

"Come in, come in!" Ruth called out. "Pardon the mess."

"What mess?" Wilma walked into the kitchen and looked around. "Your house is always meticulous, Ruth! If you consider this untidy, I'd hate to have you stop into *my* house unexpected!" She laughed as she said this.

Ruth gave a soft smile at the compliment, but Catherine knew that her mother didn't agree. She was always cleaning, sometimes twice a day. With eight children, things could quickly get out of hand if she didn't. Catherine, being the oldest daughter, helped out as much as she could and did her best to school her younger siblings on the virtues of picking up after themselves. A daunting task if one would ask her!

"*Kum*, Wilma. Sit for a spell. I still have warm coffee from breakfast." Ruth gestured toward the kitchen table.

"And I made some coffee cake yesterday," Catherine added.

"Oh, Catherine! You do know how I love your coffee cake." Wilma set down her bag and readjusted the white strings from her prayer *kapp*. "I'll take you up on that offer, but only if you join us. It's actually both of you that I've come to visit with."

Catherine hurried over to the far counter to help her mother gather the coffee mugs and little plates to set on the table.

Her mother sat down next to her friend while Catherine heated up the coffee. "What a nice surprise, Wilma! What brings you this way on a Monday morning?"

"Duane and I spent the night at Sister Anna's. To

see Mother, you know. And since we didn't have time to visit after church yesterday…" She didn't finish the sentence. Normally, after the worship service, everyone gathered for fellowship over a small meal. However, with her mother being ill, a bad summer flu, the Andersons had left early to travel to her sister's farm in the next town.

"She's doing well then?" Ruth asked the question with a hopeful expression on her face.

"Oh, *ja*, much better. The doctor feared she would get pneumonia, and at her age…" Wilma shook her head and clicked her tongue. "Well, she surprised him for sure and certain! She'll outlive us all, I reckon!"

Outside, a rooster crowed and Catherine glanced out the window. While the coyotes hadn't bothered much with the chickens since early spring, the hawks were still troublesome. But she didn't see any shadows on the driveway nor did the hens scatter for cover. She heard her mother ask about Wilma's mother, but she didn't listen to the response. After all, Wilma was visiting and with a happy smile on her face. That was all Catherine needed to see in order to know that her mother was fine. Ruth, however, tended to worry about everything and everyone.

"Where are the little ones?" Wilma asked, looking around the kitchen as if expecting to see the other children hiding somewhere. On most days, they would have been. After all, unless they were doing chores or playing, the smaller *kinner* had a tendency to linger wherever their mother was.

But not today.

Catherine picked up the plate of coffee cake and carried it to the table. "James took the boys fishing, and

Sarah took the girls over to see cousin Betsy. They have a new foal. And *Daed* took George with him. They rode to town for grain." She didn't add that it was nice, for once, to not have her younger brothers and sisters underfoot, especially six-year-old George, who was the youngest—and loudest!—of all the children. With any luck, Catherine might find time to steal away and read her new book without anyone interrupting her or, even worse, teasing her about her unconventional reading habits.

"*Ach*. So, you have a little peace and quiet then!" Wilma winked at her as she took a sip of her coffee. "A rare opportunity, indeed!"

Ruth laughed and joined them at the table. "Peace and quiet is a *gut* thing once in a while, I reckon. Gives a body time to think a spell."

Wilma gave a firm nod of her head and set down her cup. "That's exactly the main reason why I'm here."

"For peace and quiet?" Catherine asked. "You didn't know the *kinner* would be gone!"

"Clever girl!" Wilma laughed and waved her hand at Catherine. "*Nee*, I did not come here seeking solitude. I've plenty enough of that without any *kinner* of my own."

Unlike most men in their community, Duane was not a farmer. Instead, he had started and run a dry goods store for over thirty years before he sold it to one of his nephews. Now, retired and living in a smaller *gross-dawdihaus* on the same property as the store, Duane often helped out at the store just for something to do.

"You remember Susie Troyer, right?" Wilma asked, watching as Catherine cut the coffee cake and placed a piece onto a plate for her. "Duane's niece. Well, they live in Banthe by Moreland Lake. It's a pretty little town set in the woodland, and there's an Amish farming community surrounding it."

"That does sound lovely," Ruth said.

"We're going to visit them for a few weeks."

"A few weeks! Everything all right there?" Ruth asked, the typical hint of panic in her voice.

Wilma nodded. "Oh, *ja*, right as rain. You might remember Susie's husband, Vern, don't you, Ruth? Well, they're having a work frolic at their place for their new chicken house, and another neighbor's having one for his new shop. The community decided to have the frolics during the same period of time, you see. So more people can come and help out."

"Isn't that smart?" Ruth raised an eyebrow.

Wilma nodded. "It's a beautiful place. Just an hour or so away from here by horse and buggy, although we've hired a driver. Vern has a small cottage on the far side of his farm that overlooks the lake. And you know how Duane loves to fish and all."

Ruth laughed. "How could anyone not know about Duane's fishing? Why, I believe we ate fresh fish every week last summer, thanks to your husband!"

It was true. Catherine remembered how Duane stopped by almost every Friday evening after spending the day at the large pond on a neighboring farm. A nearby stream fed it so it was always full of trout, especially in the summer months. Without fail, he would have a small red and white cooler full of fish that he often offered to her mother. After all, he would explain, it was only himself and Wilma and they couldn't eat so many fish in a week.

While her older brother James often spent his free

afternoons fishing, it was a pastime that she had never been introduced to. She wondered if she would like to sit by the edge of a pond or lake for hours, waiting for a fish to bite her line. Listening to the birds chirping while a gentle breeze blew through the trees? Yes, she could definitely see herself liking to try her hand at fishing.

"The lake's a rather special place, a nice mixture of farm community with woodland relaxation. A lot of Amish vacation there. I'm surprised you haven't!"

Catherine almost rolled her eyes. Farmers with eight children didn't take vacations. Surely Wilma knew that. Then again, Catherine realized, without having her own children, Wilma probably didn't.

"Well, with so many people gathering to help out, we thought that, mayhaps, Catherine might enjoy accompanying us."

Catherine caught her breath. That sounded like a wonderful idea, and she said a quick little prayer that her parents would agree. It wasn't as though her father needed her help on the farm just yet. The crops had been planted several weeks ago, and with seven children left on the farm, he had plenty of help. But she knew better than to get her hopes up. Being away from the farm for such an extended time was not something she had ever done before.

And, truth be told, Catherine wouldn't mind traveling with Wilma. She had always got along well with the older woman. Several times Catherine had volunteered to help her with spring cleaning or fall canning; it was only fair since Wilma often helped at the Miller house. When they were alone and working, their conversations were lively, and Catherine loved that Wilma seemed quite willing to listen to her stories about whatever book she was currently reading. No one at home would do that.

"That is a kind offer," her mother said, glancing at Catherine and giving her a quick smile. "I'm sure she'd love to accompany you, but I best check with Martin first."

"Of course, of course," Wilma cooed, picking at the coffee cake. "I told Duane to ask Martin about it as well. We'd be leaving on Saturday so we've plenty of time to plan."

"What's the name of that town again?" Catherine asked, hoping that her voice didn't sound too anxious. She wanted to ask her brother James if he had ever heard of it.

"Banthe, which is right on Moreland Lake. You'll find it to be rather quaint, Catherine. And the people are *most* unusual." The way Wilma stressed the word *most* made Catherine's imagination kick into high drive. "Folks from all different areas are there. Some are full-time residents that farm just outside of the town proper, and then there are summer vacationers that stay at little lake houses. The mix of people just adds to its charm."

Moreland Lake? Banthe? Catherine couldn't recall ever hearing about an Amish community by such names. Of course, she hadn't much reason to travel outside of her own little town, and *her* family had never taken a vacation anywhere. Still, she made a mental note to look at the address directory of church districts after Wilma left to see if she knew any of the names.

"There's always so much to do there, Catherine," Wilma continued with great enthusiasm. "You'll certainly have a wonderful time with the other youth. They like to boat and fish, even camp overnight on a small island on the north end. And Vern and Susie have a son and daughter just about your age. I know they'd be tickled to meet you."

Catherine felt the color creep into her cheeks.

"That does sound like a right *gut* time indeed," Ruth said with a soft sigh. "Why, I think I'd like to go along with you, too!" She gave a small laugh at her own joke. With seven other children and a farm to run, that was an impossibility.

Wilma stayed to visit for another thirty minutes, the discussion turning to conversations that were less exciting for Catherine, such as gardening and new babies born to cousins, nieces, or other people that she had never met. Catherine didn't mind sitting with them, though. Her mind was already preoccupied with what a vacation at Banthe might entail.

It wasn't long before Duane and Martin appeared in the doorway.

"Well, Mother, I reckon it's time to head on home," Duane said to his wife. He glanced at Catherine and smiled. "Did Wilma talk to you about traveling with us to Banthe?"

"Oh, *ja*! *Danke* for asking me, Duane," she gushed. And then, looking first at her mother and then her father, she waited patiently to see if a decision had been made.

"I told Duane that it was fine with me if you went," Martin said in a slow voice. "Unless your mother has any objections."

Immediately, Ruth shook her head. "*Nee*, there's nothing going on over the next few weeks that requires Catherine's presence. And Sarah can step up a bit. Besides, it's high time that Catherine had some fun. She's been quite the blessing to me over the past years, and she deserves to go."

From the heat that rushed to her cheeks, Catherine knew that she was blushing. She never thought twice about herself when it came time to work around the house. She saw her mother tackling chores, and without being asked, she always assisted her. To hear such a compliment meant more to Catherine than anything in the world. It was something she had never expected to hear, but was awfully touched to have heard it.

"Well, then, it's settled!" Duane grinned at his wife. "You'll finally have your own *dochder*, Wilma, even if only for two weeks!"

The adults laughed and Catherine smiled, still trying to come to grips with the reality of the situation. When she had awoken that morning, she had thought this would just be another typical day. Now, however, it had become something much different. She almost felt as if she were a character in one of those romance books that she loved to read. *What adventures await me?* she pondered as she half-listened to Duane explain to her parents the details of the trip. She could only imagine that it would be the best two weeks of her life.

Chapter Two

"Now, Catherine," Ruth fretted, "you keep track of any expenses, *Dochder*. We'll need to know how much to reimburse the Andersons. Don't trouble them so."

Catherine folded her burgundy dress and laid it in the small suitcase, careful to smooth out the wrinkles. After five long days of waiting and preparation, today at last she was leaving for Banthe, and she could hardly wait. "I know, *Mamm*. And I've my own money from selling that quilt I made last year. I can always pay them back if need be."

"And here." Ruth handed her a small package wrapped in plain white paper. There was a sticker holding the paper together that read *Harper's Store*.

Surprised, Catherine took the package from her mother and carefully examined it, turning it over in her hands before she looked at her mother. "What's this?"

Her mother suppressed a smile as she raised her eyebrows. "Perhaps opening it might be a way to find out?"

Quickly Catherine unwrapped the package. Inside the paper, she found a small journal and a pen. The cover looked like leather, although she was fairly certain that her mother would not have spent money on such an extravagance. But the pages inside were lined and blank, just waiting to be filled up with stories and details of her adventures at Moreland Lake. She had never had her own journal, although she knew that her mother kept one. She had never thought to ask for one, but now that she held this in her hands, she knew that she would treasure it.

"*Danke, Mamm,*" Catherine whispered as she stared at the unexpected gift for a moment.

"I…I don't suppose you'd mind if I use it for a diary?"

Her mother smiled and patted her arm. "Of course not, Catherine. It's yours and you can do with it what you'd like. I'm pleased that you want to keep a diary, though. I'm sure you'll want to remember everything that you do while you're away. Your sister Sarah will be anxious to hear all about it."

Catherine highly doubted that was true, but she remained silent on *that* particular subject.

Her fifteen-year-old sister hadn't said much about their parents' decision to permit Catherine to travel with the Andersons. But Catherine suspected that Sarah felt a little jealous, although not necessarily in a sinful way. With Catherine leaving, it would be up to Sarah to step up and help their mother with the cleaning, cooking, washing, and gardening. And while Sarah might not think that was such a good deal, Catherine knew that her sister would benefit from some time as the eldest daughter in the house. After all, regardless of Sarah's preference for working in the fields, all Amish women needed to learn how to do housework in order to take care of their future families.

"And be careful of the youth out there," Ruth continued. She rubbed her hands together, a nervous tick that she had developed years ago, when her first child had begun walking. If anyone had a tendency to overthink and panic too much, Ruth Miller was that person. "You know that not all of the Amish communities have good youth. Some of them are quite wild!"

Catherine laughed. "Oh, *Mamm*! You said that about the Amish youth in Holmes County and Lancaster County! I'm sure that Moreland Lake has just as fine youth as we do."

Her mother made a sound that indicated uncertainty regarding Catherine's statement.

"Besides, *Mamm*, you know I have no interest in running around with youth."

This much was true. Catherine rarely attended the youth gatherings in their own district. While she enjoyed the singings and volleyball games, she wasn't partial to riding home with any of the young men. Accepting an invitation of a buggy ride home from one of the young men at the gathering would indicate a mutual interest in initiating a relationship. Catherine was definitely not ready for that. And as far as game nights? She avoided those evenings when the young women played board games and the single men cruised by to "check them out." Catherine had no desire to settle down with any of the silly men from her own district. Most of them were too young, and not necessarily just in age.

Besides, Catherine's favorite pastime had always been losing herself in the pages of a good book. For quite a few years, she had enjoyed reading the classics she borrowed from her teacher and the very few people who, like her, indulged in the unconventional pastime of reading fiction. And then she had discovered an author who rewrote those classics set in Amish country. Oh, how Catherine could devour those novels!

To many in the *g'may*, reading Amish romance novels was still considered a waste of time and even frowned upon; but times were changing.

Her mother leveled her gaze at Catherine and pursed her lips as she said, "It would do you good to spend some more time socializing. I sure hope you'll attend some singings and other functions while you're there."

Catherine knew what her mother was really saying: plainly said, if Catherine didn't socialize, she'd never get married. And no one wanted a *maedel* in the family. But, at nineteen years of age, Catherine didn't want to just settle for just anyone. She wanted to live a life of romance, just like in the books that she read. Oh, when she read about Lizzie and Daniel in that popular Amish romance book published by the *Englischers*, *Lizzie*, Catherine knew…just knew!…that there was someone special out there for her. That was what she wanted: a man that connected with her on many levels, just like Daniel did with Lizzie, even though they didn't care much for each other when they had first met.

But Catherine didn't speak a word of this to her mother. Instead, she quietly reached for her freshly laundered cobalt blue dress and folded it, carefully placing it on top of her other dress in the suitcase.

"Wilma says that you're to stay at a small lake house that the Troyers own. You make certain to help her with everything," Ruth reminded her. "Laundry, cooking, even shopping."

Catherine fought the urge to roll her eyes. Of course she knew she must help Wilma. Her mother didn't need to remind her about that! Catherine had never been one to sit around and let others do the work. And she had listened to her father complain far too often about how the people in the *Englischer* communities tended to focus more on their own needs than on the good of the community. From what little Catherine knew about the non-Amish world, people didn't help others with farming or gardening, unless there was something in it for them. How much nicer the world would be if people could just step outside of their own self-centered world and realize that helping others made life better for all!

Instead, Catherine glanced over her shoulder, watching as her mother paced the floor. "Oh, *Mamm*, you know that I'd never behave poorly. You needn't worry."

For a moment, Ruth paused. She stared at her daughter as if seeing her with fresh eyes. The tension left her shoulders and she managed to smile. "Of course. You're right." She paused just long enough to sigh. "Sometimes, Catherine, I forget that you're all grown up now."

Catherine returned the smile and gently said, "Never too grown for reminders, but, then again, I *have* learned from the best *maem* possible!"

This time, the smile on Ruth's face broadened and she stepped forward to embrace her daughter, a rare treat in a family that, just like the majority of Amish families, did not often show physical affection. "I will miss you so," she whispered into her daughter's ear. "I've never been apart from my children for even one day! These two weeks will seem like a lifetime, for sure and certain."

A lifetime for her mother but an adventure for Catherine.

A half hour later, Catherine and her mother were in the kitchen. Catherine sat at the table folding the laundry while her mother prepared the evening meal. The porch door opened and her father walked inside. With a small smile, he walked over to the sink to wash his hands. "Getting all ready then?"

Catherine nodded her head, not realizing that her father couldn't see her. "*Ja*," she said. "I'm almost finished with the packing."

He shut off the water and took the hand towel that his wife gave him. "*Danke*," he said as he dried his hands and the back of his neck before walking over to the table. "Now Catherine, I'm sure your *mamm* has told you to behave proper."

"*Daed*!"

He held up his hand to stop her. "*Nee*, Catherine, it's better to just say it outright and be done with it. I know that you aren't the kind to do anything silly or rash. But you haven't been away from home before so I just feel better reminding you. That's all."

Quietly, she looked down at the floor and sighed.

"And you won't know those youths there so you best listen to the Andersons. People come from all over to vacation at this lake place, and not all of them Amish. That means that the Amish youth that live there year-round are a little worldlier than the youth you usually interact with, here at home." Her father leveled his gaze at her, his steely gray eyes studying her face. "Use prudence and caution."

"And it gets cold at night! Make certain you pack your heavy coat!" her mother added.

Catherine took a deep breath and bit her tongue from fear of making a sassy remark.

"And don't go walking around alone," her father went

on. "Lots of tourists in that town, I'm sure. They won't be as mannerly as the *Englische* around here."

She tapped her toes against the floor, waiting for the litany of instructions and words of caution to finally end.

"And one last thing," her father said at last. He waited until she looked up before he reached into his back pocket and withdrew an envelope. Slowly, he slid it across the table toward her, his fingers still on the edge. "Figured you'd need some pocket money. You'll certainly want to buy a new book or two, *ja*?"

Her eyes followed the envelope. When he left it in front of her, she lifted her eyes and stared, wide-eyed, at her father. "Oh, *Daed*!" She reached out for the envelope, hesitating before she pulled it closer.

He cleared his throat. "Now, that's more cash than you're used to having, so I want you to be careful."

"Use that journal!" her mother added. "It's best to keep track of your spending!"

Catherine felt a lump in her throat and nodded. With eight children, money was not something that came easily to the Miller family. She knew that any extra cash given to her was much more than a gift; it was a sacrifice. She hadn't expected such a contribution. In fact, she hadn't thought about spending money at all. "*Danke*," she whispered. "I…I'll be careful for sure and certain."

Satisfied, her mother smiled and returned her attention to the kitchen chores. She needed to bake bread for the family, a daily task for her but one that Catherine usually helped her with. Today, she would not be helping her mother. Instead, she would finish packing, for the Andersons were coming to fetch her in just another hour, for the drive to the lake.

"Hey, now!" Her oldest brother James walked into the kitchen, pausing to kick off his dirty boots at the door. Removing his hat, he hung it on a peg on the wall and shook his head, his sweaty brown hair still sticking to his forehead, the blunt cut making him look like a young boy, though he was almost twenty-two. "*Wie gehts*?"

"You're back a day early now, aren't you? You must be hungry!" Ruth hurried to fix him a plate of food.

"*Ja*, we finished the barn building early so the driver fetched us this morning." He plopped down at the table and sighed. "And *nee*, I'm not hungry but a coffee would hit the spot, for sure and certain."

Unlike the other Miller children, James didn't work on the farm. With so many children per family, land in their community was becoming scarce and pricey. As a result, many a young Amish man had taken to apprenticing in more worldly trades. Some used complicated machinery requiring computer skills to calibrate and fabricate metal parts shipped around the world. Others chose more traditional trades, working in leather shops or building buggies and carriages, mostly for their local communities. James had a job with an Amish man who had a construction company. They built outbuildings and barns in nearby towns, but as their reputation for quality work grew, they were asked more and more frequently to erect a barn, a garage, or a large pole building in a different state. Sometimes James spent days or even weeks away from his parents' farm. The younger children, especially the boys, thought that it was exciting, but Catherine could tell that the time away from home and the travel were draining on her brother.

He glanced at his sister and kicked at her foot under the table. "Everything all right around here, then?"

"Your *schwester*'s getting ready to leave us," Ruth responded as she placed a cup of coffee in front of James. "For Banthe."

"Banthe?" James gave his sister a half-hearted grin accompanied by a small laugh. "Oh, *ja*? What for? Your *rumschpringe*?"

Carefully, Catherine folded and then tucked the envelope against her palm. It was better that no one knew about the envelope of money. She didn't want any of her siblings accusing her parents of playing favorites.

Before Catherine could answer, her father ran his fingers through his hair, leaving it standing up on end. "The Andersons are taking her. They invited her last week."

"They're vacationing for a few weeks on the lake since their niece lives there, and her husband is having a work frolic," Catherine added in a soft voice. "Wilma wanted some company and invited me to come along."

"Huh! Don't that beat all. A lot sure happened in the week I've been gone, now don't it?" He drummed his fingers against the table top. "You deserve a little fun, Catherine, for sure and certain! Always working…or with your nose buried in a book!" he teased.

She made a face at him and he laughed again.

"Who are the niece and nephew?"

"Troyer's the name, Vern and Susie Troyer," his father answered before he glanced at his wife. "Any coffee left in that pot for me, too, Ruth?"

Within seconds, Ruth handed him a cup of hot coffee in a chipped yellow mug.

"Troyer, you say?" James looked up toward the ceiling as if thinking about something. "Related to John and Ida Mae Troyer, who are about my age?"

Catherine frowned and stared at James, curious as to how her brother might know the family.

"One and the same. Vern and Susie are their parents."

Catherine could no longer contain her curiosity. "How would you know them, James?"

For a moment, her brother looked at her with a sheepish expression on his face, as if admitting the acquaintance was an admission of guilt to some dark secret that he had hidden from her. It struck her as odd because James never kept secrets from her. He was only two years older than her and they were as close as a brother and sister could possibly be.

He shuffled his feet and looked down at the ground. "Oh, at one of the nearby youth gatherings I met them. A few summers ago, I reckon."

"Do you keep in touch with John then?" Catherine asked.

"*Ja*, a bit. During the off-season, there's not much to do in Banthe, so his youth group sometimes comes to ours, especially when we are gathering in Chelsea. That's only thirty minutes from Banthe, you know."

Perhaps she would have met John Troyer, too, if she were more inclined to go to the youth gatherings that sprung up from time to time in different districts. But she wasn't as partial to those events, preferring the quiet of the house to read. And that was what she was looking forward to: reading. She would have fewer chores at the lake, and she could envision herself sitting on a pretty porch, a glass of cool lemonade or meadow tea on the arm of an Adirondack chair and with a book on her lap as she listened to birds chirping and cicadas buzzing. In her mind, that would be the best day possible: peace and quiet to lose herself in one of her Amish romance novels.

"If you know the Troyer's nephew, I'm surprised you didn't know about the frolics." Her comment was meant innocently, but from the way his cheeks reddened, she wondered if, perhaps, he actually *had* known about them.

"Enough talking, I suppose," Ruth said over her shoulder. "You best go finish packing now, Catherine."

"Okay, *Maem*," Catherine replied as she stood up, the envelope of money in her hand.

"And don't forget that coat! Remember what I said about the cool evenings. No sense in you getting sick while you're there. You don't want to be a burden to the Andersons."

"Alright, *Maem*." Catherine hurried to the stairs and quickly ascended, her mind wandering over which books to bring and completely forgetting the coat.

Chapter Three

"Oh, Catherine!" Wilma said when the young woman emerged from the small bedroom where she had left her suitcase. "Isn't this just wonderful?"

She stood at the large picture window and stared outside at the lake. It was only a few hundred yards away and the sun shimmered on the glasslike surface. The reflection of the blue sky was beautiful, and Catherine stood beside Wilma in silence for a few minutes, appreciating the gift from God.

"And I didn't realize that the *dawdihaus* was so far from Susie's! Why, it feels as if we are all alone here at the lake!" From the tone of her voice, it didn't sound as if Wilma was unpleased with the situation.

The door opened and Duane walked in, his arms filled with firewood.

"Oh, dear!" Wilma hurried over to him. "It's too warm for a fire, Duane, don't you think?"

He nodded and gestured with his head toward the back door. "There's a fire pit out there. We can cook on that. Easier to bring it through the house than around," he explained. "And won't heat up the house."

Without being asked, Catherine hurried over to open the back door.

Wilma, however, commented on the dirt that was tracked into the house.

"I saw Vern just now," Duane said when he returned to the house. He slapped his hands at his chest and belly to loosen any lingering dirt. Ignoring Wilma's scowl, he headed toward the counter and sat upon a stool. "Susie's gone to visit a sister-in-law who just had a baby. Apparently, she won't be back till tomorrow."

That bit of news did not sit well with Wilma.

"Oh! That's awful. Didn't she know we were arriving today? Why, I had hoped that she'd show us around a bit. Perhaps take us to the store to fetch some food. Surely she thought of that?" The question did not warrant an answer. "She could have introduced us to people. We know no one here." She glanced at Catherine. "And who will take Catherine to meet some of the young folk? She can't just barge in on their gatherings!" She paused and, with a tilt of her head, asked, "Could you?"

Catherine shook her head. She'd no sooner do that than break one of the commandments! Without a proper introduction, she'd have no choice but to wait until Susie's return. In truth, she didn't want to mingle with people she did not know. Nor did she really mind a delay. It just meant more time lingering in the shade of the back porch that overlooked the lake. And with her new book, *Emma*, beckoning to her, Catherine thought that a day of reading sounded appealing, indeed!

"This is terrible, Duane," Wilma continued and began pacing the wide plank wooden floor, which squeaked under her weight.

"Susie's absence is not going to harm anyone,"

Duane replied with a weary tone to his voice. "And the two of you can certainly bicycle to the store to pick up anything you have forgotten to pack, although I dare say from what I unloaded, you seem to have packed quite a bit."

Wilma shook her head and mumbled some more about how people didn't seem to have any common sense when it came to how they treated friends and family. After a few minutes of listening to this, Duane sighed and stood up, informing his wife that he wanted to walk over to Vern's house and take a look at the place. His escape did not go unnoticed by Catherine, who wished, for just a moment, that he had asked her to accompany him.

Instead, she was left with Wilma, who continued her diatribe about not knowing anyone and how could her husband's niece be so insensitive and self-serving?

"Let's bike to town," Catherine suggested at last. She hoped that she could redirect Wilma's attention because she knew, without a doubt, that she could not tolerate two days of listening to these lamentations. "It's a beautiful day and the breeze will make it feel even more refreshing. Perhaps you might let me treat you to some ice cream at the store that the driver pointed out?"

And so, fifteen minutes later, Catherine pedaled a bicycle up the dirt lane and toward the paved road that ran past Vern and Susie's farm. The farther they rode from the lake, the more the woodlands opened into pockets of small farms, each one about forty or fifty acres and mostly used for dairy cows to graze. But each farm also had a large field for growing hay. In between the farms were more pockets of woods so that the area was not completely open and just farms. It was an interesting topography, and Catherine enjoyed seeing the small white houses, set back from the roads, along with their pretty red barns and gray silos.

The other thing that Catherine could not help noticing, merely by its absence, was the lack of traffic on the road. While her own hometown of Fullerton was still very rural and away from the commercialism and tourism that thrived because of the nearby Indiana community of Shipshewana, it was shared with Mennonites and *Englischers*, and traffic, while not substantial, was moderate but constant. Moreland Lake was just the opposite. Tucked into the gentle hills and woodlands, the lake presented a hidden cove for the local Amish farmers to enjoy during their down time, when crops had been planted but were not yet ready to harvest. And the Troyers' property, a massive two-hundred-plus-acre farm, abutted the lake.

Once in town, Wilma and Catherine set their bicycles against a large tree near the first store. The street was narrow and there were few signs of automobiles. There were also very few buggies, which Catherine thought was interesting. It appeared that most of the people who lived in the area used their bicycles and scooters for transportation.

Nearby, at an old picnic table, a group of young women sat and talked. The ease of their communication certainly indicated a close friendship, and Catherine watched them with a touch of envy. Wilma touched her arm and nodded toward them. "*Mayhaps* you should go talk to them?"

Horrified at the idea, Catherine shook her head. "I'd feel rather…uncomfortable," she admitted.

Wilma nodded and the two of them walked on, approaching the closest store to see what it offered.

It was a natural food market with bulk items for sale. The vegetables and fruit looked wonderful, an aroma of freshness filling the air. Even in Fullerton the stores did not carry such an abundance of produce.

"Oh, my!" Wilma looked around as Catherine retrieved a cart from the entrance. "Have you ever seen such a collection of goods?"

Catherine laughed. "I can't say that I have! Why, I don't even know what some of these items are!" She was staring at a small bag of green fruit, and out of curiosity, she picked it up and lifted it to her nose. Wilma began to wander farther down the aisle, and Catherine quickly set down the fruit and followed after her.

Several other Amish women gathered at the back of the aisle, standing together and talking. They glanced up as Wilma and Catherine approached, but not one of them greeted the newcomers. Instead, they watched the two strangers with guarded curiosity, which made Catherine feel even more uncomfortable. She averted her eyes, hurrying past them. To her surprise, the other aisles were equally as crowded with even more women and a few men. She began to realize that the food store was more than just a place to shop; it was also a place for socialization.

The crowded aisles were hard to navigate, and she frowned when Wilma started putting items into the cart. Up ahead, Catherine could see how long the line was for the single cash register near the last aisle. Two young women stood there, staring in her direction. She saw one of them say something to the other and then both laughed. For some reason, Catherine had the suspicion that they were making fun of her. Perhaps it was her stiff prayer *kapp* that was shaped a little different than theirs, or maybe it was the dull color of her dress, which contrasted sharply with the bright red dresses that they wore. Either way, Catherine hurried to catch up to Wilma, feeling more comfortable in the older woman's presence.

"There are so many people here," Catherine whispered to Wilma.

"I just wish I knew someone," Wilma replied. "If only Susie hadn't gone away to visit her sister-in-law and the new *boppli*!" The irritation in Wilma's voice was more than apparent, and Catherine had to agree that Susie was rather unthoughtful for leaving them alone during their first days at the lake, even if a new baby trumped all.

By the time they finished shopping and waited their turn at the checkout line, Catherine was beginning to think she had made a mistake in wanting to come to the lake with the Andersons. What she had thought would be an adventure, perhaps even filled with some romantic elements like the ones those authors wrote about in her beloved novels, was turning into a trying ordeal filled with uneasiness. But she also knew that the best novels often started out that way, so she held out hope that a grand experience could still await her.

Outside of the store, Catherine carried the box of food toward the bicycles.

"Oh, Catherine! Look! There's a fabric store. I might just pop in there to get some floss for my cross stitching," Wilma said.

For a split second, Catherine considered going into the store with Wilma. Perhaps she could use some of her father's money to buy brightly colored fabric to make herself a new dress. But as exciting as that thought was, Catherine knew better than to waste her father's hard-earned money when her own dresses were as good as any other, even if they were plain and dull colored. So, instead of joining Wilma, Catherine glanced toward the empty picnic table. "I'll just sit here a spell, if you don't mind."

Alone at last, she sat at the picnic table and sighed as she looked around the small town. She noticed a young man standing near a carriage as if waiting for someone to leave a store. When she caught his eye, he leered at her and Catherine quickly looked away. But she could feel that he was still watching her. She felt uncomfortable under his constant and steady gaze so she dug into her cloth bag to retrieve her book and flipped to the page that she had dog-eared the previous evening. Quickly, she escaped from the lake and returned to Lancaster County, where Emma was talking with her father's friend, Gideon. Catherine could almost envision the way that Emma flitted around the kitchen, preparing coffee while chatting with Gideon, completely unaware that, deep down, Gideon favored her.

"Well, that must be one interesting book," a voice said from beside her.

Startled, Catherine shut the book as she quickly turned in the direction of the voice.

He was a handsome young man, a bit willowy in the frame, which made her presume that he was not a farmer. His dark hair poked out from beneath his straw hat, and his dark eyes stared at her from behind narrow glasses. And a smile lit up his face as he studied her in return.

"I would hate to think of anyone wasting time reading a book that wasn't interesting," Catherine said lightly.

"Ah, good point." He glanced at the cover. "*Little Amish Women?* Is that a romance?"

She blushed.

"And an Amish romance at that!" He reached out his hand, a silent inquiry to examine the book closer. Reluctantly, she handed it to him. She watched as he flipped the book over and quickly read the back of the book. "Ah, an adaptation of Louisa May Alcott's classic!" He looked up at her, his eyes sparkling from behind those lenses. "Have you read Louisa May Alcott herself?"

The way he asked the question insinuated that she should have read it. Embarrassed, she shook her head that she had not.

"She's a wonderful author. From the 1800s. Her writing style is classic, for sure and certain!" He handed the book back to her. "I'd be curious as to how this book compares."

Catherine tucked the book under her apron. "Are you a reader then…?" She hesitated, realizing that he had not yet introduced himself and she didn't know how to address him.

"Henry," he offered, extending his hand for her to shake. "Henry Tilman. My family is vacationing here for a few weeks."

"Catherine Miller," she said. "Tilman isn't an Amish name, is it?"

He shook his head. "*Nee*, it's not Amish."

She tilted her head. "So…?"

"My great-great-grandfather was Mennonite. But, like the hero of all good Amish romances," he said, gesturing toward her book, "he fell in love with an Amish woman. Lucky for me that he did, *ja*?" When he smiled, his whole face lit up.

For a moment, Catherine tried to imagine an *Englische* man falling in love with an Amish woman. How hard it would have been for him to convert to not just the Amish religion but the Amish way of life! She could envision the emotional turmoil as Henry Tilman's great-great-grandfather had made the decision to leave his family and join with an Amish community. The pain, the indecision, and ultimately, the determination that his love for the Amish woman was worth any and all sacrifice.

"He must've loved her very much," she said with a dreamy sigh. "I bet it was just like those romance novels."

Henry gave a soft, but not offensive, laugh. "It was *very* much like those romance novels, Catherine Miller, of that I'm sure and certain."

Oh, she could imagine everything: the courtship, the hand-holding, the long walks on quiet roads under starry nights.

"So, Catherine Miller, are you here to help with the frolics?"

"The frolics?" Her thoughts broken, she had to shake her head a little to realize what he was actually asking. "Oh, *ja*, I am. I came with friends of my family, Duane and Wilma Anderson. They're related to the Troyers." She paused before she added, "We're staying at a small lake house on the south side of town."

"Let me guess. Near the lake?"

For a second, Catherine looked at him, a blank expression on her face. Then, when she realized that he was teasing her—for of course the lake house was south of Banthe!—she blushed. There was a moment of silence after he spoke, so, feeling uncomfortable, she asked him the same question. "And you? Do you live here or are you visiting to help, too?"

He hesitated before he responded. "I live at Newbury Acres." He paused as if waiting for her to respond. However, she did not know that place, and when she did not indicate any familiarity, he quickly added, "That's my father's farm and woodworking shop."

"So, you are visiting then?" she asked. "For the frolic?"

"Many hands do make light the work," was all that he responded, leaving her question unanswered, which she thought rather odd. After a pause, he said, "You asked earlier if I read. Yes, I do. I believe that reading is a wonderful pastime. I confess I do not read Amish romances, though." Unlike some other people, he did not sound dismissive, however, of the idea.

For a moment neither spoke, and Catherine began to feel that uncomfortable feeling once again.

As if sensing this, Henry placed his foot on the picnic table's bench and leaned forward. "I have been rather remiss. I should have asked how long you've been at the lake, whether you have attended the beach volleyball games, and whether or not you have participated in fishing at all. If you have a spare moment, I will correct that immediately!"

"Oh, that is not necessary…" she started to say, but Henry placed his hand upon his chest in mock horror.

"*Nee*, Catherine. There is a sense of propriety that must be followed," he said with an over-exaggerated air of correctness. "Now have you attended any of the volleyball games?"

"I have not," she said, trying to hide her smile.

"I see. Well, I suggest you put that on your list. What about the fishing?"

"*Nee.*"

He raised his eyebrows. "When did you arrive at Moreland Lake, then?"

"Just this morning," she responded, quick to add: "Had you asked that question first, you would have spared yourself the trouble of the other two."

He laughed. "Well, now that we have had proper introductions and proper conversation as good etiquette demands, we can abandon the need for practicality!" he exclaimed, to which Catherine bit her lower lip, trying to suppress a smile. "Ah, I see what you are thinking!"

"You've only just met me. How could you possibly know what I'm thinking?" she laughed.

"Let's see now." He studied her intently. "You are thinking that I'm an odd man."

"I do not think that at all." But, in truth, she had been thinking that he was unlike any man she had met before. And that was not necessarily a bad thing. She found Henry Tilman to be a breath of fresh air, light in conversation and a bit witty. There was nothing threatening about him, however, and she felt an immediate yearning to know him better, a fact that made her feel warm and tingly.

Henry pressed his lips together and raised an eyebrow as if in disbelief. "I imagine I will make a fun description but poor addition to your journal entry for the evening."

"My journal!" Catherine couldn't help but laugh again. "What if I have no journal?"

This time, Henry shook his head. "Impossible to

fathom! A young woman on a trip to the lake? Someone as fond of reading romantic novels as you are? Of
course, you would have a journal to document all of
the new and exciting experiences that, undoubtedly,
lie ahead of you."

"We're only staying here but two weeks."

Henry smiled at her. "And that is plenty of time for
adventures, don't you think?"

Catherine didn't have time to respond. If she had,
she would have told him that she hoped for nothing less
than a wonderful adventure. Life in Fullerton was so
predictable and, at times, downright dull, especially
when she compared her daily life with the exciting tales
that she read in the evenings. But just then Wilma came
out of the store with a bag clutched in her hand, a smile
lighting up her face when she saw Henry speaking to
Catherine.

"Oh, my," she said as she joined them. "You are already making friends, Catherine! How delightful."

Catherine blushed, understanding the underlying
hint in Wilma's voice.

Henry introduced himself and Wilma seemed even
more delighted by his manners.

"Did you find your floss?" Catherine asked.

"I did, although I'm not so certain that it is of similar
quality to what I am used to using," she asked, opening the bag and withdrawing a few of the different colors of thread.

Henry peered at it, a serious expression on his face.
"I dare say you are correct."

Wilma's eyebrows knit together as she stared at him.
"And you speak from experience?"

He laughed. "My sister, she loves to embroider and

cross-stitch. But she brings her own floss from home at Newbury Acres because she is not a fan of the floss sold here. I believe she mentioned that it bleeds when washed, so you might want to wash it before you use it."

Catherine found his knowledge of thread intriguing. It was something of little to no importance to men. However, she suspected that it spoke highly of his relationship with his sister. And suddenly, she decided that she quite liked this Henry Tilman.

Long after they parted from Henry, with smiles and "it's been a pleasure" on both sides, Catherine and Wilma commented on how the little town of Moreland Lake was delightful and that their two weeks would be most engaging if more of the people proved to be as friendly and polite as the young man they had just met.

Chapter Four

The following day started early with the Andersons and Catherine walking up the long lane and past the Troyers' farm. Church was being held at another farm, and with no horse and buggy to use, the threesome was forced to walk. But the cool morning air felt refreshing and the backdrop of birds singing kept them interested during the forty-five-minute trek.

"I believe I just heard a Baltimore oriole!" Wilma declared with great enthusiasm. "Did you hear it, Catherine?"

"I'm sure I wouldn't know." Catherine wouldn't know the song of a Baltimore oriole unless the bird sat in front of her and sang to its heart's content.

Wilma redirected her attention to her husband. "Did you, Duane?"

"I did not." He seemed even less interested than Catherine.

"Just listen to those birds singing! God has blessed them with the gift of song, wouldn't you agree?"

Catherine smiled at that comment. "God has blessed all of us with special gifts, indeed."

In her mind, as they continued walking in silence, Catherine wondered what her own special gift was. While she loved to garden and to cross-stitch, she didn't consider either one of them to be *her* special gift. If she could, she would have loved to write books. Perhaps that was her gift, but it was untapped. Nevertheless, she could imagine the stories that she would write, if permitted and able. They would be romances, much like the ones that she enjoyed reading so much. But the only experience she had with romance and love was from the pages of the novels, not from real life.

Her mind wandered to Henry, and she wondered if she might see him today at church. His humor and wit had stayed with her long after she had parted company with him. The previous evening, Wilma had commented more than once about how kind Henry was. Duane, however, seemed about as interested in the mysterious Henry Tilman as he was in the Baltimore oriole.

When they arrived at the farmhouse where church was being hosted that week, Catherine looked around, hoping to catch sight of Henry. But he was nowhere to be seen. She did, however, meet several young women. As was the custom at her own church district, all of the women greeted each other with a handshake before they exchanged a holy kiss. When Catherine and Wilma reached the end of the line, they stood there in order to greet other women as they made their way through the line. That was when one woman approached Wilma and introduced Catherine to her two daughters, neither of whom appeared overly excited to meet her. But at least she now knew two young people to sit with. Reluctantly, she followed them to a bench quickly filling with other young women.

"There's a singing tonight," one of the sisters said while they waited for the bishop and preachers to enter the room. "Jared Troyer's family is hosting it."

"I don't know Jared Troyer," Catherine responded.

"They are cousins with the other Troyers, your friends' niece's family."

"Ah." That didn't surprise Catherine. In most Amish communities, everyone had some relationship with the other families, or so it seemed.

The other sister sighed. "It's going to be hot in here today. I can tell already."

The banal conversation bored Catherine, but she tried to remain cheerful and open to dialogue. The only problem was that she didn't care for the dullness of their exchange.

Exhaling through puffed lips, Catherine glanced around the room, watching as the older women began to sit at the benches in front of them. She didn't like the way that this church district was so informal about the seating arrangements. Back home, the women walked single-file into the worship area and sat down all at once, not like this *g'may*, where it seemed so willy-nilly. Her eyes caught on Wilma, who was talking with a woman, both appearing very animated and happy. Catherine wondered who the woman was when she saw Wilma peering around the room in the direction of the benches. Once they made eye contact, Wilma waved frantically for Catherine to join them.

Relieved to be rid of the two dull sisters, Catherine politely excused herself and hurried over to where Wilma stood.

"Catherine! *Kum* now! Look who is here! Susie

Troyer!" Wilma laughed in a frivolous sort of way. "We've been saved!"

As Catherine joined them, she greeted Duane's niece with a smile. With Amish families typically being rather large, it wasn't unusual for aunts and uncles to be close in age to their nieces and nephews. Catherine suspected that Susie was almost the same age as Duane. However, she did not resemble her uncle in the least. Unlike Duane, Susie was a tall woman with almost white hair and a willowy figure. Her eyes were pale, almost gray in color, and her skin wrinkled around her eyes, but nowhere else.

Wilma reached for Catherine's hand and gave it a friendly squeeze. "This is our dear Catherine," Wilma said, smiling at her ward before returning her attention to Susie. "Such a tolerate companion she's been. I must confess we both felt rather lost without knowing anyone the other day."

Empathetically, Susie clicked her tongue.

"I'm so relieved to see you here. Why, I didn't know what we would do during fellowship. We've no one to introduce us to the people in Banthe! It's a terrible feeling when you're an outsider."

"Never fear. We're home now." Susie Troyer glanced around and waved at another woman before she continued talking. "Truly, I felt awful that I wasn't here to greet you, but I trust that you settled in nicely, *ja*?" She didn't wait for an answer but turned her attention toward Catherine. "And you, Catherine, why, you simply must meet my *dochder*, Ida Mae."

Wilma leaned over to Catherine. "She only has the one *dochder*."

"And she's more than enough!" Susie laughed. "She must be just about your age! What are you? Twenty?"

"Nineteen."

Dismissively, Susie waved her hand. "Close enough. Why, my Ida Mae knows just about everyone in this town. So many people coming and going all the time. The poor dear. It's hard to live in a town that caters to so many vacationers."

Catherine hadn't thought about that. How could Ida Mae, or anyone else, have any real friends in a town with limited year-round residents? How lonely it must be, she thought and made a mental vow to befriend Susie Troyer's daughter.

"Ach! Perfect timing." Susie raised her hand and waved it over Catherine's head. "Here she comes now!" With a warm smile, Susie greeted her daughter and gestured toward Catherine. "Ida Mae, meet Catherine. She's here with the Andersons." Susie took a step backward as if to open up the space between the two young women. "You both are just about the same age. I reckon you have tons in common, *ja*?"

"Catherine? Catherine Miller?" Ida Mae asked as she extended her hand. Her pale gray eyes peered at Catherine from beneath thick eyelashes. "From Fullerton?"

Catherine shook Ida Mae's hand, knowing instantly that she would like this young woman. From the way her eyes sparkled, to the softness of her voice, there was clearly nothing to dislike about her. "*Ja*, I'm from Fullerton. How did you know?"

Ida Mae glanced at Wilma, who was now deeply engrossed in conversation with a small group of women. "Aren't the Andersons from Fullerton?"

Feeling a bit foolish for not having made that connection, Catherine changed the subject. "Have you visited there?"

Ida Mae gave a soft smile, almost coy in nature. "*Nee*, but I intend to."

Catherine wasn't quite certain how to interpret that comment.

Ida Mae placed a finger to her mouth and looked up toward the ceiling as if thinking of something. "And I seem to recall that I've met your *bruder* James. He's friends with my older *bruder*, John."

"*Ja*, James mentioned that he had met you at some youth gatherings."

Instantly, Ida Mae dimpled. "Did he? I'm so glad he remembered us!"

Catherine could see why her brother would remember Ida Mae. Catherine found her to be a lively young woman with a pretty face, even if her eyes were pale and her nose sunburned, most likely from helping outside on the family farm. Her dark blond hair was neatly tucked under her prayer *kapp* and she wore a dark peach dress, a color that Catherine had not seen before. Clearly, she was adventuresome and energetic, perhaps even someone who might become a good friend.

After the introductions, Catherine and Ida Mae moved toward the benches to claim their places while the rest of the women began to filter to their own rows and take a seat. It wasn't long before the bishop and preachers entered through another door and made their way along the seated women, pausing to shake their hands when it was physically feasible.

"How different this is!" Catherine whispered to Ida Mae.

"Oh? How so?"

Catherine shrugged. "I just never realized that church districts that were so close in distance might have different manners of gathering. In our church, the bishop and the preachers greet the women while they are still standing. Only when they sit down do the women occupy the benches."

Ida Mae laughed. "That seems rather strange to me!"

One of the older women glanced over her shoulder at Ida Mae, giving her a stern look that instructed her to be quiet and stop laughing. Ida Mae covered her mouth with her hands and giggled into Catherine's shoulder. Even though she knew better, Catherine couldn't help but smile at her new friend's antics.

Almost three hours later, by the time the last sermon had been given, hymns sung, and prayers prayed, Catherine's back ached and she felt fidgety, as if she were still a child and not a young woman. For some reason, the different style of worship at this service made her restless. She had even dozed off for a minute or two during the silent kneeling prayer. In her own district, ten minutes was the longest they knelt to pray. But this preacher had them kneel and pray for almost twenty minutes, and that was ten minutes too long for Catherine.

"My word!" Ida Mae whispered to Catherine as the congregation dispersed, the men to convert the benches into tables for the noon fellowship hour and the women to organize the food distribution. "That second sermon was rather long, don't you think?"

Catherine wasn't certain how to respond. She didn't want to say anything negative about the preacher, but she certainly agreed with Ida Mae. However, she didn't know the people and their relationships to each other.

And she did not know Ida Mae well enough to complain that it was, indeed, boring, not from content but from delivery. "I…I suppose I've sat through longer ones," she said at last. "At least it was interesting."

"What. Ever!" Ida Mae waved away Catherine's comment as if she swatted at a pesky fly. "Every time he preaches, he says the same thing…about the dangers of the world and how technology is just no *gut*! He drones on and on and on in that same monotone." She rolled her eyes. "And he stares at the boys, barely addressing any of his sermon toward the women!"

"*Mayhaps* he thinks the boys are more likely to be tempted by worldliness," Catherine offered.

Ida Mae made a scoffing noise and rolled her eyes. "Man and woman are more equal than Preacher gives us credit for, *ja*? I've seen just as many young girls fall into temptation as boys. Just the other week I saw something glowing from within the front pocket of Alice Burkholder's apron!" She leaned over and whispered into Catherine's ear, "She had a cell phone!"

Even though she didn't know who Alice Burkholder was, Catherine understood the implications of what Ida Mae shared. She gasped and leaned backward. "No!"

Ida Mae nodded. "And she didn't look none the sorrier for having been caught. Can you imagine such a thing?"

Indeed, Catherine could not. "Who on earth would she call?"

Once again, Ida Mae leaned forward, lowering her voice so that no one else could overhear. "She's not the only one in the district with a cell phone. In fact, several other young women have them. And, of course, many among the boys!" Straightening up, Ida Mae brushed some imaginary dust from her sleeve. "So, you see? The preacher might focus his words on the young men, but he should realize that the young women are just as wicked when it comes to worldliness."

Back in Fullerton, there were very few opportunities for young people to interact with *Englischers*. Most of the youth lived on farms, and while there were some non-Amish families that lived scattered throughout their neighborhood, most of them either kept to themselves or were considered friends. The *Englischers* that caused trouble tended to be the tourists who snuck photos, asked silly questions, or invaded their privacy. Fortunately, Fullerton did not have many tourists. Indeed, the tourists tended to flock to Shipshewana instead, thus leaving the Amish in Fullerton to live in a more secured environment without external intrusions.

During the fellowship hour, Catherine stayed with Ida Mae, mostly because Ida Mae remained glued to her side. They talked about everything under the sun, leaving no stone unturned. Or, rather, Ida Mae talked about everything. Catherine seemed to do no more than nod her head and say "*Ja*" once in a while. Several times, while Ida Mae continued to chatter, Catherine caught herself looking around for Henry Tilman, but each time, she silently scolded herself. She knew that he wouldn't show up for the noon meal since he hadn't come to the service, so hoping otherwise was senseless.

Until, of course, Ida Mae finally paused to take a breath after asking Catherine what she did for fun in Fullerton.

"Oh, me?" Catherine was almost startled that Ida Mae had asked her anything at all. "Oh, I…well…it's much quieter than Banthe, I'm sure. Not many tourists."

"Uh huh." Ida Mae didn't sound impressed. "But surely you must do *something* for fun!"

"Well, I help my *maem* at home and we do have quilting parties in the winter." Catherine felt as if she were disappointing Ida Mae with descriptions of her simple life in Fullerton. "Of course, there are singings and I do like to read."

At this, Ida Mae perked up. "Read? What types of books do you read?"

"Romances." She said the word in a whisper, which clearly delighted Ida Mae.

"Oooh. Romances." Ida Mae tucked her hand into Catherine's arm and leaned closer. "I've read a few. I love a good *Englische* romance."

Horrified, Catherine withdrew her arm. "*Nee!*" She would never read an *Englische* romance. That was far too worldly and her parents—not to mention the bishop!—would surely object. "I read Amish romances. I am partial to this one author who retells classic literature."

Ida Mae's excitement died and her eyes glazed over. "Classics? I see."

From the lack of enthusiasm in Ida Mae's voice, Catherine suspected that she *didn't* see and, even more telling, probably didn't even really care. "She's written an entire series. *Lizzie*, *Emma*, *Maryann and Eleanor*, *Fanny*. They're based on Jane Austen's books, but all of them take place in Amish communities."

"Never heard of her," Ida Mae said, clearly uninterested, as she glanced around the room. "So, tell me. Have you met anyone since you've been here?"

Catherine hesitated. For some reason she didn't understand, she didn't feel like telling Ida Mae about having met Henry Tilman. While she knew practically nothing about him, she almost preferred it that way. In her mind, she could imagine all sorts of things pertaining to him. It was like having her own private friend. But she wasn't one to lie so she finally responded with a simple, "Not really. Just one fellow, Henry Tilman. When I was in town with Wilma," she quickly added.

Ida raised an eyebrow. "Henry Tilman, you say?"

"We only spoke for a minute or two."

Ida shrugged in a bored sort of manner. "When his family vacations here, he usually attends this service, but maybe he's visiting another church today."

A deep sense of disappointment washed over Catherine, and immediately she scolded herself. She barely knew the young man, and certainly not well enough to miss him already.

With a wave of her hand, Ida quickly changed the subject. "Well, anyway, you'll have lots more fun here at Banthe and you'll meet tons of new people. There's always something to do and new people to meet!" She started to laugh and talk about some of the frolics and youth gatherings from earlier in the summer. It seemed several of the young men liked to race their buggies along the backroads, something that Catherine thought sounded dangerous but seemed to delight Ida Mae.

"Oh, Catherine!" Ida Mae cooed, tucking her hand once again into the crook of Catherine's arm. "Here comes someone I'd like you to meet!"

A young man, no more than three or four years older than Ida Mae, approached them, a broad smile on his face. While he wasn't entirely unattractive, there was something off putting about his appearance. Catherine couldn't quite put her finger on it. Perhaps it was his too broad of a nose or his wide, thick-lipped mouth. But his eyes, so similar in color to Ida Mae's, danced in a mischievous way.

"This is my *bruder*, John," Ida Mae offered.

He sauntered up to them and gave Catherine an unruly grin. "And you are…?"

"Catherine. Catherine Miller." She noticed the way he looked at her, his grin changing to a playful smirk, which she found odd since she had no previous acquaintance with him.

"I had the pleasure of seeing you in town the other day," he said.

Catherine suddenly remembered having seen him as well, the leering man by the carriage. Surely, he had seen her talking with Henry, although Catherine could not recollect having paid any attention to how long John had stood by his carriage watching them converse.

As if reading her mind, he chuckled. "I look forward to having the pleasure of getting to know you better myself."

The heat rose to her cheeks and she gazed toward the floor.

Sensing the awkward silence that was to ensue, Ida Mae cleared her throat before speaking. "We were just going to take a short walk, weren't we, Catherine? The air is so fresh and there isn't much more to do here."

"Were you now? Well, I'd be happy to walk along with you then!" he exclaimed, inviting himself to join them.

Catherine glanced over her shoulder at Wilma. "I…I really should return to the Andersons," she said. "I am, after all, their guest."

John made a dismissive noise. "*Ach*, Cathy! They

will surely not mind one bit. Guest or not, Sunday afternoons are meant for young people to socialize!" Lightly, he touched her elbow and began guiding her toward the open doors, his sister quickly falling into step beside him. "Now tell me, Cathy…"

She quickly interrupted him. "It's Catherine."

He laughed. "Catherine, Cathy. They're both beautiful names to my ears."

Uncertain how to take that, Catherine remained silent. She didn't want to be rude to Ida Mae's brother, but she simply detested the abbreviated version of her God-given name. She had *never* been called Cathy.

"Now tell me, Catherine," he said, enunciating her name in a teasing way, "have you explored the countryside yet? In particular, the area on the far side of the lake?"

"I have not. We've only just arrived."

"Is that so?" He looked surprised. "Well, I would be remiss if I did not invite you to accompany my sister and me on a ride one day. No one should ever leave Banthe without seeing Moreland Lake from all angles! The view on the far side is much more superior than from this side."

Catherine caught her breath. "You're most kind!" she exclaimed.

Again, he laughed. "You sound surprised."

Once more she felt the heat rising to her cheeks. She hadn't meant it that way. However, she was a little taken aback by his offer. After all, he had only just met her and he must certainly have his own obligations, since the Troyer family were not vacationers in Banthe. Taking her with Ida Mae on a carriage ride around the lake was a generous offer indeed.

"I suggest we go for a ride this evening. What do you say, Catherine?"

She looked around for Wilma. Having just arrived, she wasn't certain it would be proper to accept such an invitation. "I…I must decline. My plans were to stay in and read this evening."

"Read?" John tossed his head back and laughed even harder. "Read what?"

Embarrassed by his reaction, Catherine remained silent, but Ida Mae leaned over and whispered in a loud voice, "Romances, my dear *bruder*. Amish romances."

John turned his head to stare at Catherine, his eyes blazing with mirth. She didn't care one bit for the way he seemed to be mocking her when he said, "I see! Amish romances. Looking for pointers, then?"

She turned her head away, her initial impression of John Troyer having quickly been solidified. If she had thought she didn't particularly care for John when she first saw him leering at her, she was now fairly convinced of it. He was far more worldly than she preferred, and therefore, Catherine remained as guarded as could be in his company until she finally saw Wilma and Duane preparing to leave.

For Catherine, their departure didn't come a moment too soon.

Chapter Five

On Monday, Catherine found her day starting with one disappointment after another.

Shortly after morning prayers and breakfast, she walked into town, hoping that she might run into Henry Tilman. She didn't know where the Tilmans' cottage was located, but she had learned from Ida Mae that they worshipped in the church district, so they must have lived nearby. So why hadn't Henry been in church? Had he decided to visit another church district instead? While their acquaintance was brief, she certainly would have thought Henry might have mentioned if he was leaving town right away. Where could he have gone?

She glanced around the shops in town, her gaze stopping and lingering on the picnic table where they'd met, secretly hoping he might be sitting there. But there was no sign of Henry.

Several times, Catherine went over their conversation and tried to remember what he had specifically said about the frolic. From his mysterious comment that gave no direct answer, she had presumed that he was, indeed, going to be helping. However, it appeared that he was, in fact, gone from the town of Banthe.

Her first disappointment of the day.

And then the second came: John Troyer bicycling along Main Street. To Catherine's dismay, when John spotted her, he immediately abandoned his bicycle, leaned it against a tree, and fell into step beside her. While she wasn't opposed to John's company, she did wonder how having him walk with her might appear to other people that they passed on the street. She certainly didn't want people thinking that she was sweet on John Troyer. Plus, she still worried that Henry might show up in town and notice her walking with another man.

While John was too eager to her taste, today he seemed a tad more pleasant and conservative. In fact, the young man proved himself to be amusing company. As he walked beside her, he pointed out various people that he saw, telling her silly stories about each one's background and family.

"And there," he said, leaning close to whisper so that no one else could overhear, "is Noah Bontrager. He's on his third wife, can you imagine!"

"Third wife!" she exclaimed and quickly covered her mouth with her hand. Fortunately, Noah Bontrager was too far away to have witnessed her overstated reaction.

With a very somber expression on his face, John nodded his head. "That's right. And the first two died under the most suspicious of situations."

"Oh, you don't mean…!" She gasped.

But he did not offer any more of the story, merely walking in silence, his heavy boots crunching the gravel beneath with each step.

A few seconds dragged out and Catherine could not

stand the suspense. She touched his arm and leaned over. "Tell me, John! I want to know."

"*Ach*, of course you do!" He winked at her, clearly delighted with her interest in his story. "And so does the entire town. Even the best of Christians want to know the worst of gossip, *ja*?"

Immediately, Catherine sobered. His comment stung, even though she suspected he meant it in jest. Still, she wished she could take back her request for more information about Noah Bontrager and his first two wives. How could she have fallen victim to John's trickery?

Unaware of the change in her mood, John continued talking, demonstrating that even the best of Christians also wanted to *spread* the worst of gossip. "*Ja*, quite the mystery. The first wife was in an accident in the fields."

Silence.

"That's it?" Catherine couldn't mask her disappointment. "I admit that I'm sad to hear that, but there is nothing mysterious about it. Unfortunately, it happens quite frequently."

Artfully, John raised an eyebrow, just one, and peered at her in an off-hand type of way. "Really? How about if she was found under the *front* of the baler!"

As if on automatic pilot, Catherine stopped walking as soon as she heard his words. "The front of the baler? Why, that's rather unusual, *ja*?"

"Noah claimed she was driving the mules while he loaded the baler. But still," John said, lowering his voice again, "how would she have fallen forward unless, perhaps, she was pushed?"

Catherine gasped.

"No one thought much of it, you see, until his second wife fell from the hayloft. She was in the hospital for quite some time."

Catherine tilted her head. "Was he with her then?"

"Oh, *ja*! Every day, never left. Not once." He glanced around to make certain that they were not near anyone. "As if he was afraid she might wake up and speak. Perhaps, Catherine, she might have told that he pushed her!"

Another gasp and she turned her head to look at Noah Bontrager, who stood outside of the small post office, sorting through his mail. "Why would anyone marry him with such a past?" she asked in a hushed voice.

"Indeed." John said this with staunch conviction, lifting his head in such a way that he appeared confident that the third wife would find herself in the same situation as his wife number one and wife number two: dead.

The thrill of the possible scandal, however, was short-lived. After Catherine and John reached the only restaurant in town, he paused.

"Mayhaps you'd care to join me for a coffee or soda?" he asked, gesturing toward the restaurant.

But Catherine was quick to shake her head. "*Danke*, but *nee*. I've some errands and then I best be getting back to the cottage." The truth was that she wanted to stop at the small store next to the restaurant, for Wilma had heard tell that they offered a nice selection of suitable books for purchase. However, even if she hadn't wanted to peruse their bookshelves, she would have declined his invitation anyway. After all, Catherine knew better than to let John think she might be interested in courting him.

"Then I shall be on my way, I reckon." He sounded

disappointed, thrusting his hands into his front pockets and taking a few steps backward in the direction where he had left his bicycle.

"Please tell Ida Mae I said hello," Catherine added before she turned around and headed for the store. Despite suspecting that John was still watching her, Catherine refused to look back, fearing that such a gesture might be misinterpreted by John. Instead, she hurried into the store, welcoming the respite from his unruly tongue.

The bell over the store's door rang as Catherine shut the door and looked around. There were aisles of yarn and fabric, even floss for embroidery. The assortment of bright colors immediately comforted Catherine and she wandered over to a table full of clearance cloth patches. Oh! How she could make such a pretty quilt from the different pieces, she thought.

"May I help you, then?" a dark-haired young woman asked.

Startled, Catherine shook her head to clear her thoughts, trying to remember why, exactly, she was there. "Oh, *ja*, please. I heard you sell books here?"

The woman pushed her wire-rimmed glasses further up the bridge of her nose and pointed down the back aisle. "All along that back wall is our book section. If you can't find something in particular, my *maem* can order it."

Thanking the woman with a pleasant "*Danke*," Catherine hurried in the direction that she had pointed. The aisle was long with tall shelving on both sides, each filled with beautiful books. For a moment, Catherine shut her eyes. She took a deep breath and felt her lungs filling with the wonderful smell of books. Oh, how that made it so much easier to forget John's story about Noah Bontrager and his tragic past marriages!

When Catherine opened her eyes, she began to walk down the aisle, taking her time to examine the different titles. She raised her hand and let her fingers run along the spines of the books, wondering what mysteries, adventures, and romances they contained.

There was a large section of Bibles and hymnbooks. Catherine passed by those quickly. Next was a very healthy young adult and children's section. That, too, was not what she wanted to read. But as she approached the last third of the aisle she spotted it: the romance section.

"Oh!" she gasped to herself as her eyes scanned the different titles.

Each book was arranged in alphabetical order, and she scanned each title by every author. Some of the names she recognized; others were new to her. She paused and pulled out a small Amish novella, quickly flipping it over and reading the description on the back cover.

"Oh!" she gasped when she realized the little novella was part of a six-book series and each book was only a hundred or so pages for seven dollars each! Catherine rolled her eyes and shoved the book back onto the shelf. "Who would ever pay almost fifty dollars to read a six-hundred-page book!" she said aloud to no one in particular. Why, *she* could think of many better things to do with her money…such as buy eight or nine full-length novels!

"So you like the Amish romances, eh?"

Catherine looked up and saw the store worker approach. For a moment, Catherine panicked, wondering what the woman would think. Had she heard her comment? Or would she think less of her because she liked reading Amish romances? So many people among the Amish clicked their tongues and shook their heads at the Amish romance books. But, just as quick as she panicked, she realized that the shelves were stocked full of those books for a reason, and that reason was far greater than *just* Catherine Miller's interest. Obviously other people enjoyed reading them, too.

"Does anyone buy those little novellas for so much money?"

The woman shrugged. "Not particularly. Frankly, I don't care for that author." Disapprovingly, the woman shook her head and frowned. "I met her once. She came to Banthe a few times to hold book signings. Why, the tourists that came flooding into town!"

Catherine cocked her head. "But that's a good thing, *ja*?"

"*Ja*, right *gut* for business. But she wasn't very kind to my *aendi*, Jennifer Esh, who hosted a dinner for her and her *Englische* readers. Word spreads quickly when one of those authors doesn't know anything about us or isn't kind to the Amish communities."

This was surprising news to Catherine's ears. She had never thought of it that way.

"Oh, *ja*, there's a dark side to the writing world, especially those authors who write Amish romances," the woman said. "Why, we have a computer connected to the Internet. Up front, you know? For ordering stock?"

Catherine nodded, hanging onto every word that the woman was saying. She had known others who used the computer and her father preached at home and the bishop at church about the dangers of the Internet. But she had never personally seen one in use.

"*Ja*, vell, you should see the garbage that's out there. Pure junk!" The woman waved her hand dismissively. "Why, these *authors*! They just copy other authors, using their names and book titles and the images on the covers. They're just pure silliness. For instance, I saw a whole series about goats!"

"What. Ever!" Catherine gasped in disbelief.

"Uh huh!" The woman shook her head. "Amish goats. What on earth do people need to know about Amish goats! And the woman on the front wore an Indiana prayer *kapp* but was supposed to be from Lancaster County, Pennsylvania! And then there are some about mail-order Amish brides! Have you ever heard of such ridiculousness? And who would want to read such rubbish?"

"Oh, help." Catherine felt a wave of disappointment at what the woman was telling her. If what she said was true, and Catherine had no reason to suspect otherwise, Catherine could not blame people for mocking Amish romance books. She felt dispirited that such unscrupulous people would try to write deceitful stories about the Amish, most likely to just try to make some money rather than because they truly held a passion for the people about whom they wrote.

For many years now, Catherine had found Amish novels so interesting and entertaining. She had discovered a great relevance in the books, enjoying them for their light messages of faith and hope as well as their emphasis on family, community, and God, all values shared by her Amish community. The fact that there was, indeed, a dark side to this left her disillusioned.

The woman sighed. "We try to limit our inventory to the *good* books from *real* authors, even if they aren't always kind to the Amish communities, you see." She motioned toward a section of books farther down the aisle. "Have you read any of these?"

"Oh, *ja*. I used to enjoy that author, but her latest books…" Catherine pretended to yawn.

The young woman laughed. "Same stories over and over, ain't so." She took a few more steps, contemplating the books farther down. "Ah, these are right *gut* ones! I sure do like this one author. Good, clean, light, and accurate." She pulled out a paperback book with a red cover. A pretty woman in a light blue dress stood before a barn, her stiff prayer covering properly adjusted on her head and a smile on her face. On her arm, she held a basket filled with fresh vegetables and behind her stood a small herd of Holstein cows. "This just came out and I enjoyed it!"

Catherine took the book from the woman, glanced over the back of the cover. "I'll try her. I'm almost finished with my latest book, and I'm always looking for new authors." But, based on what the woman said, Catherine knew that she would have to be much more selective in what books she selected to read. She certainly didn't want to read authors who didn't care about corrupting impressionable, eager minds who might not know better than to question the material they read.

"*Ja*, just got to be careful what you pick up to read. I like my money to go toward the good authors, not the ones who know next to nothing about the Amish way of life but claim to know it all!"

Catherine couldn't agree more. She glanced a little farther down the aisle. "Oh! Here's the book I'm reading now!" She pulled out the novel from her bag, showing it to the woman. "What do you think of this author?" She was eager to know that one of her favorite authors was held in high regard by this like-minded young woman.

"Oh, *ja*, I enjoy her writing." The woman smiled. "A kind woman, for sure and certain, and rather knowledgeable about the Amish. She always writes with respect."

Relieved, Catherine sighed. "Oh, I so agree! Why I love her Jane Austen adaptations in the Amish setting. *Lizzie* and *Emma* are my two favorites!"

"Did you know that she has a new book? *Maryanne and Eleanor*, I believe it's called. Care for me to set aside a copy for you when they arrive?"

Without any hesitation, Catherine nodded.

After she finished browsing the aisles, Catherine paid for the book, thanking her new acquaintance, Naomi Mast, for such sage advice.

With her book tucked under her arm, Catherine stepped outside, eager to head back to the cottage. She had spent far too much time in the store, as any avid reader is wont to do, of course. But she'd have to make haste on her walk back so that she could help Wilma with chores, and bumped into none other than Noah Bontrager himself. For a moment, she caught her breath and could do nothing more than stare. With his deep-set wrinkles and long white beard, he looked as menacing as John Troyer had made him out to be.

Catherine pushed herself against the doorframe, her back against the hard wood, so that he could pass. She feared that he might actually brush against her, but instead he merely tilted his head and looked at her.

"You're that Miller girl, *ja*? Visiting with the Andersons?"

She swallowed and nodded her head slowly.

The older man squinted his eyes as he looked at her. "Duane and Wilma Anderson?"

Again, Catherine nodded, her heart pounding. After what John Troyer had told her, she felt frightened to be near this man.

But just as she began to inch away, the man smiled and his blue eyes twinkled in delight. "I grew up with Duane Anderson!" He laughed, the noise sounding like a good-hearted guffaw. "We ran with the same supper gang." He winked at her. "Not a finer man walks the earth, I tell you. I sure will look forward to catching up with him." He glanced over Catherine's shoulder and seemed to make eye contact with someone. "Edith! *Kum esse!*"

A middle-aged woman wearing a magenta-colored dress with a black apron pinned at the waist emerged from behind a display. When she noticed Noah standing with Catherine, she lit up and hurried over to join them.

"This young gal," Noah said, "is staying with the Andersons. Duane Anderson. You remember me telling you that I heard he might be coming this a-ways to help with the frolics?"

"Oh, *ja*!" She smiled and nodded.

"We must invite them to grill one night, don't you think?"

Edith beamed at the suggestion. "That's a fine idea, Noah. Perhaps tomorrow evening since the work frolic is on Thursday?"

Catherine's mouth opened, just enough that she could not hide her surprise. The joy shared between these two elderly people could not be denied, but she wondered how, exactly, Edith had come to marry Noah, especially given the circumstances of his previous wives' demise? And now, would Catherine be expected to have dinner with them, too? Surely she would learn more about John Troyer's story then!

As soon as Noah and Edith left the store, Catherine found she was shaking. While they seemed like nice enough people, given their past, certainly something dark and mysterious must lurk beneath the surface. Perhaps, she thought, if I go to dinner there, I'll learn more about Noah Bontrager's tragic past!

On her walk back to the lake cottage, Catherine held her newly acquired book pressed against her chest. She hadn't seen Henry Tilman and she had learned more than she wanted to know about the books she loved so much. However, she knew that she would only need to sink into a plush chair, curl up, and lose herself in the pages of her new book—written by a reputable author!—in order to forget the earlier disappointments of that bright and sunny Monday.

Chapter Six

"Tell me, tell me, Catherine!" Ida Mae gushed as she hurried to the table where Catherine sat shelling peas. "What did you learn about Noah Bontrager last night?" She slid onto the bench and positioned herself across from her friend. "I'm all ears!"

Catherine gave a soft laugh and looked up at Ida Mae. Her eyes were wide and bright with expectation as she leaned forward, her hands clasped in front of her. The eagerness with which Ida Mae wanted to learn about Noah almost made Catherine chuckle, but she kept a stoic and stern face. "*Ach*! It was the most astonishing of visits!" she confessed, tossing the empty shells of a peapod into a bowl. She furrowed her brow and scowled playfully. "The most troublesome of discoveries was made!"

Ida Mae clapped her hands, delighted with the hint of some good gossip.

As Catherine had simultaneously feared and desired, she had been invited to the Bontragers' house for supper Tuesday evening. Earlier in the day, Ida Mae had sent word that Catherine should join her for some cross-stitching on that same afternoon—a message sent by none other than her brother John! Catherine had no choice but to reply that she could not, and she made John promise to let Ida Mae know that she had been invited to join Duane and Wilma at the Bontragers.

"Noah Bontrager!" John had exclaimed. "Aren't you worried that you might be his next victim?"

While she had known that John was partially teasing, she had also felt a thrill at the idea of such an adventure.

Now it was Wednesday afternoon. Not even five minutes earlier, Ida Mae had showed up at the Andersons' door, eager to learn all about her visit with the Bontragers. She even told Catherine that she had hurried through her chores just so that she could visit with her.

"Please do tell me!" Ida Mae demanded impatiently, learning forward. Her eyes, so light and gray-green, just like John's, practically glowed in anticipation as she waited for Catherine's story.

"We arrived," Catherine started, her voice full of mystery and suspense. She hesitated and lowered her voice. "The farm yard was cluttered with debris and weeds. The laundry had yet to be taken in from the line. And the hinge on the screen door was in dire need of being oiled."

Ida Mae leaned forward, her eyes growing even bigger as she stared at Catherine. "And?"

Catherine glanced around as if to ensure that no one was nearby, even though she knew that Duane and Wilma had walked to the grocery store and wouldn't be back for another hour. "Well, inside the house—which is very dark, by the way!—that Noah Bontrager sat in his chair, his wife doing all of the work in the kitchen. She worked by herself, refusing all help from me and Wilma. In fact, she kept glancing furtively at Noah as if she feared that he might reprimand her in front of us!"

Ida Mae pressed her lips together disapprovingly. "I knew it! He's an awful man! Probably yells at her all the time!"

"And then..." Catherine interrupted her, glancing around once again in an overly exaggerated manner and lowering her voice. "... When Edith called us to the table, he arose from his seat and slowly crossed the room to take his place at the head of the table." She paused, giving Ida Mae time to catch her breath in anticipation of the next part of the story. "You wouldn't believe what he did next!" she whispered.

Ida Mae practically fidgeted in her seat. "What?" she breathed in a husky voice. "What did he do, Catherine?"

"Well, he bowed his head for the silent prayer before starting to pass around the food. Can you imagine? Such a scoundrel!"

"Oh, Catherine!" Ida Mae couldn't help but laugh. She tossed a nearby hand towel at her friend. "You're teasing me, I reckon!"

Catherine laughed as she caught the towel. Yes, she had entered the Bontragers' house afraid of what she might learn, but, as it turned out, it wasn't what she had expected at all. Noah had been the perfect host, telling funny stories about when he and Duane were younger, and the four adults sat together and laughed for the greater part of the evening. "Honestly, Ida Mae, the Bontragers are lovely people. Noah is the most delightful of men and appears truly devoted to his wife. In fact, I was surprised to learn that they have been married almost ten years! The way John told it, I'd have thought he cycled through wives every few years!"

"To be fair," Ida Mae said somberly, "Edith is his third wife!"

But Catherine shook her head, not at the memory but at what she had initially thought about the innocent man. "Your *bruder* told a tall tale, I fear. And if he hadn't been so kind as to keep me company during my walk into town, I might find myself upset with him. But I'm sure that people talk and stories spread. I, however, will not be a part of that cycle, so you must correct your *bruder* at once."

Ida Mae pursed her lips, her dimples becoming more pronounced, and rolled her eyes toward the ceiling. "Now what fun is that, Catherine? Life is so much more interesting with a little mystery in it!"

But Catherine did not agree. "Not if it injures someone's reputation, I dare say. He's a fine man, and here I would've avoided that man for the rest of our time here at Banthe! Just because of your *bruder*'s idle talk."

Ida Mae stiffened at the reference to John and tilted her chin in defiance. "Perhaps you should still avoid him, Catherine. Noah Bontrager certainly is not as engaging as my *bruder*, wouldn't you say? Unless, of course, you are interested in becoming the fourth *fraa* of Bontrager."

At that comment, Catherine glanced toward the window as if looking for something or someone, anything to avoid giving a response.

But Ida Mae remained persistent. "Catherine? I asked you a question," she said in a light but unwavering tone.

"Have you?"

"About…my *bruder*?"

For a long moment, Catherine paused. She had no interest in John Troyer, especially after his gossip about Noah. A man who would spread rumors, regardless of whether they were grounded in some degree of truth, was not a man to be trusted. Yet she did not want to say this to her new friend. After all, Ida Mae clearly held her brother in high regard. "Oh, Ida Mae!" she sighed in an exasperated tone. "I'm not in a position to comment on your *bruder* John. I spent no more time with him than I did with Henry Tilman!"

"Henry Tilman?" Ida Mae looked taken aback. "Has he returned, then? To Banthe?"

There was a look in Ida Mae's eyes that matched the acerbic tone of her voice. Her words may have been innocent on the surface, but there was an undercurrent to them, a not-so-gentle reminder that Henry Tilman was gone from the town and, therefore, not available as a suitor. Her brother, however, was in Banthe.

"*Nee*, he has not returned," Catherine admitted. "At least not that I am aware." She knew that she couldn't hide the disappointment from her voice and averted her eyes from Ida Mae's.

"So, *mayhaps* you should tuck aside your silly romance books and read some of my favorite books," Ida Mae said, a gay tone to her voice once again. "They are fun and light-hearted mysteries set in Amish communities! I've brought some for you to read, Catherine."

"Mysteries?"

The tone of the conversation shifted. For the next few minutes, Ida Mae continued to comment on several books by one of her favorite authors, telling Catherine about the plots and characters, the issue of Henry Tilman clearly forgotten. At least by Ida Mae. By the time Catherine's spirits began to lift, Ida Mae was finishing her description of her fifth favorite book.

"My word, Ida Mae! And you read all of those books in the past month?"

Her friend nodded. "I did indeed!"

"When do you have the time?"

Ida Mae shrugged. "I've had plenty of spare time, Catherine, since I've stopping running with that Anna! You know her, *ja*? You sat with her at church before we met."

Truth be told, Catherine hadn't remembered the names of either of the two women from church. She wasn't even certain she had been introduced to them. But, rather than sidetrack Ida Mae, Catherine merely nodded her head.

"Well, you see, she accepted a buggy ride home from a youth gathering with Paul Troyer—a distant cousin of mine, I believe—but, after three weeks of riding with him, she rode home with Aaron Hostetler. Just like that!" The expression on Ida Mae's face bespoke her disapproval. "Can you imagine? Why, everyone was rather upset by how she dismissed one suitor for another with hardly any thought to their feelings or her reputation!" Ida Mae lifted her chin and adopted a stern look. "She's not well thought of by the men now, I can assure you of that. And the other women are hard pressed to speak to her for fear that people might start thinking that they, too, are like-minded."

"Oh, help!" Catherine muttered, shocked by Ida Mae's confession, although she wasn't certain whether her distress came more from Anna's behavior or Ida Mae's propensity to spread gossip!

"But don't you worry none," Ida Mae said, a fresh smile on her lips. "If anyone were to speak about you in a similar manner…"

"Me!" Catherine gasped, shocked at Ida Mae's comment.

"…I'd defend you, Catherine!" she continued nonchalantly.

"Why would anybody speak about me? I haven't accepted a ride home from anyone," she gushed, her voice full of anxiety. "Nor do I intend to!" The last thing she wanted to do was create any sort of problems, especially in a community foreign to her. Neither she nor the Andersons would want to offend anyone. And despite her one exchange with Henry, Catherine had no real desire to actually *live* one of her romance novels. Oh, she longed for a bit of adventure, yes, but romance? The thought scared her a little. It was much safer to live vicariously through the pages of a good book!

"Well, you were seen talking with Henry Tilman on one day and then walking with my *bruder*, John, on another." Ida Mae gave her an innocent look when she paused as if to let her words sink in. "But, as long as we're friends, no one would dare speak against your character. I wouldn't let it happen!" She gave a light laugh and added, "It simply wouldn't do for you to have a soiled reputation!"

Upset by Ida Mae's comment, Catherine began to wring her hands as she kept them on her lap and out of her friend's sight. How could her reputation be tainted just from talking with Henry and walking with John? Yet, Ida Mae's reassurance helped alleviate some of the stress. Catherine knew that her friend was well thought of among the youths, and if Ida Mae spoke to Catherine's character, not a person would question her.

For a few moments, they sat in silence. Catherine concentrated on shelling the peas while Ida Mae merely observed her working.

"All of this talk about suitors and courting," Ida Mae said at last. "That Anna truly ruined her chances of being courted by any reputable man. I wonder what type of man she will wind up with after what she did." Leaning forward, Ida Mae stared at Catherine until she had no choice but to look up and meet her gaze. "And what about you?" she asked. "What type of man do you like?"

"Me?" When it was obvious that Catherine had not misunderstood Ida Mae, she gave a nervous little laugh. "Oh, I'm sure I wouldn't know."

Ida Mae seemed to ponder her response for a long, drawn-out minute. "I suppose I can envision you with someone adventurous. Perhaps a bit aloof in person but rather lively and dedicated in private."

Catherine made a face at her. "Dedicated? Lively? Those are terrible unromantic adjectives!"

"Ah, so you like romance!"

Flustered, Catherine felt the color rise to her cheeks. She had never really given much thought to her preference in men. She knew that she favored Henry Tilman. He was, after all, tall, witty, and rather handsome. But Catherine held no false illusions that their acquaintance could develop into any more than just a casual friendship, especially with the little time she had remaining in Banthe. She would return to Fullerton and he remain in Newbury Acres, wherever that was. As for John Troyer, he was far too worldly and brash for Catherine's taste.

In a perfect world, however, she would find herself one of those men like in the books she read. A man who was older and wiser, yet enthralled with her because she was younger and less worldly. Perhaps, as in that last book she read, he would be broody at times like Frederick was. They would have a conflict, perhaps a misunderstanding, that would separate them until the truth was discovered. He would meet up with her when she was walking and profess his love. His ardent passion for her. And then, only then under the shade of the overhanging trees, he would propose to her, waiting for her response before kissing her.

"I...I suppose romance is important for a good match," she managed to admit.

Yet she couldn't help but wonder if that was true. Her own parents were a wonderful example of what a solid match should be. They were kind to each other, respecting each other's opinions and desires. On a few occasions, Catherine caught them laughing over something when they thought no one was looking. Her father treated her mother like a special treasure, making certain that he never bossed her around like some husbands did. He always included her in the decision making and never once scolded her when she disagreed with him. And her mother sought nothing more than to keep her husband comfortable, making him his favorite foods and always having a pot of fresh coffee ready for him.

But was that romance?

"Perhaps your ideal romantic interest is in someone you already know?" Ida Mae teased. "Dare I suggest someone you have met in Banthe?"

"The only romantic ideal that I have is the characters in my books," Catherine responded right away. She did not want to confide her tender feelings for Henry for fear of giving Ida Mae further fodder for gossip. "Anyone I might have met in Banthe is nothing more than a new friend that will soon be parted from my company."

"Characters in a book?" Ida Mae laughed out loud. "Well, reading is a wonderful pastime—you know how I like mysteries!—but I do prefer the company and conversation of a real man, not just one stuck on the pages of a book!"

Catherine didn't want to confess that she knew too few "real men" so her only other option for romance was the fictitious kind. The only men she ever really interacted with were the young men from her own youth, and she had a hard time remembering them as anything other than boys from her school years. Besides, she felt safe letting her heart fall for the heroes in her novels. She was in no hurry to get married, not unless she fell in love first.

Chapter Seven

On the morning of the barn frolic, Ida Mae walked beside Catherine up the lane toward the farm. She had insisted upon sleeping at the lake house the night before so that she could assist in baking bread and pies well into the evening. Now, as they walked, each of them carried the handle of a large wooden crate which contained ten loaves of bread and twelve pies. Walking was difficult, but the crisp morning air kept them cool and their spirits light.

"I wonder what surprises will be in store for us today!" Ida Mae exclaimed. "So many people have arrived in town that I could hardly navigate my way to your house yesterday afternoon. I was almost hit by a horse and buggy, twice!"

"Oh, Ida Mae!" Catherine clicked her tongue and shook her head, playing along with her friend's obvious exaggeration. "You must be more careful!"

"You would think that one of those people might stop to ask if they could give me a ride," she said out loud. "But they all seemed to be in quite the hurry and barely lifted their hand to wave at me, even the two drivers who ran me off the road."

As they approached the main section of the road that led into town, Catherine peered ahead and noticed that there was a lot of activity near the stores. Dark bay horses pulled wagons through the town, each one filled with young men and boys and only a few carrying young women. For the most part, they were all headed in the same direction: toward the barn frolic.

"They appear to have a good turnout, wouldn't you say?" Catherine asked.

"*Ja*, indeed!" Ida Mae stopped walking. "I need a rest, Catherine. This box grows heavier as the morning air lifts."

But they barely set the box upon the ground when a familiar voice called out to Catherine.

Startled, she looked up and squinted, trying to see who might have recognized her. To her surprise, she saw a wagon approach with two young men sitting in the front: Ida's brother, John, and her own brother, James.

"James?" she asked in a happy but confused voice. "Whatever are you doing here? I didn't know you were coming all this way."

As soon as John stopped the horse on the side of the road, James jumped down and, with a sheepish grin, looked from Catherine to Ida Mae. "I thought that more hands would help raise the barn faster, *ja*?"

It was the way that James looked at Ida Mae that caused Catherine to shift her gaze from her brother to her friend. Ida Mae gave a coy smile to James and glanced away, but only for a moment. "You two know each other?"

James nodded. "We've met. Through John."

Catherine accepted his explanation. After all, when

she first met Ida Mae she had learned that John and James were friends.

"Now, girls," John called out from the wagon seat. "Let's hurry along, then! James, put that box in the back. Ida Mae, you help him. And Catherine, you come sit up here. I want to hear all about your visit with the Bontragers this week." He stared at her, his eyes sparkling with delight. "I hear that your impression of Noah differs greatly from mine!"

"It does," she admitted as she placed her foot onto the iron step and pulled herself up. She swung her other leg around and started to climb into the back of the wagon, but John reached for her arm, indicating that she should sit next to him. Startled, she hesitated for a second too long. James and Ida Mae took the back seats, leaving Catherine no choice but to sit beside John.

Once she was situated, John stepped off the foot brake and slapped the reins onto the horse's back. The wagon lurched forward, and Catherine fell against John's arm.

"How do you like my new horse and wagon?" he asked, already forgetting about Noah Bontrager and his request for Catherine to tell him about her opinion of him. "I just bought them this week."

Catherine let her hand remain on the metal bar that acted as an arm rest. The wagon jostled as he drove the horse toward the barn frolic. "It…it's lovely."

"Lovely?" He spat the word out as if it was an insult. "Lovely? I'll have you know, Catherine, that this horse comes from one of the best horse breeders in this area. I had to pay twice the sum that normal boys pay for a new horse. *Mayhaps* even thrice!"

For the briefest of moments, Catherine shut her eyes. With her face directed toward the road, she doubted that John had witnessed her silent rebellion against his prideful remark.

"And this wagon?" He glanced at her and grinned. "It's just the latest model that Aaron Wheeler is making!"

Catherine had no idea who Aaron Wheeler was, but she wasn't about to admit that.

"He made this one just for me, he did! Based on my own design." John glanced at her as if waiting for her reaction. When none came, he added, "It's extra-long, *ja*? Good for hauling things as well as people!"

Pretending to be interested, Catherine glanced over her shoulder. To her surprise, it was longer than most other wagons used by the Amish in her community. In the section behind where Ida Mae and James sat, she could see that John had several buckets and two tool boxes. "So it is, I reckon," she commented as she redirected her attention to the road ahead.

"Figured it was worth spending the extra money." He paused, his hands handling the reins with ease while he looked at her. "Better to spend more now and have it done right the first time around!"

His bravado was wearing thin on Catherine, so she merely looked up at a nearby tree limb and commented on a bird that she saw, hoping to distract John from more discussion about his spending and acquisitions. While his manners were clearly less than what she'd normally stand for, he was Ida Mae's brother, and if for no other reason, that forced her to give him more respect than she would otherwise.

When they pulled up the lane to the Troyers' farm, John quickly drove his buggy alongside the barn and gestured toward one of the younger boys who were managing the horses. "Here now! You!" he called out as he stepped down to the ground. "Make certain to unharness my horse and wash him down, *ja*? And put the harness in the back of my wagon so it doesn't get lost or mixed up with another."

He didn't wait for a response before he turned his attention to Catherine. He held out his hand for her to take, making her exit from the wagon easier. When she managed to stand beside him, she noticed that he hesitated before releasing her hand. In that single moment, she raised her eyes to look at him and noticed that he, too, was watching her.

"Perhaps you might permit me to drive you back home afterward?" he asked in a low voice.

"Oh, that would be right *gut*!" The thought of walking all that way to the lake after a long day of working in the sun did not entice her, and she could only beam at John for his thoughtfulness. Perhaps, she reconsidered, he was not such a bad sort after all.

They walked toward the farmhouse and parted company, the men heading toward the area where the pile of lumber and other men stood, while Ida Mae guided Catherine toward the house. They crossed the plain cement patio and were just about to open the screen door when Ida Mae paused and looked back toward the gathering of men.

"What is it?" Catherine asked.

She turned back toward her friend and smiled, shrugging her shoulders in a dismissive way. "I just think it's rather nice how your *bruder* came all this way to help my uncle."

"He's a good sort, for sure and certain," Catherine replied. Although from the look on Ida Mae's face, she suspected that she wasn't disclosing any new information.

"He's your oldest *bruder*, *ja*?"

Catherine reached for the handle of the screen door and opened it. "*Ja*, the oldest. And set on being a farmer. Like my *daed*."

For a moment, Ida Mae seemed to contemplate this as she followed Catherine into the house. But she asked no further questions about James.

Inside the kitchen, the other women were already busy at work. In no time at all, both Ida Mae and Catherine were tasked with various assignments: setting up the tables for the noon meal, taking pitchers of water to the men, minding the smaller children who played outside. There was always something to do, and time, as always, seemed to fly.

By the time Catherine thought to look up and observe the progress of the men, she was surprised to see that all four walls of the barn were already in place. Many of the younger men were busy nailing down the floor to the hayloft while the older ones were focused on the roof.

Ida Mae stopped short. Her arms were full of the plates that she had been instructed to set upon the table. "What is it?" she asked, but her gaze followed Catherine's and she caught her breath. "Oh!"

The structure was just a skeleton, the frame an outline in fresh, creamy lumber, but oh, what a sight it was! The men that crawled atop it, their white shirts and straw hats contrasting with their dark pants, almost looked like ants from where the two women stood. The feat of raising a barn was admirable, but so was the fact that the entire community had joined together to help the Troyer family.

It was a spectacular reminder of how wonderful their lives truly were.

One of the older Troyer women exited the kitchen

door and walked the length of the porch to where the large bell hung above the roofline. She reached for the thick rope that hung from it and tugged…once, twice. The bell rang out. From the paddocks behind the house, the shouts of the children could be heard as they ran toward the area where the tables were set up and waiting for them. The men began to descend from the barn, many of them wiping the sweat off their brows and almost all of them wearing smiles on their faces.

"Ah! Look at this!" Duane said as he approached the table. "Enough food to replenish our energy for the afternoon, *ja*?" He laughed at his own comment, but the two men walking beside him smiled and nodded.

After the men were seated, the women standing at the ready behind them, they took a moment to bow their heads and give silent thanks to God for the plentiful and nourishing food that he had seen fit to provide for them. And then, the prayer over, the conversation started again, this time even more animated than before, with the occasional burst of laughter. The women hovered nearby, quick to refill water cups or replenish any empty platters of food.

Catherine stood behind a row of young men, hardly paying attention when someone called out for water. She snapped out of her daydream and hurried over to the man.

"Make a fellow wait for water?" a teasing voice said.

She blinked and stared at the pleasant face that smiled at her. It took her a minute to realize that she was standing by Henry Tilman's side. "Henry!" she exclaimed, a blush covering her cheeks right away when she realized that several people had heard her and were turning their heads and their attention to her.

"It is I, indeed, Catherine," he said in a playful tone. "Or, at least, it was when I last checked!"

She took his cup and refilled it. Slowly. "I presumed you had left Banthe when I didn't see you at church."

His eyes darted to observe the slow manner in which she poured his water. A smile teased his lips. "I had an out-of-town errand," he said, returning his eyes to look at her.

"Oh?" Her hands trembled. Certainly, he had gone to church in another district, perhaps to visit with a young woman who had captured his attention. She felt a wave of disappointment wash over her, for she hadn't thought before now that he might already be courting someone.

Henry glanced behind her and his smile broadened. "And there is my errand now." He motioned with his hand, and Catherine turned to look in that direction.

A young woman, no more than three years older than she, approached them. She was tall, willowy, and with pretty green eyes that stared at Henry first and then turned to Catherine. When she smiled, her face lit up, and several other young Amish men took notice.

"Here you are!" she said in a sing-song like voice.

Catherine felt as if her heart deflated.

"Have you been looking for me then?" Henry asked. "Well, if so, you must not have looked too hard." He glanced toward the barn structure.

"You tease so!" the woman laughed. Then she turned her attention toward Catherine again. "Are you going to introduce me, Henry? Or shall I just stand here in suspense, waiting for you to show your manners?"

"Of course, Ellie." He cleared his throat and let his eyes fall upon Catherine once again.

By this time, the color had drained from her face,

and she wished for nothing more than to scurry away and hide herself in the kitchen behind a tower of dirty plates and bowls.

"Catherine, I would like to introduce you to Ellie," he said, dragging out each word much in the same manner that she had drawn out pouring his water. "Ellie is my only sister."

At the word *sister*, Catherine frowned for just a moment. She digested the word, repeating it in her mind as if to convince herself that that was, indeed, what he had said. When she realized that she had not misunderstood him, she broke into a warm, friendly grin and reached to shake Ellie's hand.

"Such a pleasure to meet you." And she meant it with all sincerity.

Ellie tried to hide a coy smirk as she shifted her gaze from Catherine to Henry and then back to Catherine. "Likewise."

Henry glanced toward his empty plate of food and coughed into his hand. "I reckon I best get some food before it's all gone," he said. "Perhaps, however, you might arrange to go walking tomorrow, Ellie, with Catherine. I know a particularly nice path from town toward the far side of the lake."

No sooner had he said that than he returned his attention to the table and platters of food that had passed by him. Ellie, however, quickly concurred with Henry that a nice walk around the lake would be the best of activities in the late morning.

Catherine could hardly believe her good fortune. Not only had Henry returned to Banthe, but his sister appeared to be particularly lovely and amiable to a friendship.

Chapter Eight

"*Kum*, Catherine! Don't be such a goose!"

Catherine stood on one side of the kitchen table with John, James, and Ida Mae standing on the other. She had been sitting with Duane and Wilma while she read her book when the trio arrived at the lake cottage. She hadn't been expecting them and was surprised when they asked her to go for a carriage ride around the lake. Duane and Wilma quietly excused themselves, leaving the four young people alone to discuss their plans.

Catherine, however, had no desire to go riding around the lake. At least not today when she already had plans. But Ida Mae insisted.

"I don't want to go for a drive around the lake," Catherine replied, politeness escaping her voice. She wasn't used to confrontational situations, but she was beginning to feel as if the three of them were ganging up on her. Their persistence was grating on her nerves. Even though it wasn't any of their business, she finally added, "Besides, I already have a commitment with Ellie Tilman. She asked me to go walking this morning."

John removed his straw hat and ran his fingers

through his unruly, and very unevenly cut, hair. "The Tilmans?" He said the name as if he were spitting.

Catherine lifted her chin. "Ellie and Henry Tilman, to be exact."

"Well, don't that beat all!" John chuckled under his breath. He shook his head and clicked his tongue three times, reminding Catherine of one of the elderly women in her own church district.

Feeling affronted by his reaction, Catherine scowled. "And I promised to go with them. How would that make me look if I wasn't here when they showed up?"

John slapped his straw hat against his thigh and turned his head so that she couldn't see his expression. Ida Mae pouted, the expression of disappointment unmistakable on her face. Even James looked downtrodden.

"The Tilmans, you say?" John turned back toward Catherine, his eyes sparkling as if he was enjoying this discussion. "Seems you have yourself a bit of a problem there."

She cringed and braced herself as she asked, "And how is that, John?"

He leaned forward and stared directly into her eyes. She had never noticed how his eyes were a light gray-green color that looked like the edge of the lake water. A bit murky and not necessarily very becoming. "Why, Catherine, I saw them not even twenty minutes ago, driving their two-seater through town the opposite way of the lake. From the looks of how they were dressed, they were going on a visit somewhere."

Catherine caught her breath and tightened her shoulders. She could hardly believe John's words. "Why on earth would they do that?"

Casually, he shrugged. "*Mayhaps* they forgot or something came up."

"They wouldn't do that!" she gasped. How disappointing! She had been looking forward to spending time with Henry and Ellie. Crestfallen, she sank down onto one of the kitchen chairs.

"Just goes to show you what type of friends they are," John quipped as he slid his hat back on his head and pushed his hands into his front pockets. "And you were worried about your reputation?"

Catherine scowled and glared at him.

Ignoring her brother's snarky comment, Ida Mae bounced on the balls of her feet as she clapped her hands together. "*Wunderbarr*! Then you can come with us!" She sounded like a schoolgirl. "What fun would it be to drive around the lake without you, Catherine? You simply must join us. What else will you do? Sit home all day?"

But she wasn't convinced yet.

One glance out of the front windows confirmed that it was a gorgeous day. The azure blue sky was crisp and clean; only a few scattered white clouds gently dabbed against the otherwise pristine backdrop to a perfect summer day. Perhaps Ida Mae had a point, Catherine thought to herself. If John had, indeed, seen the Tilmans driving away from town, it would do her no good to sit inside all day, pining for Henry when, clearly, he had forgotten about his request for his sister to arrange a walk with her.

"Please, Catherine?" James gave her a pleading look. He glanced at Ida Mae and mouthed the word *please* one more time.

With a sigh, Catherine finally nodded and reluctantly acquiesced. For her brother's sake as well as Ida Mae's, she would go with them. "I suppose you're right. If Henry and Ellie went for a drive already…"

Not even half an hour later, Catherine found herself sitting next to John in the front of a two-seater open carriage. She had argued at first that it wouldn't be proper and why couldn't they all ride in James's carriage. But John insisted for he drove his new horse, a beautiful chestnut Standardbred, and made certain to remind her repeatedly about how expensive the horse was. Behind her, in another carriage, Ida Mae sat beside James, neither one of them at a loss for words or smiles. Miserably, Catherine sat beside John, regretting her decision to accompany them.

"Now look over there, Cathy!" John said, pointing toward a low tree branch that hung over the road. "Just through the trees you can see the water's edge."

She scowled at his use of a far too familiar nickname—and one she wasn't partial to! No one had ever called her that before, and she didn't care for it one bit.

John, however, didn't seem to notice. Instead, he pointed toward the lake that could barely be seen through the trees. "We'll be on the other side of the lake, and just wait until you see the view from that ridge up there!"

Catherine squinted, barely able to see the shimmering water through the branches.

"It's beautiful, once we move beyond the town proper!" He slapped the reins against the back of the horse and made a clicking noise with his tongue. "Gid up!"

The horse tossed its head and picked up the pace, the carriage jostling so that Catherine had to hang onto the little iron railing that kept her from falling out. In the process, she pressed against John and he laughed.

No sooner had the town come into sight than Catherine noticed the man and woman walking down the road toward them: Henry and Ellie. From the looks of it, they were headed toward the house where the Andersons stayed.

"Oh!" She gasped and quickly turned around, too aware that they were staring at her as she rode past them in the open buggy next to John Troyer. "Oh, John! Stop the carriage!" She grabbed his arm. "Please! There are the Tilmans!"

But John did the opposite of her request. Instead of slowing down, he let the reins go slack and the horse ran even faster. "Whoa!" he cried out, but did nothing to actually slow the horse.

"John! I insist!" Bewildered, she sat on her knees, peering after the disappearing figures. She turned to glare at John. "Stop right now or I'll jump out!"

By this point, the horse was going far too fast, and even if he had tried, John couldn't have stopped it. Catherine had no choice but to swing around, grab his arm, and hold on. She knew that several people walking through town must have seen the spectacle of the runaway horse, the man, and the woman. Without doubt, rumors would fly, and Catherine felt as if her heart sank to her stomach. Without any intention of doing so, she had most certainly just created the very thing she had hoped to avoid: gossip.

By the time John was finally able to slow the horse, they had traveled too far away from the town for Catherine to disembark and make her way toward the Tilmans.

Distressed, she crossed her arms over her chest and pouted. "Why did you tell me they were gone?" Her anger was so great that she could barely even look at him. No one had ever deceived her in such a manner! In hindsight, she realized that she never should have trusted him in the first place. Once a liar, always a liar.

"Now, Cathy," he said in a calm voice, "I meant no harm. I did see them out. Perhaps I misunderstood their direction."

"You said they were driving out of town! Clearly that wasn't true."

He gave a casual shrug. "My mistake," he admitted without actually sounding apologetic. "But it is for the better. Would you be so selfish as to deny James the company of my sister? Clearly you can see that they are *ferhoodled*!"

Catherine pursed her lips, still angry with him. "They didn't need me to go along with them!" If she had not come along, the three of them could have made the trip in one buggy. John's mistake, if that was indeed what it was, had most certainly spoiled her relationship with Ellie and Henry, two people Catherine wanted to spend more time with for her own purposes. Judging from the way James and Ida Mae conversed, her brother needed little help in promoting his affections to the young woman.

"Besides, you have no idea about those Tilmans." John scowled as he shook his head. "An awful lot, really."

"Awful?" Despite her disappointment, her curiosity was suddenly piqued. Admittedly, she knew nothing about the Tilman family. Perhaps, like Ida Mae's Amish mystery books, there was a secret in the Tilman's closet, she thought as she turned to look at John. "Why would you say such a thing?"

He scoffed, slapping the reins against the back of the horse so that, this time, it started walking down the lane. "Why, they live in Newbury Acres, you know. Their *daed* has the largest dairy farm in the town and a rather renowned woodworking shop."

"There's nothing awful about that!" Catherine cried in defense of the Tilmans. Success did not make people sinners. It was what they did with that success that often invited evil and sin into their lives.

But John was not easily convinced. "Newbury Acres is a strange place. I've been there once and I've heard many stories. Eerie, really. It's an Amish community without really being Amish at all."

Catherine rolled her eyes. "That doesn't even make sense! Besides, you cannot hold two people responsible for an entire community!"

John gave her a blank, disinterested look. "All right then. How about this? Their *maem* died under mysterious circumstances, Cathy. Ellie had been sent away and suddenly the *maem* died, despite having no sickness. And their *daed* never remarried. Instead, he just works all the time, from sunup to well after sundown. In fact, some even say that he works on Sundays! His oldest son, Freddie, has yet to join the church and has quite the reputation. Not one to be associated with, let me tell you. Between the *daed* and son, the family is not well thought of, despite their wealth."

Catherine didn't know whether to believe John. He had, after all, made similar claims against Noah Bontrager.

"Why, you should thank me, Cathy!" John exclaimed with an air of mock offense. He pressed his hand against his chest and acted as if he were truly offended. "I saved you from associating with that family and sullying your own reputation."

For some reason, Catherine doubted his assertion. She saw it more as John tricking her in order to get his own way, like a petulant child. She was not about to let that happen again, she told herself as she crossed her arms over her chest and sank down into the seat.

"Hey, now!" James called out as he pulled up beside them, the two horses and buggies in tandem on the road. He took one look at his sister's sullen expression and looked back to John. "Everything all right here?"

John nodded. "Oh, *ja*, just the horse…was spooked back in the town. Could scarce do more than let it run out a spell."

Still angry, Catherine glanced at him, considering whether she should expose his falsehood. James gave a little laugh, but Ida Mae nudged him with her arm to silence him.

"Well, I reckon he's calm enough now," Ida Mae said, a twinkle in her eye.

They continued down the road, John leading the other carriage. He made certain to point out different birds that he saw in the trees and even a deer trail through the woods. Catherine feigned interest, not wanting to maintain her cross attitude and ruin the entire day. She would nod her head and make soft sounds of acknowledgment, all the while fretting over what Ellie and Henry must be thinking of her. She tapped her heel nervously against the floorboard of the carriage, wishing with all of her might that the drive would come to an end as soon as possible.

As if providence was supposed to always pay attention, it soon did.

Under the canopy of the trees, it was difficult to discern that the sun had slipped behind some low-lying clouds. However, when the darker clouds rolled in, Catherine looked up at the sky.

"I believe it's going to rain, John," she said, hopeful that he would take the hint and turn around.

"Oh, stuff and nonsense!" He urged the horse to continue moving forward. "There wasn't a cloud in the sky when we left. And the weather did not call for any rain, Cathy. You mark my words!"

But, sure enough, the sprinkles soon began to fall.

"It'll pass soon enough," John announced.

Twenty minutes later, a torrential downpour put an end to his argument, and with great reluctance, John agreed to turn back for town. It took almost an hour to close the distance between where the rain started and the house on the lake. Catherine dripped wet with water, shivering in the cool air that blew across the lake. But she gave a sigh of relief as she bid the other three good-bye and jumped down from John's buggy.

She ran toward the front door of the house and slammed it shut behind herself.

"My word!" Wilma jumped up from the rocking chair and hurried to fetch a large towel. "You must change right away, Catherine, or you'll catch a cold."

Duane glanced up from the table where he had been seated, reading *Die Blatt* newspaper. "For sure, and summer colds are the worst!"

Catherine accepted the towel and wrapped it around her shoulders.

"I hope you had some fun at least," Wilma said, the curiosity in her eyes indicating that she wanted to hear more about the adventure.

Catherine, however, didn't have much to say beyond, "I never should have listened to that John Troyer! Why, that was the longest two hours of my life!"

Duane tried to stifle a laugh and Wilma hid a soft smile. Clearly there was no love match between Catherine Miller and John Troyer!

Chapter Nine

The following morning, Catherine arose early, helped prepare breakfast, and cleaned the dishes before she announced that she was walking to town. Wilma cast a knowing look at Duane, but neither one said a word, merely reminding her to be home by the dinner hour at noon.

The muddy road made walking difficult. Catherine, however, persevered, despite the accumulation of mud on her shoes and ankles. If Henry and Ellie were going to be out walking, she was going to find them and apologize for the error of her judgment on the previous day. She could only hope that they'd accept her explanation that she had been deceived by a young man with very poor scruples into believing they had forgotten her.

Unfortunately, she did not spot them walking toward the lake. Determined, Catherine sat on a bench under the shade of a tall elm tree, pretending to read one of Ida Mae's books. Her eyes barely took in one full sentence before she would look up and scan the area to see if anyone approached her. For an hour, she waited and watched to no avail. Two cars drove by, one slowing down long enough so that the *Englischer* in the passenger seat could snap a photo of her. Disgusted, Catherine jumped to her feet and began her trek back toward the lake house.

After changing her clothes, she helped Wilma with the food preparation. She listened to the older woman talk about the different people she had met since their arrival, but Catherine's mind was still focused on the Tilmans. Like Wilma, she had met many different people in Banthe. Yet the only two people that she felt particularly interested in getting to know better were the same two people that she had inadvertently offended when she had listened to John Troyer and one more of his tall tales.

That afternoon, she went blueberry picking with Duane and Wilma. They walked up the lane toward town, each carrying a small plastic bucket. Catherine maintained her due diligence, watching for either Ellie or Henry. Once again, she found herself disappointed when neither appeared on the road ahead.

Near the edge of town, Duane led them down another road toward the path that meandered around the lake. Noah Bontrager had mentioned that blueberry bushes grew there, and Wilma had a hankering to make some blueberry pies. Catherine tried to empty her mind of any thoughts regarding Henry and focused instead on plucking the blueberries. She idly listened to Wilma chatter with Duane about this and that, but nothing interested her. Instead, she began to lose herself in her imagination, letting herself drift into the pages of one of her romance novels.

Oh, if she could only write a novel! she thought. As

she plucked blueberries, she escaped into a scene that was just forming in her mind.

She would be standing on the edge of the lake, collecting the blueberries, when a boat full of *Englische* tourists would pull up behind her, their lenses pointed in her direction. Duane and Wilma would hurry up the path and away from the intrusive cameras that stole their photos. But Catherine…well, she would certainly be too far away. And then she would hear the sound of footsteps crashing through the underbrush. Henry Tilman would arrive just in time. He would wrap his arm around her shoulders, and after turning her away from the *Englische*, he would help her up the hill to safety.

"Are you all right?" he would ask her, his hands pressed against her shoulders as he stared into her eyes.

"I'm…I'm fine now," she would answer in a breathless tone.

He would reach up his hand to pluck a stray bramble from her prayer *kapp*. When he did, his fingers would brush against her cheek and his eyes would stare deep into hers.

"Catherine!"

Immediately, her daydream disappeared at the sound of her name being called. She shook her head and looked over her shoulder at Wilma. "*Ja*?"

"We're finished with our buckets. Are you?"

Catherine glanced down and blushed. She had been so lost in her thoughts that her bucket was only half full. "*Nee*. I need another few minutes," she said and began to quickly pluck more berries from the bushes, not caring if stems and green berries made it into the bucket. How could she have let time slip away? Surely, they would notice that she had collected half of what they had gathered! What on earth would they think?

"Catherine?" Wilma called once again. "Are you ready now?"

"Coming!"

She grabbed three more handfuls of blueberries and hurried down the path toward where Wilma and Duane stood waiting.

For the rest of the afternoon, Catherine helped Wilma make blueberry pies as well as several jars of blueberry jam. It felt odd to work alongside Wilma when she was so familiar with working with her mother. But Wilma chattered about different people and told light-hearted stories about her youth, which helped make the time pass quickly. Before she knew it, the sun was beginning to descend in the sky and it was time to start preparing the evening meal.

After dinner, Ida Mae dropped by and implored Catherine to go on another buggy ride with her, John, and James that evening. With worship being held early in the morning, Catherine refused, and for the first time, there was no amount of coaxing from Ida Mae that could convince her to relent. Even if Henry were to see them together, something Catherine highly doubted, she didn't want him to think that she enjoyed spending time with John Troyer. Besides, she had still not forgiven John for tricking her, even if he claimed that he was trying to save her reputation.

Finally, Sunday came and Catherine found herself looking forward to the worship service. Unlike in Fullerton, the Amish in Banthe held worship every Sunday, alternating between a designated building in town and people's homes. When Catherine had asked Wilma about this, she had been told that there were so many visiting Amish families, and usually more than a few preachers, that the community held services every week during the summer.

"It's nice to listen to the preachers from different *g'mays*," Wilma had explained. "Plus, if a person is missing Sunday worship while vacationing here, they'll be able to attend a service here."

While Catherine wasn't as eager for another three hours sitting on those hard pine benches, she was excited to see Ellie again.

Upon arriving, Catherine caught sight of Ellie at the worship service. She stood at the end of the greeting line, and when Catherine approached, Ellie gave her a disenchanted look of curiosity. After shaking her hand and giving her a kiss, Catherine hesitated, wanting to say something right then and there. But other women were behind her, and Catherine knew better than to hold up the line.

It wasn't until three hours later that Catherine had a chance to approach Ellie. While the older women and men at the first seating ate their fellowship meal, a meal that consisted of bread, peanut butter, pretzels, and cold cuts, Catherine sought out the young woman and found her standing in the open doorway of the shop where they had worshipped.

No sooner had Catherine reached Ellie's side than she saw that Henry stood on the other side of the door. She paused for a moment, but decided that there was no harm in going forward with her apology.

"Catherine," Henry said in a cool voice, dipping his head slightly as he greeted her.

"Oh, you must think I am terribly rude!" Catherine

gushed, her gaze shifting from Henry to Ellie and back again. "Please, allow me to explain. There was a horrible misunderstanding!"

Henry raised an eyebrow and waited patiently for her to continue speaking.

"I…I was told that you were both seen riding out of town toward the far side of the lake. I…" She swallowed and fought the trembling in her hands by clutching them together. "I didn't want to go riding in the buggy. Believe me," she said and lowered her voice, "I would so much have preferred your company." She thought she saw Ellie smile. "But when I believed you had forgotten, I didn't want to hold back my brother and Ida Mae from being able to go."

Henry made a serious face at her. "I must admit that I was rather surprised, Catherine," he admitted. Then, with a softening of his expression, he added, "But Ellie was rather adamant that something must have happened. As usual, she was correct."

A sigh of relief escaped from Catherine. "Truly, I begged John to stop the buggy and let me out. I never would have knowingly done such a thing."

This time, Henry smiled. "Then do us the honor of attempting the same walk tomorrow, Catherine. And this time, we will be at your lake house no later than ten, weather permitting."

His eyes flickered over her shoulder, and for the briefest of seconds, Catherine thought she saw something dark and broody, like a black shadow, cloud his face. His back stiffened and he seemed to lean away from her as if preparing for something unexpected.

"And who is this young woman?"

Catherine started at the gruff voice that spoke from

behind her. Quickly she turned around to find herself the subject of study by an older man with a stern face, weathered and dark, and white hair that ran from the crown of his head down his cheeks to his long mustache-less beard. There was something earthy about him that would have been welcoming if it weren't for those dark eyes that narrowed as he appeared to scrutinize everything about Catherine. He was a tall man, much like Henry, with broad shoulders and very large hands. Each of the deep-set wrinkles in his forehead and cheeks made him look angry, and the way that he was assessing her did not put her at ease.

"Father, this is Catherine Miller," Ellie said in a soft, timid voice. "Catherine, this is our father, Gid."

Catherine stretched her hand out to shake his. He merely squinted one of his eyes and stared at it.

When he did not say anything, Ellie cleared her throat. "She is to go walking with us tomorrow."

"Miller, eh?" he said at last, his voice deep and raspy as if he had a sore throat. "You aren't from Banthe, are you?"

"*Nee*, I'm from Fullerton," she responded, hoping that her voice didn't give away how intimidated she was feeling at that moment.

"Fullerton?" He seemed to search his memory as if trying to find a link between himself and that town. When none came, he ran his tongue over his bottom teeth and made a noise. "I understand you are here with the Andersons?"

"I…I am, *ja*." She couldn't help but wonder why he would know anything about her. Even more puzzling was why he was paying any attention to her at all!

For a long moment, his eyes studied her before he

nodded his head as if giving his approval. For what, she did not know. "I see," he said at last.

Her knees felt weak. Never in her life had she encountered such a man as Gid Tilman. She felt as if she were on display, and the feeling did not sit well with her. For a moment, she remembered John Troyer's warning about the Tilman family, and for once, she wondered if there wasn't some truth to what he had told her. Something just did not seem right with Ellie and Henry's father.

Finally, he looked away from her. There was an uncomfortable silence among the four of them as Gid glanced at Ellie first and then Henry. For a long, drawn-out moment, he said nothing, just stared at Henry, who merely turned his head in the other direction. Gid returned his gaze back to Catherine and cleared his throat. "I reckon I'd be remiss if I did not invite you to have the noon meal with us tomorrow after your walk," he said gruffly. It wasn't a question or invitation, but more of a demand. "Noon sharp, of course."

Catherine bit her lower lip. "Of course." She hesitated before adding, "After I check with the Andersons first."

His eyes flashed at her last comment, whether from favoring her thoughtfulness or from disliking her loyalty, she wasn't certain. Then, with one final long look at his son, Gid Tilman turned and walked away, moving slowly to where the preachers stood in a huddle, talking. Without waiting for them to finish their conversation, Gid joined them.

Henry leaned over and in a soft voice said, "Never you mind him, Catherine. He might come across as rather stern, but he is just reserved."

She thought she heard Ellie make a scoffing noise.

"And he must be rather impressed by you," Henry continued, "to have invited you to the house for dinner. He never invites anyone to join us, except the church leaders."

"Is that so?" She couldn't help but gasp as she asked this, the color draining from her cheeks. She had never met anyone who intimidated her more than Gid Tilman. His presumption of power over strangers as well as his own children made Catherine wonder just how much truth John Troyer might have spoken the other day. She certainly didn't like feeling so overpowered. And Henry's comment about his father having been impressed by her did not sit well with Catherine. "I'm no one to impress anyone," she mumbled, embarrassed by Henry's compliment. "Perhaps I should decline. I would hate to leave false notions in anyone's head. I'm not more plain than anyone else!"

Henry laughed and even Ellie smiled at her innocent remark.

"Never you mind, Catherine," Henry said with a soft voice. "I doubt anyone could have false notions about you. You are as pure of heart as any person I've ever met."

They stood in the sun, talking some more until it was time to say the after-prayer. And then Catherine excused herself to help clear the table of plates from the second seating, which was always the younger men and women who hadn't eaten during the first meal. She managed to steer clear of John Troyer, too aware that he watched her while she worked. She gave him no opportunity to approach her, keeping herself busy with helping the other women and then promptly escaping to keep company with Wilma and her new friends, who lingered at a table by the open door, a bowl of shared popcorn before them.

Catherine also managed to avoid Ida Mae during the fellowship hour, for her friend appeared more than content to spend her time in the company of James. It wasn't until later that Wilma mentioned that neither Catherine's brother nor her friend had sat down to eat at all, preferring to talk together on the wooden swing that was set in the back by the shade.

James and Ida Mae. It was an unlikely pairing, the distance between Fullerton and Banthe being so great, but a pairing that appeared far too real. Catherine thought about that while she walked home with Duane and Wilma. Was it possible that her brother might actually consider courting Ida Mae?

Chapter Ten

"What do you mean you won't go riding with us anymore, Catherine?"

Ida Mae sat on the sofa next to Catherine, her eyes pleading with her friend. She had dropped by late Sunday afternoon to ask Catherine to go out riding that evening with John, James, and her. But Catherine held firm to her decision. She had made up her mind that she would no longer put herself in a position that could compromise her budding relationship with the Tilmans. "I just prefer not to go, that's all," she said in a soft voice. She chose her words carefully because she didn't want to offend Ida Mae, but she also did not want to speak an untruth.

Unhappy with Catherine's explanation, Ida Mae scowled. "That makes no sense! You went the other day!"

Catherine kept her eyes focused on the letter she had begun writing to her mother. How could she tell Ida Mae that both Duane and Wilma had spoken to her, encouraging her to not be seen riding in the two-seater open carriage again if she meant to protect her reputation? Besides, she was still angry with John for having lied. While she appreciated his kindness to her, she did not want him to interfere again with her budding relationship with either Henry or Ellie. A man that lies once has already proven his true character. Even without Duane and Wilma's request, Catherine knew that she wanted to limit her exposure to John Troyer, even if his sister was one of her friends.

"I just don't think it is a good idea," Catherine finally said in an even tone, still avoiding looking at her friend. "That one day, the day when I went, I didn't realize that we were taking two buggies. Besides the fact that we weren't even together anyway, you know that open buggies are for courting, Ida Mae. And I'm not courting your *bruder*, John."

With an overly exaggerated sigh, Ida Mae leaned against the back of the sofa. "Is that all? Oh, Catherine! Banthe is a vacation town. It's not like Fullerton! All of the young people ride in open carriages. It's the summer season, after all! Who wants to be stuck in a stuffy old closed-up buggy? Besides, sitting beside a young man is not a commitment to marry him!"

Setting down her pen, Catherine gave Ida Mae a stern look. "Perhaps, but when I return to Fullerton, I'd prefer that my name and reputation be as intact as when I left. After all, you're the one who warned me of how your friend damaged her reputation by being seen riding in buggies with two different young men."

Once again, her answer did not please Ida Mae, who jumped to her feet and began pacing the floor. She wore an angry expression and scowled. "I thought we were friends, Catherine. But you seem to be thinking more of yourself than about anyone else!"

"That's not fair…"

But Ida Mae wasn't listening. "Friends, Catherine. The best of friends. I had hoped we'd be more than that one day, too."

Catherine looked up at Ida Mae in surprise. Was she talking about her relationship with James? Certainly, she couldn't be jumping so far ahead, especially when they had only just met! "And how is that, Ida Mae?" she dared to ask.

"Oh, please!" She waved her hand dismissively at Catherine and flopped back down on the sofa. "Sometimes I think you're only just *acting* innocent!"

"Excuse me?" Catherine sounded as taken aback as she felt.

Leaning forward, the scowl suddenly disappearing from her face, Ida Mae gave her a sideways glance that was full of mischief. "You know that John fancies you."

"What. Ever!" Catherine forced the two words out of her mouth as she tried to catch her breath.

"And I've seen how you are around him, too. Everyone is talking about it!" Ida Mae said, a smug look on her face.

Catherine gasped. What a disastrous thought! How could Ida Mae make such a claim? If anything, Catherine had worked extra hard to avoid John over the past few days. If people were talking, certainly Duane and Wilma must have heard. Was that why they had talked to her? Would they return to Fullerton and tell her parents that she had behaved inappropriately?

"There must've been some sort of misunderstanding then," Catherine began to explain. "If that is how my behavior has been regarded…"

"Indeed, it has!"

Ignoring the eagerness with which Ida Mae so readily agreed, a new emotion overcame Catherine: regret. She tried to reflect on the past week since she had met John Troyer. She had walked with him once and gone on that horrible drive with him. But after that, she had spent little to no time in his company. Even after church, she had managed to stay away from him. So how on earth could her attentions to what she regarded as a simple friendship have been misconstrued as something more?

"Then that is all the more reason for me to refuse another ride with your *bruder*." Catherine returned her attention to her letter, hoping that her trembling fingers did not give away her true feelings of distress.

Ida Mae stood up and crossed her arms over her chest. If she had been unhappy before, she was even more upset now that her own words had been used against her. Angrily, she marched toward the back window and stared outside in the direction of the lake. "I don't understand you, Catherine! You claim to be my friend, yet you refuse to spend time with me. I think you're being rather selfish."

Selfish? Catherine fought the urge to let Ida Mae know who was truly being selfish. In her life, she had never had words with anyone, and she certainly didn't want to have them now with her friend. "I don't refuse to spend time with you, Ida Mae," she said, carefully selecting her words. "We're spending time together right now, *ja*? But you are choosing to use that time to argue rather than to have a pleasant visit together."

"It's really *you* arguing with *me*."

Determined, Catherine shook her head. "I have no

intention of arguing with you. Or anyone else for that matter."

Turning on her heel, Ida Mae rushed back to where Catherine sat and knelt before her. Her eyes widened with eagerness. "So you will go for a ride this evening then?"

Dropping her hands onto her lap, Catherine pressed her lips together and stared at Ida Mae. She didn't like the way that she was being bullied by her. No meant no. "*Nee*, I will not." The forcefulness of her voice startled even her. "And I'd thank you to stop trying to manipulate me into doing what you want, when it goes against my principles!"

Angry, Ida Mae stomped her foot like a petulant child. "That means I won't be able to go either! Oh, you *are* very selfish, Catherine Miller. And here I thought we were friends!" Without another word, she turned and hurried out the door.

As Ida Mae stormed out of the house, Catherine sat there, her hands still on her lap and her mouth agape in surprise. She had never been spoken to in such a manner, and to be truthful, she didn't know how to respond. Of course, it was too late anyway, as Ida Mae was gone. So Catherine just sat there, stunned into silence.

"Is your friend gone so soon?" Wilma asked as she walked out of the bedroom where she had been napping and entered the living room. "That was a short visit."

Catherine tried to find the words to explain what had just happened. But she wanted to avoid any more discussions about open carriages and soiled reputations. She settled for the simplest explanation. "I…I suppose she left rather angry."

Wilma frowned, glancing at the door as if Ida Mae still stood there. "Angry? About what?"

She sighed and leaned back in the chair. "Not about what but about who, and that who is me."

"You? Whatever for? Why, you have the most pleasant and even disposition of anyone I know!" Concerned, Wilma sat down beside her on the sofa. "Certainly, it was just a misunderstanding, Catherine. Nothing to fret over, *ja*?"

But Catherine wasn't so certain. While she did not know Ida Mae very well, their friendship only in its second week, she had come to think of her as a friend. But friends did not treat each other in such a way. And, the irony of the situation was that, by calling Catherine selfish for not wanting to go riding, Ida Mae was guilty of the very same thing for wanting to force her to do so. Still, it did not sit well with Catherine, and she found herself wondering if she had, indeed, wronged her friend.

"Does this have anything to do with our talk the other day?" Wilma asked in a gentle manner.

Swallowing, Catherine nodded her head. "She wants me to go riding, but I don't want to. She says she can't go if I don't."

Wilma clucked her tongue. "You know that she can do whatever she'd like to do."

"She said that people are talking about me."

Wilma appeared startled at that last comment. "Talking? About you?" She shook her head. "Seems like that young woman needs to reflect upon what she says to people, wouldn't you say? Perhaps she tends to apply to others what she fears, applies to her!"

But Catherine was still upset. "She says that people

think I'm courting John. And nothing could be further from the truth, Wilma. I've given him no indication that we are anything more than friends. And even that is only because of Ida Mae."

Wilma gave a small laugh and clucked her tongue three times. "Oh, Catherine, if anyone in Banthe is talking about you, it is only kind things. There is nothing else that can be said about such a young woman who is so pure at heart."

"I don't feel pure at heart at the present moment," Catherine grumbled.

"Well, I can personally tell you that there is not one person in Banthe that is speculating about you fancying John Troyer. Certainly Susie and Vern have no such illusions, and they're his parents."

"Well, there is one person, and that person is Ida Mae!" Catherine said grumpily as she slouched down in her chair.

"Remember Matthew 15:18. 'But those things which proceed out of the mouth come from the heart, and they defile the man.' It seems to me that she has said more about herself than about you." She bustled into the kitchen, where she began to pull things out for supper.

Catherine couldn't help but wonder about what Wilma had said. Certainly, it was true that gossiping mouths often said more about the speaker than the person being gossiped about. Still, Catherine didn't like the idea that Ida Mae believed what she had said. Did she really think Catherine had flirted with John? Could she have missed Catherine's not-so-subtle clues that she was interested in getting to know Henry better, not John?

She was still sitting there when Wilma returned, carrying a glass of lemonade.

"Are you still fretting about this?" She handed the glass to Catherine. "I know what would cheer you up, Catherine. Why don't you go outside and gather some wildflowers for the dinner table? They would brighten up this kitchen."

Catherine forced a smile and did as she was told. It would do her some good to get out of the house, and perhaps gathering flowers would put her in a better mood. After her tiff with Ida Mae, she realized just how much she enjoyed Wilma's company and all of her stories about when she was growing up and how she met Duane. There was something light-hearted and sweet about Wilma's provincial view of life. She was always upbeat and cheerful, finding something interesting about even the simplest of life's pleasures. After the unsettling exchange with Ida Mae, Catherine suddenly found herself grateful for Wilma's simple and sincere friendship.

Chapter Eleven

"You are a bundle of nerves this morning," Wilma teased as she finished drying the breakfast dishes. "One would think you'd never walked around a lake before!"

Catherine chewed on her bottom lip, staring anxiously out the window.

Duane emerged from the bedroom, shutting the door behind him. "Perhaps you should walk to town with us, Catherine? You know we're heading up there to meet with Vern and Susie."

"Oh, *nee*! *Danke*!" Wild horses wouldn't have driven her away from that window. She suspected that John and James would come around later, hoping to take her for another ride with Ida Mae. But Catherine figured she would be long gone by that time. With an empty house, they would have no one to coax and finagle into taking a buggy ride. Catherine didn't even care that her leaving meant an inconvenience for James and Ida Mae. If they were truly courting, it wasn't as if people didn't already suspect it, especially after they missed the fellowship meal the previous day, something that did not go unnoticed.

"Duane! You know she has plans already!" Wilma playfully scolded him.

He laughed good-naturedly as he went to the sink. He reached for a glass and poured himself some cool water from the faucet. "*Ja, ja,* I know that."

Catherine smiled but returned her attention to looking outside. It was, after all, almost ten o'clock.

When she saw the two figures emerge at the crest of the road, Catherine broke into a happy grin. "They're here!" She ran over to the mirror and glanced at it, pausing to pinch her cheeks and push her hair further back under her head covering.

Wilma smiled. "Enjoy yourself at the Tilmans," she said. "Your company will be missed at the Troyers, but I'm certain they will understand."

Catherine barely acknowledged Wilma's words as she hurried out the door, letting her feet race down the wooden steps in her eagerness to join her new friends.

The midmorning air was cool under the trees, and sunlight filtered through tiny gaps in the lush green leaves ahead. The sound of birds chirping was only broken by the occasional sound of a plane flying overhead.

Henry guided both women to a dirt path that led them to the walking trail. Rather than turn toward town, they walked the other direction. For the beginning of the walk, Ellie held Catherine's arm, asking her questions about Fullerton and her family. When Catherine had nothing more to tell, Ellie inquired about her relationship with the Andersons.

"Oh, they are fine people, the Andersons," Catherine gushed. "The finest there are. Poor Wilma never had any children, so she likes to say she's adopted me as her *dochder*. I try to help her as much as I can when it's time to plant the gardens and can vegetables."

"No children? Such a shame," Ellie lamented.

"And…and you? I met your *daed*, but…" She hesitated for just a moment.

"Our *maem*?" Ellie sighed and strolled a few paces before she continued speaking. "*Ja*, *vell*, she has moved on, Catherine. Called home to be with Jesus when I was just eleven years old."

"Oh, I am so sorry!" Catherine couldn't imagine such a loss. Her heart hurt for her friend. "You must miss her very much."

Ellie managed to give a soft smile, but it was full of remorse, not happiness. "*Ja*, I do. It hasn't been easy to grow up without a *muder* and, as you can see, *Daed* never remarried."

Catherine was just about to inquire further about that, for surely it was most unusual for a widower with three young children to not remarry, when, ahead of them, Henry stopped walking and turned around. "What could you two possibly be talking about with such serious countenance?"

"Family, dear *bruder*."

"Family?" Henry appeared mystified. "Why, I should think that you would have moved onto more important—and entertaining!—topics."

At this, Ellie laughed and tossed a small stick in his direction. "More important topics? Tell me, dear *bruder*, what do you consider to be a more important topic than family?"

He gave a casual shrug of his shoulders, but there was a mischievous gleam in his eyes. "Perhaps issues pertaining to gardening or sewing. The latest colors that have been put on display at the fabric store. The new rose color fabric is rather scandalous, wouldn't you agree? It's patterned!" He added with an exaggerated air of disapproval on his face.

At that comment, even Catherine had to laugh. "Oh, Henry! What would *you* know about fabrics anyway?"

"Why, Catherine! I happen to know quite a bit about fabrics!" he said, placing his hand upon his chest, feigning offense at her comment. "There is polyester fabric. All of the fabric stores carry that, of course. But some of the less conservative areas tend to include new polyester blend fabrics, some with patterns that, to the untrained eye, are rather hard to see. Take, for instance, Ellie's dress."

Catherine suppressed another laugh as she glanced at her friend.

"That, my Catherine, comes from Newbury Acres, where fabrics are a bit more expensive but tend to wear well, the color not fading even after multiple washings and line drying!"

Ellie rolled her eyes but in a good-natured way.

"And my dress?" Catherine asked, lifting the skirt just a bit as if to show it off.

"Ah, *ja*! Your dress. Well, it is rather pretty, isn't it?" Henry said with an approving look in his eye. "But I'm afraid that you have selected a fabric that will fray if proper care is not taken."

"You are…" she laughed, unable to complete the sentence.

"…a wealth of useful information!" he said, completing it for her. "And ask me about dairy cows. I will be certain to entertain you for hours on end about how to increase milk production and avoid mastitis on their teats!"

"For a dairy farmer, that is rather useful," Ellie pointed out.

Catherine frowned. "Is that what you will do? Dairy farm?"

Henry reached for a dried tree branch and snapped it so that he could chuck it down the embankment into the water. "*Ja*, dairy farm." He glanced at her. "Have you never heard of Newbury Acres, then?"

She shook her head.

"*Daed* inherited two farms, one from his own father and one from our *grossdawdi* on our *maem*'s side: the Woods farm. She had no *bruders* to pass the farm to, you see."

"Your parents grew up neighbors?"

Henry nodded, snapping another branch as he walked.

"How romantic!" she sighed.

Henry made a noise in his throat but did not comment further. "One of the farms was for dairy cows and hay while the other just for hay. That was *Maem*'s family farm. About ten years back, *Daed* built the wood shop. My *bruder* Freddie works there and will inherit that."

It dawned on Catherine that the Tilmans must have access to a lot of resources. It was a rare Amish family that could provide two large, working farms to more than one son. Her parents were not in that same situation, especially since they had eight children and a small working farm at that! And with her father being a preacher, he barely had enough time to eat and sleep, never mind grow his farm in such a way that it could provide for more than one son.

But dairy farming was hard work. Cows needed to be milked twice a day, like clockwork. Vacations were few and far between, since leaving the dairy barn meant that hired help must be brought in.

And that raised a question in Catherine's head: if he was a dairy farmer, how on earth was Henry here, in Banthe, enjoying time away from the farm?

"I see that quizzical look upon your brow," Henry teased. "You're wondering how it is that I'm here if I have cows to tend."

"The thought did cross my mind," she admitted.

"Newbury Acres is not your typical farm, Catherine. It is much larger than others and provides plenty of opportunities for other Amish men to farm for pay." He paused, glancing at the lake for a long moment. He seemed deep in thought, and both women waited for him to speak again. "Our *daed* has very conservative views, Catherine. He does not believe that Amish men should work among the *Englische*. So he has created a farming co-op, if you will. This way, rather than one family working so very hard to make ends meet on a smaller farm, he has two very large farms, and other Amish men farm it together."

"How clever!"

She almost wished that her family lived near such a community. As it was now, their own small farm was surrounded by several modest *Englische* homes and non-Amish farmers. Both of her parents were increasingly concerned about the future of their children. Only one of their sons would inherit the farm, most likely one of the younger ones. And the property was not large enough to house more than one other house and possibly a shop for trade. What would then become of the other children? The daughters would be married off, but to whom? And the sons would have to find a trade to work in the hopes that, one day, they might have enough money to purchase their own farm. However, with the ever-increasing cost of land, so much time might pass before enough money was saved that they might no longer wish to farm at all.

Henry nodded his head. "I suppose it is clever," he admitted, his voice drawn out as he spoke those words. "However, he has very high expectations of those workers...and for his own children."

She thought she noticed a slight shift in his voice when he added that last part to his sentence. "How is that?" she asked.

Ellie reached out and touched Henry's arm. She gave him a pleading look as she said, "Let's talk about other subjects, shall we?"

It was clear that the subject matter was tender at its core, and, while curious, Catherine did not wish to pursue a topic that, for some odd reason, appeared sensitive to both brother and sister.

Half an hour later, they rounded a bend in the path and there was a small bench. Ellie sat down to remove a pebble from her shoe and told Henry to keep walking; she'd catch up to them in a few minutes.

Alone at last, Catherine felt rather grown-up walking with Henry. Even though he was taller than she was, he maintained a steady pace beside her, his hands clasped behind his back. He stared into the trees, pointing out different birds and pausing when he spotted a deer in the woods ahead, pointing it out to Catherine.

"They're such beautiful animals," he said. "I never was one who liked hunting, not like my *bruder* and *daed.*"

She was surprised by his statement. Her own brothers loved to hunt for deer and pheasants. She, however, felt the same way as Henry. "I always thought that all men liked to hunt."

Henry laughed and nudged her with his arm. "Not all

men are alike, Catherine. We aren't any more cookie-cutter people than women are."

She blushed at her naive statement and averted her eyes.

She hadn't thought of it in that way. However, she certainly recognized that Henry was completely different than John Troyer or even her brother James. They were more like the typical Amish men that she avoided on the rare occasion she attended the youth social gatherings.

As if reading her mind, Henry bent forward so that he was on eye level with her. "For instance, had you truly thought I was so like John Troyer?"

"Oh, no!" she exclaimed. "You are nothing alike."

"Uh-huh," he said with satisfaction.

"I suppose you know him well," she said. "He seemed to know an awful lot about your family, anyway."

Henry gave a small laugh. "And let me guess… I'm sure my rival was not charitable."

Catherine stopped short. "He is not…"

Henry gave her a smile.

"You're teasing me!"

They continued walking.

"I have found that people who gossip about the affairs of others are usually small-minded, and often their news is unkind or inaccurate, to say the least," Henry said.

"I know he doesn't always tell the truth," Catherine retorted quickly. "But he's been kind and attentive to me."

Raising his eyebrows, Henry gave her a taunting look.

"What? Do you think he's not trustworthy?" she asked in surprise. While she certainly thought that very thing about John Troyer, she had not realized that her opinion might be generally shared by others!

He chuckled and smiled once more. "I think," Henry said, returning his gaze to the path ahead of them, "that you should realize that I'm not the best person to consult with regarding matters involving you and John Troyer."

For some reason, it took Ellie quite a while to catch up with Henry and Catherine. During that time, Henry asked Catherine questions about her family and their farm. She wasn't used to having so much attention drawn to herself and felt flustered at first. Gradually, however, she started to feel more comfortable, especially when Henry replied to her comments with genuine interest.

"Henry!" Ellie called.

They both stopped and turned around, Catherine feeling a slight pressure on her elbow. She glanced down and realized that Henry's hand gently held her arm. His touch made her skin tingle and she felt almost giddy with joy. Was it possible, she wondered, that Henry was as interested in her as she was in him?

Ellie hurried along the trail, smiling at the two of them. "We really should get going, don't you think? We don't want to be late for dinner with *Daed*."

It dawned on Catherine that, if Ellie was with them, who would be preparing the dinner meal? She wanted to ask but sensed an urgency in their steps as they began to walk back in the direction from which they had come. What was it, she wondered, that made everyone seem so nervous about Gid Tilman? Rather than voice the question, she decided that she would most likely find out on her own as she would be in his presence for at least an hour, if not more, that very afternoon.

Chapter Twelve

She sat with her hands folded on her lap, her back far too straight and her eyes staring at a spot on the floor before her. Dinner at the Tilmans' house, while an honor, had not been a pleasant experience. She couldn't wait until she heard the clock chime twice so that she could make her excuses and leave.

When they had arrived, Gid Tilman had been standing in the doorway of their small cottage. It sat on a hill that overlooked the lake. He scowled at them, for they had taken longer to walk home than they anticipated. Once inside, Catherine's eyes wandered to the table where four places were set. Bowls and platters of room-temperature food were set out already, and she realized that he had been waiting for them.

Five minutes later, the four of them sat at the kitchen table, Catherine seated next to Ellie and diagonally across from Henry. She was thankful that she sat the farthest away from Gid, who ate without speaking to anyone at the table. In fact, the entire meal was eaten in silence, just one more reason that Catherine couldn't wait until she could leave.

Even after the meal was over, Catherine found herself the object of Gid's scrutiny. While she stood beside Ellie as they washed the dishes, Catherine found a moment of respite—Gid's attention being distracted as he engaged in conversation with Henry—to lean over and whisper, "Is your *daed* always so…" She couldn't finish the question, for she feared offending Ellie.

"Stern? Opinionated? Controlling?" Ellie gave a soft laugh. "*Ja*, he is. And more so since our *mamm* passed away."

Catherine risked a look at Gid. "He must miss her terribly."

"He mourned, *ja*."

"Henry told me that your parents practically grew up together. With three children to raise, he must have felt her loss twice as much, don't you think?"

But Ellie merely shook her head. "I gave up thinking about such things a long time ago, Catherine. Life is not exactly the same as those romance novels that you like so much."

Confused by Ellie's words, Catherine tried to concentrate on drying the plates. The oppressive nature of the Tilman's house was more than she could bear.

Now Ellie sat quietly in a rocking chair, her head bent over the pillowcase she was embroidering while Gid sat across from Catherine. She felt small and insignificant on the sofa and wished that Henry had not left so soon after the meal. All during the meal, Ellie seemed withdrawn and aloof, not unpleasant but not forthcoming in the kindness that Catherine had felt during their morning walk.

"You are enjoying Banthe, *ja*?" Gid asked her as he rocked gently in the large recliner.

"*Ja*, it's very nice here," she replied, glancing around as if her desire for Henry's return would make him magically appear.

"I find that it is refreshing to get away from Newbury Acres from time to time." Gid tapped his fingers on the arm of the chair as he studied her. "But business must continue, and therefore, we will be returning Saturday."

Catherine swallowed, feeling more than uncomfortable under his hard but steady stare.

"When are you to return then?" he asked her.

"Whenever the Andersons return, I reckon. They talked about leaving next week Monday. They had told my parents we'd be gone for a little over two weeks."

Gid made a noise in his throat.

Glancing at Ellie, Catherine wished that her friend would say something. Anything! She began to feel as if she were being interviewed by Gid Tilman, and she did not like that feeling one bit.

"Your parents. They farm, *ja*?"

Catherine returned her attention to Gid. "*Ja*, they do."

"You must have many siblings to be able to leave without impacting the workload." It was stated as a question, and Catherine realized by the way he watched her that he anticipated a response.

"I have seven siblings, one of whom is here in Banthe, but he is staying with the Troyers," she admitted.

"Seven!" Gid slapped his hand against the chair. "Plus you? Why, that's eight children!"

She didn't feel as if her comment warranted such a reaction.

"How on earth does your father expect all of those

children to earn a living?" He scowled and shook his head, clearly irritated by this news that she had shared with him.

"I'm sure he will leave the farm to one of my *bruders*," she said softly.

"And the others? What will they do?"

Stunned by his line of questioning, she glanced once again at Ellie, who was watching their exchange with furtive eyes. When Catherine realized that Gid was waiting for her to respond, she turned back toward him. "I imagine Richard and John will take up a trade," she managed to say.

Again, Gid slapped the arm of his chair, his face contorted in a fit of rage. "Exactly! And that is the problem! It's farming that holds the Amish communities together, I tell you."

Catherine felt an unexpected tension fill the room. A glance at Ellie brought her no comfort or sense of escape as Gid continued ranting.

"All of these large families. They do a disservice to our community if they cannot provide enough land to keep their children and grandchildren working the land. We must remain stewards of the earth and not slaves to the *Englische*!"

"I was under the impression that you have your own trade business," she heard herself say. She thought she saw Ellie stiffen her back and immediately knew that she should have kept her comment to herself.

Gid stopped rocking. "Indeed, I do. It would seem to be a conflict of interest if it were not responsible for paying the salaries of almost twenty Amish men in our community who would otherwise be employed by the *Englische*."

Catherine heard footsteps at the door and stared in the direction of the entrance to the kitchen. While Gid continued to ramble, Catherine silently willed Henry to enter the house.

"You are most fortunate, Catherine, that the Andersons have taken you under their wing, to have access to their land."

"Excuse me?" she said when she heard Gid's last comment.

The kitchen door opened and Henry entered the room. Immediately distracted, it was all that Catherine could do to contain herself. She wanted to jump to her feet and greet Henry with a broad smile. If he had been gone thirty minutes, it felt as if it were more than an hour. But the look of irritation on his father's face helped her remain seated.

"And where have you been?" Gid snapped at Henry.

Henry hung up his straw hat and lowered his head demurely. "My apologies, *Daed*. I told you that I wanted to run into town to fetch the newspaper."

His father glanced at the clock in an exaggerated motion to indicate that he felt his son had taken too long to return.

"I was delayed by Benjamin Esh. There was a message to give to you."

"And what's that?"

"Freddie will be arriving later this week."

The message did nothing to soften Gid's expression. "Then we must begin preparations to return to Newbury Acres. We cannot all be gone at the same time for long."

Catherine felt as if her heart fell at their father's words. She had known that the Tilmans would be leaving at some point, but she had hoped that it would be after she had returned to Fullerton. The thought of staying at Banthe without Henry and Ellie Tilman depressed her even though she felt intimidated by their father.

As she walked down the road that led from their cottage toward town, she breathed a sigh of relief. Such strange people, she thought. There were no smiles or laughter all afternoon. Even Henry had remained quiet and withdrawn during the visit, his only sign of interest that he stole a quick peek at her when his father was looking the other way.

"Catherine!"

She stopped and turned around at the sound of Ida Mae's voice, and Ida Mae smiled and waved at her to wait. "What are you doing out here?" Catherine asked as her friend caught up with her. They had not spoken to each other since Ida Mae's sharp criticism yesterday afternoon, and Catherine wondered that Ida Mae would even approach her, much less be all smiles and waves.

"I wanted to find out how your visit with the Tilmans went," Ida Mae said, still smiling.

Confused, Catherine stared at Ida Mae. How did she know that Catherine had visited with the Tilmans? Besides, was this smiling, happy, and concerned person the same one who had stormed away, angry and hurt because Catherine wouldn't go riding in an open buggy? "That's very kind, Ida Mae, but I thought you were angry with me." It was more of a question than a statement.

"Oh, that?" Ida Mae laughed and waved at the air in a dismissive manner. "Don't be silly, Catherine. I was just upset for a moment. Disappointed, really. Besides, everything worked out. My cousin went with us so no one was left behind. All's well that ends well, *ja*?" Another little laugh and her eyes lit up. "So, tell me about your visit at the Tilmans! I ran into Wilma in town, and she told me you were having dinner there. I'm simply dying to hear what happened!"

While Catherine didn't quite know how to take this sudden change in Ida Mae, she was eager to talk about what had happened at the Tilmans. Besides, she did like Ida Mae and knew that sometimes people argued. She decided to forgive and forget and began to share her story, picking and choosing her words carefully so that nothing that she said could be construed as gossip. But she didn't try to hide the fact that the entire time spent at the Tilmans had felt uncomfortable and created an uneasy cause for question: Why had Gid Tilman wanted her to visit in the first place?

"It's pride," Ida Mae ranted as they walked on the road. "Just plain old pride. That whole family is rather fond of themselves."

Catherine frowned. Her complaint was mostly with Gid, not with the rest of the family. "That's just not so, Ida Mae. Why, Ellie and Henry were nice as can be the other day! They even quickly forgave the misunderstanding with your *bruder* when he told me they had left without me when they hadn't."

But Ida Mae was not to be convinced easily. "To barely speak to you while a guest in their house? Does she think she is superior to you?"

Horrified, Catherine shook her head. How could Ida Mae put any of the blame on Ellie? "It wasn't like that, Ida Mae. Honest. I mean…" She paused, trying to pick her words even more carefully than before. "Ida Mae, perhaps you misunderstood me. She was more than civil toward me. I felt no sense of unhappiness toward me, not from anyone in the Tilman family."

"Then what, exactly, did you feel?"

Catherine could tell that Ida Mae was losing interest in the conversation. "Tense. Something seemed amiss between the father and the children."

"And Henry? Was he talkative to you?"

Embarrassed, Catherine shook her head to indicate that he had spoken barely one word to her.

"Oh, Catherine!" Ida Mae cried out in dismay. "This family is completely unworthy of you and your attentions. I'm going to pray that you realize that and stop thinking about them this very instant! Especially that Henry! He is the most unworthy of all!"

"Unworthy?" Catherine could hardly believe her ears. How could Ida Mae make such a declaration? She had never spoken two words to either Henry or Ellie. "I doubt that he thinks of me at all!"

"And that is exactly what I mean! He doesn't think of you! If he did, he certainly would have been a better friend to you and engaged you in conversation instead of permitting you to be mercilessly interviewed… interrogated!…by his father!"

Catherine held up her hand to stop Ida Mae from talking. "There's no doubt that I've given you the wrong impression. Gid Tilman was more than pleasant, in a harsh kind of way. He asked me questions and engaged me in conversation, even if it was not the typical conversation I would expect to hear from someone I know so little of."

Ida Mae rolled her eyes as they approached the house. "My reproach is more for Henry and Ellie than the father. Why, John thinks that Gid is quite a decent man. He said that he met him just a few days ago, at the store."

Catherine frowned. The information that Ida Mae had just shared with her was completely different from what John had told her. In fact, there was a large gaping hole in their two stories. Hadn't John told her that he wanted to save her from the Tilmans and their bad reputation? Yet, if she were to believe Ida Mae, John had only just met Gid Tilman a few days ago. Perhaps, like Noah Bontrager, this was just one more of his tall tales, she thought.

"Well, I shall see how Ellie and Henry behave toward me tomorrow afternoon," Catherine said at last, trying to keep her tone neutral. "We're to meet up and go walking once more."

"And not go riding again?" Ida Mae all but gasped. "Why, I'm beginning to think that you're avoiding me!"

Catherine tried to persuade her otherwise, although bothered as she was by Ida Mae's flirtatious ways with James and her constant attempts to push Catherine toward John, there was some truth to Ida Mae's statement. She began to wonder if there was a bit of jealousy that fueled her friend's criticism of Henry and Ellie.

"I thought you were angry with me," Catherine said dryly. "And I didn't have plans when they asked."

Forcing another light-hearted laugh, Ida Mae reached for Catherine's arm and linked hers with it. "Of course. Silly me! Well, you are certainly getting your exercise with all that walking! I confess that I prefer riding. Something about the wind on my face."

They walked farther down the road, and when they arrived at the lake house, Ida Mae hesitated as if waiting for an invitation to come inside. But Catherine didn't feel compelled to do so. Something seemed off with Ida Mae, with her too-strained attempts to placate Catherine.

"I promised Wilma that I'd spend some time with her this afternoon," Catherine finally said, feeling obligated to give a reason for not inviting her inside. "The Bontragers are coming for supper, so I need to help with the meal."

"Well then," Ida Mae said at last when she realized that an invitation was not forthcoming. "Since you're busy tomorrow with the Tilmans, I suppose I will see you at the shop frolic on Wednesday?"

"I almost forgot about that!"

"It should be a lot of fun. Much less work for us women than at the barn raising."

As she watched Ida Mae walking up the lane toward town, Catherine couldn't help but frown. She wasn't afraid of working hard, and she loved the sense of community at those frolics. She enjoyed being with so many people all lending a hand to help others. Taking part in such community activities gave her a sense of belonging. She never considered it work, and she certainly never tried to get out of doing it. Nor had she ever considered that other Amish might not feel the same way.

Apparently, she'd been mistaken.

Chapter Thirteen

Late Tuesday morning Catherine was walking up from the lake's edge when she heard the laughter of James, John, and Ida Mae approaching the small cottage. The sound of their light-hearted voices made her smile, even though she was still sore at them for constantly pressuring her to ride in those open carriages.

"There she is!" Ida Mae sang out, raising her arm to wave over her head. The way she smiled, so radiant and happy, made Catherine wonder what was going on.

James started to run ahead to greet his sister but stopped short, thinking better of it, and ran back to Ida Mae. He grasped her hand and dragged her toward Catherine.

"*Wie gehts*?" Catherine asked as she neared, confused by her brother's behavior. "Not another buggy ride, I trust."

Ida Mae jumped up and down like a child, clapping her hands together. Her eyes sparkled. "Oh, Catherine! The best of news." She held out her hands for Catherine to take, and when she did, Ida Mae skipped in a small circle, forcing Catherine to do the same. "I told you that we were the best of friends, remember? And I told you that I had hoped for something more, did I not?"

Even though she was smiling, Catherine couldn't help but frown. Certainly Ida Mae was not bringing up the subject of her relationship with John again, was she? But, with John standing just a few paces away, Catherine knew better than to ask such a question. She just said a quick little prayer that Ida Mae would not put her on the spot right then and there.

"We're to be sisters!" Ida Mae said, her voice shrill and high. She squeezed Catherine's hands and then pulled her into a warm embrace. "True sisters. Oh, I'm the happiest of girls!"

"Sisters?" Catherine freed herself from Ida Mae's arms. "I...I don't understand..." Her eyes trailed to her brother who stood beaming, rocking back and forth on his heels. "Oh! I see."

In hindsight, Catherine knew that she should not feel surprised. After all, James seemed to be constantly in the company of Ida Mae. While Catherine had known that the two of them were fond of each other, she hadn't realized just how fond. What was surprising was that her brother would propose after only knowing Ida Mae a short period of time.

"That...that seems rather sudden, don't you think?" she managed to say, her eyes staring at her brother and not Ida Mae.

"Oh, you goose!" Ida Mae laughed. "Do you really think that?"

James beamed at his soon-to-be bride. "Catherine, I've known Ida Mae for quite a bit of time."

That was when the fog cleared from Catherine's head. Of course, she thought. James knew John and, consequently, had met his sister. His visit to Banthe was not entirely at John's invitation but most likely Ida Mae's as well. Once again, she felt an odd feeling that Ida Mae had used her, knowing all along that she was courting and planning to marry Catherine's brother.

"I've come to tell you that I'm returning to Fullerton to inform *Daed*," James announced. "It's to be an autumn wedding."

Catherine smiled, even though a dozen questions whirled through her head. "How *wunderbarr*!" she managed to say at last. "Surprising, but just right *gut* news."

If Ida Mae sensed Catherine's continued hesitation, she did not let on. Instead, she began to gush about the wedding preparations. They would need to begin thinking of food and dresses, invitations and guests lists. It was all too mind-boggling for Ida Mae to handle on her own, and would Catherine mind helping her organize everything?

"We'll have to use one of those wedding trucks," Ida Mae announced. "You do have those in Fullerton, *ja*?"

"Wedding trucks?"

Ida Mae nodded. "Oh, *ja*. They are just *wunderbarr*! They supply a trailer that has a full working kitchen in it, enough to warm up multiple platters at once! And all white plates, cups, and saucers! No more of the hodge-podge assortment of dishes! And no more cluttered and overheated kitchens."

Catherine's eyes bulged out of her head. She had never heard of such a thing. "Really?"

"Really! How genius, *ja*?" Ida Mae sounded genuinely impressed. "And just think, Catherine, when the wedding is over, we can truly be the best of friends and sisters! Why, I'll be living on your farm!" She paused and glanced toward the sky. "Hmm, mayhaps, James, you should talk to your parents about having the wedding there. Surely your farm is much larger than my parents' and therefore can accommodate all of our wedding guests!"

For a moment, Catherine wasn't certain how to respond and was just about to comment when James stepped forward. "That's why I'm going to talk with *Daed*," he said as if that alone should explain his rapid departure. "I shouldn't be more than a few days. John's coming with me. So, I wanted to ask that you look after Ida Mae during my absence." He didn't wait for his sister's response. "And John will help me pick out a clock for my soon-to-be wife."

Once again, Ida Mae jumped up and down like an eager child. James extended his hand for her to take, and, once she accepted it, he led her to the side so that they could talk for a moment before he departed.

"And you," John said, stepping toward her so that he could close the distance between them. "What do you think of the clock?"

Clock? Well, she knew that many young men purchased a clock to give their fiancée but she had no idea what that had to do with her. "I'm sure I have no idea what you mean," she said in a firm voice.

"Do you care for them?" he asked in a firm voice.

"Of course I do!" she exclaimed, laughing at the ridiculous question. "All houses need to have one! Otherwise, how would you possibly know what time it is?"

"So, you would like one, too?" There was a gleam in his eye that made Catherine feel uncomfortable.

She took a step backward as the smile faded from her face. "Young couples all need a clock when they start out. I presume that, one day, I will be in such a situation, John."

He broke into a wide grin. "Oh, Cathy! How I had hoped you would say such a thing!"

Before she could comment further, James called out for his friend. "Let's go, John! I want to get home before the sun sets!"

John turned toward Catherine and said, "I shall look for the most beautiful, expensive clock for you, Cathy."

"That's really not…"

He ran toward James, not listening to her.

"…necessary," she whispered to herself as she watched John climb into the carriage next to James. Both men waved at the two young women before the horse started to move forward, the carriage lurching and then rolling along the lane.

Ida Mae rejoined Catherine, her face beaming and bright. "Isn't this the most wonderful of news?" she asked, not really expecting an answer.

But Catherine forced a smile upon her face as she stood beside her friend who stared after the disappearing buggy. "I'm happy for you and James," she said, her voice full of sincerity. "You will love Fullerton as well as our family."

"Just think," Ida Mae said with a dreaming sigh. "We'll be sisters, Catherine. How fortunate am I to have the most wonderful of men want me to be his wife? And to have his own sister be my very best of friends makes everything even better!"

She linked her arm with Catherine's and began to walk toward the house. "Now, tell me," she said in a serious voice, "tell me everything that I should know about the farm. I'm so anxious to see it and to meet the rest of your family. I do hope they will like me."

As they disappeared inside, the screen door slammed shut behind them, echoing out across the lake.

It wasn't until much later in the afternoon, the sun hiding behind the trees above, that Catherine met up

with Henry and Ellie once more to begin their walk
around the lake. She wondered why they had invited
her for an afternoon stroll instead of the morning, but
she knew better than to ask. It wasn't her place to make
such personal inquiries. If there was a reason that they
wanted to share, they would have.

"And your *daed*?" Catherine asked. "He is well?"

Ellie straightened her back and remained silent.

Henry, however, cleared his throat. "He is, Catherine.
Thank you for inquiring."

"It was quite kind of him to invite me over yesterday," she managed to say.

Neither one of them spoke.

"And such a shame that you'll be leaving the lake
so soon."

Henry coughed into his hand and looked away from
Catherine. This time, Ellie turned toward the younger
woman and smiled. "We still have the shop frolic tomorrow, and that will be quite a lot of fun, don't you think?"

Fun or not, Catherine wasn't looking forward to saying good-bye to her two new friends. She had grown
fond of Ellie and her quiet, comforting manner. As for
Henry, well... She could barely contain herself when
he teased her or engaged in discussion with her about
things no one else ever did. Newbury Acres was far
too distant from Fullerton for her to visit on a regular
basis. And that thought made her dread, not anticipate,
the shop frolic, for it would be the last time that they
would see each other.

"And what are you reading of late?" Henry asked,
clearly changing the conversation.

With a big smile, Catherine began to tell him about
the latest book that she was devouring: *Anne*. "Oh, it's
such a lovely story," she gushed. "A love long lost that

is suddenly rekindled. After so many years, who would have thought that neither one had remarried? And, after Anna refused him the first time, to think that he gave her another chance!"

Henry laughed. "You are quite the romantic, aren't you, Catherine Miller?" he asked, watching her from the corner of his eye.

She blushed at the way he looked at her.

"But life is not a romance book," he said, his tone suddenly somber. "In the real world, your hero would have most likely married long before he met up with Anna again. And poor Anna would marry an older man who needed a wife for his *kinner.*"

At this comment, she pouted. "Oh, I certainly wouldn't want to read *that* book!"

Again, Henry laughed and gently pressed his arm against hers as they walked. "I suppose you're correct! I wouldn't either. I'd much prefer reading about your long-lost lovers rekindling their courtship."

Ellie grew unusually silent, neither commenting nor contributing to the discussion. At first, Catherine didn't notice as she kept talking about the story, describing the horrible younger sister, Mary, and how she was a self-ish woman and self-centered mother. But as they continued to walk, she began to wonder why Ellie seemed so melancholy.

"Oh, it's nothing," she said when Catherine inquired about her silence. "I just enjoy listening to you so. You have such energy and passion for life."

Whether or not that was true, Catherine couldn't be sure. But Ellie's words alleviated her concern.

"When you return to Newbury Acres," Catherine asked, "what will you do for the rest of the summer?"

Ellie sighed and her shoulders drooped a little.

"Cook, I suppose. Make cheese and macramé to sell to the *Englische*. Manage the garden and all of the regular chores that I have. It's a rather lonely place at times, although I suppose I shouldn't complain."

"Lonely?" Catherine couldn't imagine ever feeling lonely at her parents' farm. There was always someone running around, especially in the summer when school was on break. But, as soon as she repeated that word, she realized that Ellie did not have a mother or younger siblings to keep her entertained and busy. "*Mayhaps* you should start a quilting circle? Invite your friends and the other women in the area to come over."

An awkward silence fell among them, and Catherine wondered if she had said something wrong.

"I'll have fine memories of our walks to keep me company," Ellie said at last.

"And the shop frolic tomorrow!" Henry pointed out in a cheerful voice. "I'm looking forward to that."

Ellie gave him a kind smile.

"Oh, help!" Catherine stopped walking and glanced at the sky. "I better head back. I promised Wilma I'd help her bake some fresh blueberry pies to bring along tomorrow. I almost forgot!"

Henry did an about-face, waiting for his sister to do the same. "Then we shall walk you there. Can't have you going back on your word to Wilma, can we now?"

Holding both of his arms at an angle, he waited for Ellie to link her arm with his. Then he looked at Catherine, nudging her with his elbow until she did the same. The three of them walked, arm-in-arm, back on the path in the direction from which they had just come, Catherine relishing her last few moments with her new good friends.

Chapter Fourteen

Unlike the barn frolic, the gathering for the shop frolic was much smaller. Many of the older people, including the Andersons, sat on folding chairs under the shade of a large oak tree, drinking meadow tea and snacking on small pretzels. Nearby, the younger men worked on building the shop, which was going to be used for making harnesses. From what Catherine could see, it was going to be three rooms, two in the front of the building and one large room in the back. The inner wall would be removable so that, if needed, the building could be easily converted into a larger room for worship services or weddings.

The framing of the building was already erected when Catherine and the Andersons arrived. Children played in the large open field behind the house, and the younger women prepared the food. With the sun shining in the cloudless blue sky, it was the perfect summer day, a cool breeze keeping the heat at bay.

Now that Catherine had been introduced to some more people in Banthe, she found herself laughing and chatting with the other women as they prepared the noon meal. The pies that she had made the previous day with Wilma were already on the long table that several men had set up outside. She carried platters of cold cuts and bowls of chow chow to set in the center of the table. Other women were bringing sliced pickles, canned beets, and cooked ears of corn to the table. By the time everything was set up, it looked like a feast fit for Thanksgiving.

"Who is that man?" Ida Mae whispered into her ear when they had finished.

Catherine paused long enough from pouring water into the cups to glance up. "Which man?"

With a nod of her head, Ida Mae indicated the tall man standing beside Henry. They spoke with their heads bent together, their conversation obviously private and of great consequence. Other men were beginning to walk from the shop to the table, but Henry remained in deep conversation with that one man.

"Well, I'm sure I have no idea," Catherine whispered back. "I haven't seen him before."

"Neither have I," Ida Mae said with a slight catch in her throat that caused Catherine to turn toward her.

What she saw startled her. Her friend openly stared at the stranger, a slight smile on her lips. Catherine noticed that the man glanced in their direction, his own eyes assessing both young women. Henry leaned forward and said something to the man, who then studied Ida Mae, his eyes actually moving from her head to her toes and back again.

Rather than act insulted, Ida Mae lowered her eyes demurely.

"Ida Mae!" Catherine hissed and reached for her friend's arm. "You should look away from him!"

"Oh, hush and bother, Catherine! A little admiration from a stranger never hurt anyone."

Scarcely able to believe her ears, Catherine's mouth opened agape. How could Ida Mae openly flirt with a complete stranger? Or anyone for that matter! Catherine's temper flared and she said in a not-too-soft voice, "I reckon my *bruder* James would feel otherwise. You are, after all, engaged!"

With a petulant expression, Ida Mae glowered at Catherine. "You say that as if I've forgotten!" Then, just as suddenly, Ida Mae softened her expression and forced a small smile, batting her eyelashes. "Why, Catherine Miller, you know that your *bruder* James is the only man for me! It isn't as if I asked that strange man to notice me. He did it of his own accord."

But Catherine knew what she had seen and she didn't like it one bit. "Encouraging his attention is just as bad as openly seeking it."

Once again, Ida Mae narrowed her eyes and scowled at her. "Interesting words from my future sister-in-law, who just yesterday went walking during the day with that Henry Tilman!"

Catherine made a face, stunned by what Ida Mae had just said. There was nothing improper with taking a walk with Henry Tilman, especially since Ellie was with them. Their time together had been innocent enough. What bothered Catherine, however, was how Ida Mae was trying to turn the subject around to find fault with her, rather than take responsibility for her poor judgment in flirting with that strange man. "And what does that have to do with your engagement?" she asked in a bold voice.

"Nothing." Her admission came fast and furious,

along with her next comment. "But it does have something to do with yours."

Catherine couldn't help but laugh. "Mine? I'm not engaged to anyone."

Suddenly, Ida Mae's expression changed. She smirked in a way that made her appear sinister, and for a moment, Catherine found herself not caring for this new friend at all. The thought came to her in a flash, as she suddenly realized how many times Ida Mae had twisted situations for her own benefit.

Ida Mae raised an eyebrow and gave her a haughty look. "That's not what my *bruder* John says. Why, he left me a letter at home. He told me that he had made you an offer to marry him, that you did not deny it, so he's intending to speak to your *daed* along with James."

Nothing could have shocked her more. Catherine gasped out loud and pressed her hand against her chest. How was it possible that John could come to such a conclusion? Not only did she barely know him, she wasn't even certain if she liked him!

"Then there was a terrible miscommunication!" she said rapidly. "You must contact him at once, Ida Mae, before he says or does something that might make him feel foolish later!" She reached out and grabbed Ida Mae's hands. "Please promise me! Surely he will contact you while he is away?"

Before she could question her friend further, someone called Catherine's name. Momentarily distracted, Catherine turned in the direction of the voice and smiled when she saw Ellie hurrying toward her.

"Oh, there you are!" she said with an eagerness to her voice that caught Catherine off-guard. "I've been looking for you."

"I've been in the kitchen the whole morning. You must not have been looking very hard," Catherine teased gently.

Ellie gave a soft laugh. "Well, we have only just arrived fifteen minutes ago. We were waiting for my *bruder*, Freddie."

Ah, Catherine thought as she glanced toward Henry once more. "So that's who Henry is talking to, then?"

Nodding her head, Ellie continued talking, as Ida Mae edged away. "*Ja*, that's Freddie. He's come for a few days since we are leaving Saturday. That way, the farm will not be unattended for long."

Once again, Catherine looked at Freddie. In some regards, he resembled Henry. They were both tall with dark hair and bright eyes. However, Freddie appeared more aged than Henry, his skin a creamy brown with deep wrinkles on his brow and under his eyes. The weathered appearance surprised Catherine for she knew that Freddie likely worked inside his shop during the day. And his mouth. It was set in a permanent scowl softened only by his tendency to raise just one eyebrow in a perfect arch.

She could not understand why, but she knew at once that she didn't care for him.

"I spoke with my *daed* about something last evening," Ellie said, redirecting Catherine's attention to her. "And I had rather hoped…" She paused and her cheeks turned pink. Clearing her throat, she started talking again. "Well, I had an idea that I wanted to share with you. You see, it would make me rather happy…"

Her sentence remained unfinished as a deep male voice approached from behind. "Ah, Ellie!" Gid said in what could almost be called a cheerful manner. "I see that you have found Catherine." Behind him came Henry and Freddie, Henry watching her intently while Freddie looked around with a bored expression on his face.

"I'd like to introduce you to my oldest son," Gid said.

Catherine glanced at Freddie, who merely raised an uninterested eyebrow at her and walked away. She made a face and thought she heard Henry stifle a laugh.

Gid, however, didn't seem to notice his son's rude behavior. "So, Ellie has spoken to you then, *ja*?" He didn't wait for a response as he stared at the young woman. "And what say you to spending some time at Newbury Acres, then? Is that something that you might find of interest?"

Ellie lowered her eyes. "I hadn't asked her yet, *Daed*," she said in a soft, non-accusatory tone.

"Indeed?" Gid looked as surprised as Catherine felt. "Well, I reckon that I've just done that for you!" He turned to Catherine and forced a slight smile. "You see, Catherine, our time at Banthe is over for the summer. I'm prevailed upon to return to Newbury Acres to oversee the shop while Henry returns to the fields. I cannot leave Ellie here in the company of her older *bruder*, Freddie…it simply would not be proper."

Catherine couldn't help but wonder why that was so.

"Her one regret of leaving this place was that she'd have no more time to spend with you. So, if your parents could spare you for just another two weeks—and, with all those children, I imagine they could!—we'd like to invite you to be our guest at Newbury Acres. I've already checked with the Andersons, and they've given their consent that you may travel with us and not return to Farmington with them, if your parents agree."

The misunderstanding with John Troyer was quickly forgotten as Catherine focused on this new, and much more pleasant, surprise.

"Why...why I'd be delighted to!" she managed to say. She glanced over Gid's shoulder to see Henry standing there, his hands behind his back and a secretive expression upon his face. When their eyes met, he feigned a serious look, but she saw through it immediately. At once, she returned her attention to Henry's father. "I mean, of course, I must speak with my parents for their approval to not return to Fullerton," she said, politely correcting Gid of his error in regard to the name of her home town.

He didn't appear to notice, or care. Instead, Gid nodded approvingly. "I imagined as much. I'm sure that Henry would be delighted to accompany you to the phone shanty down the lane so that you can make your inquiries. If there are no objections, we will look forward to departing from Banthe with you by ten o'clock sharp on Saturday morning."

He waited for no further response. Turning on his heel, he wandered over to where some of the men were working on cutting boards for framework on the shop's interior. He disappeared into the crowd, leaving Catherine speechless at the stroke of good fortune that had just befallen her.

Ellie gave her a soft smile. "I do hope your parents will agree," she said. "How much fun we would have continuing our friendship from the comfort of our home."

Of that, Catherine could not disagree.

Henry cleared his throat and took a step toward the road. "Shall we, Catherine?"

She looked at him in a questioning manner. "Hmm?"

With his hands still behind his back, something that had now become a familiar gesture to her, he shifted his eyes in the direction of the phone shanty. "Your phone call? I've been instructed to escort you." He leaned over and whispered, "Cannot risk having you swept away by any wayward tourists or mischievous Amish men!"

"Oh! *Ja!*" Sheepishly, she suppressed a laugh, knowing that her cheeks flooded with color as she began to walk alongside Henry. Behind her, she thought she heard Ellie chuckle under her breath, but she was too embarrassed to look over her shoulder.

They walked in silence, the sounds of hammers and sawing slowly fading as they put some distance between themselves and the shop frolic. The farther away they walked, the louder was the noise of the gravel beneath their shoes.

"I must apologize for my *bruder*'s behavior," Henry said at last.

"It should be Freddie apologizing, not you."

He nodded his head once as if agreeing with her. "His ill manners shouldn't be taken personally. It's just how he is. He was just as disagreeable as a baby. It probably runs in the family, I reckon!"

"I'm surprised to hear that. Both you and Ellie are the most agreeable people I know!" Then, after his words hit her, she stopped walking. "Wait a minute. How would *you* know what Freddie was like as a baby? *You* weren't even born yet!"

Henry laughed. "True. Very true! You've caught me!" He gestured for her to continue walking. In a more somber tone, he explained himself. "The truth is that my mother told me. Freddie was born early, had colic, and never seemed to learn how to get along with others."

"Oh, dear!" She couldn't imagine growing up with someone like that. It sounded as if the family had simply accepted Freddie's poor behavior rather than try to correct it.

Taking a deep breath, Henry clutched his hands behind his back as they walked. "*Maem* always said that Ellie and I were her rewards for daring to have more children after experiencing Freddie."

Catherine smiled at his jest.

"Ah, now here we are!" He gestured toward the small building that housed the neighborhood telephone. "The phone shanty!" He opened the door for her. "Take your time visiting with them. I'll just wait out here."

She was apprehensive about making the call. What if no one answered? What if her parents said that she could not go to Newbury Acres? She had, after all, been away for almost two weeks already. She lifted the handset and glanced over her shoulder at Henry. He stood on the other side of the door, staring into the distance. With a small sigh, Catherine dialed her parents' phone number and said a silent prayer that someone was nearby.

Fortunately, one of her younger brothers happened to answer the phone, and after a long five-minute wait, her mother picked up the receiver.

Catherine explained the situation and posed her question, reassuring her mother that both of the Andersons approved of the Tilmans. However, as soon as Catherine mentioned Newbury Acres, she heard her mother catch her breath. Clearly, she was familiar with the name.

"Why…of course you may go visit with your new friend," her mother said in a stiff voice. "Your *schwesters* have been helping out, and with the hay cut just before you left, there isn't as much to do until the next cutting."

"Oh, *danke, Mamm*!"

As Catherine hung up the phone, her hand lingering on the receiver, she could hardly believe that so much had changed in one day. Just an hour before, Catherine had been dreading the morning when the Tilmans would depart for Newbury Acres. She had several sleepless nights worrying about how she might stay in contact with both Ellie and Henry. The distance between their homes was far too great to travel by buggy, and it would be impractical to hire a driver. Now, however, time could not move fast enough for Catherine.

She stepped out of the phone shanty and faced Henry. She noticed that he watched her with more than simple curiosity. For a long moment, he stared at her, making no move to return to the gathering.

The intensity of his gaze caused her to catch her breath.

"She said I might go," Catherine whispered, unable to look away from him.

"So, then it is settled." His voice sounded deep and husky, as if he was saying one thing but meant something quite different.

Inside of her chest, her heart began to flutter and she felt a rush of warmth flood her body that, undoubtedly, colored her cheeks once again. She wanted to tear away her gaze, but she was transfixed. His blue eyes held hers, and if she didn't know any better, she wondered if he might be thinking of reaching for her hand.

The noise of horse's hooves and the rumbling of buggy wheels interrupted their moment. Catherine looked up, both relieved and disappointed by the distraction. To her shock, she saw Freddie and Ida Mae in the open-topped buggy. Freddie drove it down the lane, one of his boots on the dashboard as he slapped the reins against the horse's back and clicked his tongue. The horse lunged forward and Ida Mae squealed out, raising her head to touch the top of her prayer *kapp* as she laughed, which only encouraged Freddie to urge the horse to run even faster.

"Oh!"

Henry watched his brother, a dark shadow covering his face.

"Oh, no! Ida Mae!" Catherine cried out. She turned to look at Henry. "She shouldn't be riding with him! My *bruder*, James…" She let the sentence trail off, unfinished in words but not in understanding.

Henry took a deep breath and gently reached out to touch her arm. "There are some things that are better left to the discretion of the people involved, *ja*?"

Or lack thereof, she thought. But, knowing what he meant, she nodded her head. Still her heart sank at the thought of her dear brother James talking with their father in Fullerton about his future with Ida Mae at the very moment that his beloved fiancée was enjoying the company of another man.

Chapter Fifteen

"A letter?" Catherine asked. She sank into the sofa as Ida Mae paced the floor in front of her, the small envelope clutched in her hand.

Ida Mae had shown up at the Andersons' cottage just a few minutes after ten o'clock Friday morning, distressed and pale. Catherine had barely had time to dry and put away the breakfast dishes. Fortunately, Duane and Wilma had left the house already. They were fishing that morning down at the edge of the lake closer to town. While they had invited Catherine to go along with them, she had politely declined. She had never gone fishing before and knew that she was too anxious to sit still for a long period of time. It was better for her to stay at the house. After all, she needed to wash her clothing and pack her bag for the following day's journey to Newbury Acres.

"James sent you a letter?"

Ida Mae nodded her head. The white strings from her prayer *kapp* fell over her shoulders and Catherine realized that her friend had not tied them. "I…I thought he might just call me, but he sent this letter to my house instead. A driver dropped it off this morning."

"A driver!" Catherine exclaimed. "Oh, help! Is something wrong? My parents?"

"That's what I thought." The sadness in Ida Mae's voice caught her off-guard. "But it has nothing to do with your parents."

Relieved, Catherine clutched her hands together and kept them folded on her lap. "What news did he have that was so very important that he sent a letter with a driver? Nothing bad, I presume?"

For a moment, Ida Mae hesitated. She moved over to the reclining chair and sat down. With great drama, she extracted the letter and unfolded it carefully. "*Nee*, not bad, I suppose." She glanced at Catherine while she held the letter in her hand. "He wrote that he is not returning to Banthe for a while. He has to stay and work on the farm."

That was no surprise. Despite having other siblings, James was the oldest and strongest for farm work. Richard was only thirteen and couldn't do half as much as his older brother. Plus, school was starting soon for the younger children. Their father would need help with cutting and baling hay whenever it was ready again. And with the cows, no doubt. A man's help, not just a thirteen-year-old. Certainly, that news could not have upset Ida Mae so much. "And…?"

The color drained from Ida Mae's cheeks. Whatever news was contained in the letter, it was clear that she was unhappy about it. With an exaggerated sigh, she said, "Seems that he spoke with your *daed* about our marriage."

Catherine fought the urge to shake Ida Mae. She was

purposefully delaying sharing the news that had created her distress. The over-the-top drama was irritating her. "Surely there were no objections to that."

"*Nee*, no objections." Ida Mae raised her eyes to meet Catherine's. "But there is an issue regarding our future."

Raising her eyebrows, Catherine stared at her. "Your future? What on earth?"

"It seems we won't be able to marry in October."

That caught Catherine off-guard. Why would their marriage have to be delayed?

"There is no place for us to live," Ida Mae explained.

Catherine blinked. "I don't understand."

"Your *bruder* doesn't have the money to buy a farm."

She had known that. But that still didn't explain the delay.

Ida Mae's shoulders fell and she played with the letter in her hands. "He hasn't saved enough money to buy a farm, and your *daed* doesn't have extra to loan him. James will continue working for your *daed* to save money."

"I still don't understand the long delay." Frowning, Catherine pursed her lips as she waited for Ida Mae to explain.

"Apparently, your *daed* says that we could live in the *grossdawdihaus* until…" She paused as she lifted the letter so that she could read his exact words. "'…until such a time as we can afford our own place.' That's what he said. But James says that he needs to fix it up and that he couldn't start until the winter."

Once again, Catherine was confused by Ida Mae's unhappiness. "That's *wunderbarr gut* news, then! You could marry in the spring, I'm sure."

But Ida Mae did not look as pleased as Catherine

thought she might. "It could take three or more years to see the money for a farm…if we could even find one in the area. Both of us would have to work to earn money for the deposit." Ida Mae shook her head. "I hadn't known that your *daed* intended to pass the farm down to one of your younger brothers."

The look of disdain on Ida Mae's face startled Catherine. "And that's upsetting you? That one of the younger ones will inherit the farm?" Wasn't that usually the case? Older siblings usually left the farm, striking out on their own. Once he had turned nineteen, James had been paid to help with sporadic carpentry jobs and, when he wasn't doing that, he helped his father on the farm. A few more years under his belt and he would easily be able to afford his own place. "Or are you upset about having to work outside of the farm?" Neither explanation made much sense to Catherine. It wasn't uncommon for the older children to live in a *grossdawdihaus* after they married. Nor was it uncommon for newly married women to work outside of the house until their firstborn child arrived.

Taking a deep breath, Ida Mae raised an eyebrow and finally said what was on her mind. "James had led me to believe that he would be running the farm when your *daed* retired."

At this comment, Catherine gave a short laugh. She couldn't imagine James purposefully misleading Ida Mae. Surely, she had misunderstood her brother. "I'm sure James will work there for as long as he wants. But unless you intend to raise your children in that two-bedroom *grossdawdihaus*, you'll have to move somewhere else. My parents still have to raise their own family. My youngest *bruder* is only six years old!" It would be twelve years or more before young George married. And, at that time, her parents would retire to the *grossdawdihaus* while one of their younger sons took over the farm. "That's the way it is on most Amish farms, Ida Mae. Did you expect something different?"

Quickly, Ida Mae averted her eyes and shook her head. "*Nee*, of course not. That's not it at all, Catherine."

Her words were not convincing.

"I…I just feel bad for James, that's all. Such an enormous amount of pressure on him now. I mean…" She lowered her eyes. "I had thought he would be better situated if we were to marry. A *grossdawdihaus* is fine, I'm sure. But he'll have to work and save every penny in order to buy his own farm. And you know how expensive they are around here! I didn't want it to be so difficult for him, you know?"

If she believed Ida Mae, Catherine might have been more empathetic with her suffering. But she didn't. Instead, Catherine was beginning to understand exactly what Ida Mae was insinuating. There would be a lot of sacrifice in their initial years as husband and wife. Sacrifice and hard work. "Are you having second thoughts, Ida Mae?"

"Oh, no! Not at all!" she gushed far too quickly. "You know that James is my everything! I couldn't imagine not marrying him. I just wish we didn't have to wait so long."

"You are young yet, and you haven't even met our parents or the rest of the family," Catherine pointed out. "Waiting might be for the best."

"True, of course."

"My *daed*'s offer to live in the *grossdawdihaus* is what he can afford to do," Catherine continued, trying to pick her words carefully so that she did not offend Ida Mae. "And I know that James will take care of you and your children. He'll make ends meet, and you'll have your own farm eventually."

While she understood Ida Mae's concern, she did not understand her hesitation. Marriage was work, regardless of the financial situation. Even though romance was delightful, the true glue that kept a marriage together was friendship, and that was something that James and Ida Mae certainly seemed to have.

"Everything will work out," she reassured her friend. "Now, why don't we walk to town and I'll treat you to some ice cream? It's our last day together for a while, *ja*? We should have some fun."

As they sat on the bench near the center of town, their ice cream cones dripping in the increasing heat of the day, they watched the people coming and going. Most rode bicycles while a few used their horse and buggies. It was the one thing that Catherine would miss about Banthe. Unlike Fullerton, Banthe's town center was truly the heart of the community. On any given day, most people passed through it.

So she wasn't surprised when she saw a familiar face driving an open carriage. While she had not spent any time to speak of with Freddie Tilman, she would never forget meeting him the other day at the shop frolic.

"Oh, help and bother!" she muttered under her breath.

But Ida Mae had seen him, too. Suddenly, she sat upright and tossed her ice cream into the trash bin beside the bench. "Do I look alright?" she whispered to Catherine.

"Of course. Why?"

Catherine only needed to follow Ida Mae's gaze to figure out why she had asked.

"Ida Mae! You're to be married!" she hissed.

"I'm just being friendly."

"Too friendly, if you ask me."

Ida Mae ignored Catherine's reprimand. "Freddie!" she called out, waving her hand in the air. "Have you come to town looking for something special then?" she asked as the buggy slowed to a halt before them.

There was no mistaking the roguish way that his eyes looked at Ida Mae. "Indeed, I have! And it appears that I have just found it! And now, if that something special would care to go for a ride...?"

"Oh!" She giggled in a flirtatious way that angered Catherine.

"Your fiancé would not approve," she said loud enough so that Freddie would hear. Unfortunately, he didn't even blink at the mention of an upcoming wedding. Instead, he jumped down from the carriage and held out his hand for Ida Mae to take. He then held her hand far too long before he guided her to the little round step on the side of the carriage. Furious, Catherine dropped her ice cream cone and crossed her arms over her chest. She glared at Ida Mae.

"Oh, don't be a spoil sport," Ida Mae said in a light-hearted manner. "I need to get home anyway. I have wedding preparations to make." She dragged out the word in such a way that it sounded almost mocking. "Have a great time in Newbury Acres, Catherine!" she called out as Freddie climbed up beside her and quickly urged the horse away from town.

Catherine clenched her teeth as she watched the buggy disappear down a road that led to neither the

Troyers' farm nor the Tilmans' cottage. Her brother would be devastated, and Catherine knew that she would have a hard time forgiving Ida Mae for this blatant slight toward James.

Once they were gone from sight, Catherine wandered over to the store where she had purchased her book the previous week. She didn't want to return home yet, her head being too full of worry about Ida Mae and James. While she couldn't do anything to change Ida Mae's poor decision to ride off with Freddie, she could try to find a new book to read so that she could forget about it.

She lingered near the bookshelves, taking one book after another off the shelf so that she could read the back cover. When she was on the fifth book, she felt someone walk up behind her.

"Are you going to select a book or just read them all here?"

Startled, she spun around and collided with Henry. He placed his hands on her arms and steadied her.

"Whoa now! Easy does it," he teased.

"You frightened me!" But she smiled.

He glanced down at the book in her hand. "A mystery?"

She blushed and put the book back on the shelf. "Just something to bring with me to Newbury Acres."

"Ah! Of course! Newbury Acres is the perfect place to read a mystery book! There are so many secrets lurking in the shadows!"

Her eyes widened. "Are there really? Like what?"

He leaned forward and whispered, "Large buildings with dark corners and shadows that conceal passages."

"Do you think you might speak with your *bruder*?" she asked in a timid voice. She had not expected to ask

Henry for this favor, but the words had blurted out of her mouth. "About Ida Mae, I mean."

Henry seemed puzzled by her request. "Why would I do such a thing?"

"Well… I thought…" She stopped and tried to figure out what, exactly, she had thought. "Oh, I don't know."

Patiently, Henry tried to coax it out of her. "What is it you thought, Catherine?"

"That maybe you might talk to him about Ida Mae's engagement. That it's inappropriate for her to be riding around with him. If he paid her less attention…"

Henry held up his hand, stopping her in midsentence. "Say no more, Catherine."

A feeling of relief washed over her. "Then you will speak to him?"

"I will not."

She hadn't expected to hear that from him. "You won't?"

He shook his head. "*Nee*, I will not. She is a grown woman, and she is making her own choices. If I were to interfere and ask Freddie to leave her be, one of two things will occur." He held up one finger. "He becomes more interested in her because she is the forbidden fruit or…" He held up a second finger. "… If that is her true nature, to succumb to temptation, she will find someone else to interest her while James is away."

"Oh, help!" Catherine muttered. She hadn't considered those two outcomes, but she realized that it made sense.

"In my life, I have learned that when you tell someone 'No,' that very prohibited thing becomes that which is most ardently desired."

His words took her by surprise. She hadn't thought of

it in that way. But he had a point. If Ida Mae was willing to risk her engagement and reputation by flirting with Freddie, then he was not the problem: she was. And she knew very well how hard it was to tell her younger siblings that they could not have something, such as a cookie or piece of fresh-baked bread. Once she said no, that was all that they wanted.

"Come now, Catherine," Henry said. "I'm sure that everything will be just fine with Ida Mae and your *bruder*. You shouldn't worry about their romance, especially when you have your own."

Her eyes widened.

He gestured toward the bookshelf. "See? Tons of romance at your disposal. Let's select your novel, and if you would not mind, I'd enjoy walking you home, Catherine." He glanced through the titles and selected a book. "Ah! *Maryanne and Eleanor*! Based on Jane Austen's lovely romance, *Sense and Sensibility*, I see." He held up the book for her to admire the pretty cover while he read the description on the back of the book with exaggerated drama, which made her laugh. When Henry finished, he looked at her and raised his eyebrows as if inquiring whether or not she wanted that particular book. "What do you say? Should we find out what happens to those two sisters? Will they find romance after they are forced to move to Devontown?"

Charmed by his ability to make her feel better, all that Catherine could do was nod her head. While she suspected that both Maryanne and Eleanor would find romance in Devontown, she could only hope and pray that a certain young woman named Catherine Miller would find it in Newbury Acres.

Chapter Sixteen

Unlike the Andersons, the Tilmans had driven their horse and carriages to Banthe. When they arrived to pick up Catherine Saturday morning, she was surprised to see Gid, not Henry, come to the door for her bags.

"Good day, Wilma. Duane," he said with all manner of politeness.

"Take good care of our girl." Wilma already had a tissue clutched in her hand and was dabbing at her eyes. Even though Catherine was embarrassed by the overly exaggerated display of emotion—for they were returning to Fullerton on Monday and would have had to part company then anyway—she went over and gave Wilma a quick embrace. "Oh, help," Wilma sniffled and gave a little laugh. "I've grown even fonder of you these past few weeks! I didn't think it was possible. I'll miss having you around."

Extracting herself from Wilma's arms, Catherine gave her a kind smile. "*Danke* for having me. It's been *wunderbarr*!"

And just as quickly as Gid had walked into the house,

he exited. Catherine hurried and followed him, pausing at the road to wave at Wilma and Duane.

"Now, Catherine," Gid said as he tossed her bag into the back of his buggy. "I hope you don't mind if I ask you to ride with Henry. Keep him company, *ja*?"

While she didn't mind one bit, she was, however, curious as to why Gid Tilman would make such a request. Rather than ask, she merely nodded and hurried to the second carriage, the same one that Freddie had driven the other day with Ida Mae.

Henry greeted her with a big grin and reached down his hand to help her jump into the carriage. "What a pleasant trip home this will be!" he commented jovially.

"I hope my companionship lives up to your great expectations," she teased back.

No sooner had they pulled away from the lake house than Catherine understood why she was seated beside Henry. The back of Gid's buggy was filled with bags, and there was no room for her in the back seat. Ellie looked miserable as she rode beside her father. She stared into the distance, and neither one of them appeared to engage in any conversation.

Henry, however, kept enough distance from his father's buggy that they could converse without any fear of being overheard.

"I hope you like Newbury Acres," he said. "It's a bit different than most Amish farms."

"Oh?" She stared at him while he drove. "How so?"

The reins moved in his hands and the horse snorted, trying to speed up, but Henry held it back. "It's an older farmhouse. Been in the family for generations now. Over the years, it's been added onto several times so it's rather…" He paused and glanced at her. "Large."

She laughed at the serious expression on his face. "It's large? And that's why you think I wouldn't like it?" She leaned over and lowered her voice. "I'm not afraid of large houses," she whispered.

He leaned toward her so that their shoulders touched. "I didn't think you were," he whispered back, and she laughed.

"So, tell me about this large farm of yours." She straightened up and leaned back against the seat.

"It's five hundred acres," he started to say.

Catherine gasped, cutting him off from continuing. "Five hundred acres! Why, that's not large! It's monstrous!"

He glanced at her and winked. "Afraid now?"

"Not even one bit! But that is far too large to farm, Henry."

He nodded his head. "*Ja*, indeed. Part of the property is wooded. *Daed* and Freddie go hunting there sometimes, and in the winter, we tap the trees for syrup. It's a good time when everyone comes together to boil down the syrup. We bring our grill and cook food while we work."

That sounded like fun to Catherine. "I've never done that before!"

"And of course, we have the dairy barn. We have almost a hundred cows."

Once again, Catherine gasped. "A hundred! Even with a machine, that must take you hours to milk them!"

He held up his hand, pointing toward the sky. "Very astute, Catherine. Indeed, it would take hours. But we have two milking pits and we also have workers. Remember I told you about my father creating the farming co-op? Without those workers, I never would have the chance to get away to Banthe, and I certainly would not have the pleasure of making new acquaintances such as yourself."

She was starting to understand what Henry meant when he had told her that Newbury Acres was a bit different from other Amish farms. She couldn't imagine the amount of labor required to manage it on a daily basis. "Why does your *daed* want to have such a large herd of cows? That's an awful lot of work, even if you have workers."

"And don't forget that we have the wood shop. Freddie runs that. They make furniture that is shipped to almost every state in the country. Tables. Chairs. Beds. Dressers. You name it. He also has workers that help him." He paused, looking at her once more to see if she was still listening. "And, of course, we grow corn and hay."

"With the help of more workers, I take it?" she asked.

He nodded. "Most of the community works at Newbury Acres. Besides our farm, there are just a scattering of small gentleman's farms where the other Amish live. Just enough property to grow their gardens and graze their horses."

Catherine frowned as she tried to digest what Henry was telling her. From the sound of it, Newbury Acres wasn't just an Amish farm. It was more like an entire Amish community. Only the Tilmans owned the majority of it, which meant that the workers were at their beck and call. While she knew that sometimes Amish families needed help with their financial situations, they still remained independent. She couldn't imagine a life where she was beholden to one family in order to put food on the table.

"Personally, I prefer working in the fields. There's something about working the soil," Henry continued. "I'm glad that so many young men in the area can take care of the cows so that I can tend to the crops. But even that is a bit cumbersome for just one person. I've been resisting my *daed* on hiring workers. I'd much rather tend to it myself, you see. But he's adamant that I need help."

"And does your *daed* always force his opinions on others?" she asked in a genuinely curious tone.

"He does."

Catherine made a face. "I wouldn't like that one bit."

Henry chuckled under his breath. "I imagine you wouldn't, Catherine. And I can assure you that I don't either."

For a long moment, Catherine remained silent. Her mind was spinning as she realized that there was much more to the Tilman family than met the eye. "And what else does your *daed* impose upon you?" she asked.

"What else is there?"

She hesitated, knowing she was about to bring up an intimate topic. But her curiosity overcame her. "None of you has married yet. And Freddie's much older than you. I would think that he'd have a wife and children by now."

"Freddie is…" Henry hesitated, searching for the right word. "Well, let's just say he's not ready to settle down, I imagine. As for Ellie and myself, well, our *daed* does have expectations of who we should marry."

"Expectations!" Catherine turned to face him. "I should think that the only expectation he would have is happiness!"

Henry gave another soft laugh. "Oh, Catherine. If only happiness were enough for *Daed*."

"But he was happy with your *maem*, wasn't he? Shouldn't he expect no less for his own children?"

"Was he happy with *Maem*?" Henry glanced at her and she noticed that there was a sad look in his eyes. "I suppose he was happy. After all, he acquired her parents' farm when he married her."

This was more than Catherine could accept. "Happy because he acquired her parents' farm? Didn't he love her?" When Henry did not respond, Catherine wrung her hands on her lap. "I can't imagine a marriage without love!"

"Unfortunately," Henry said in a somber voice, "love does not make the list of his expectations. Money. Land. Those are the two qualifications that top his list, at least for his sons. In fact, he has gone so far as to threaten us with the loss of Newbury Acres if we do not marry a 'worthy' woman." He said that with mockery in his voice. "As for Ellie, I'm not certain he has any expectations. He might very well prefer that she remain an old *maedel* so that he doesn't have to worry about her leaving. After all, who would cook his meals if she wasn't there anymore?"

Distressed, Catherine slumped in the seat next to Henry. She couldn't imagine living in such a family. How depressing for Ellie, to know that her father preferred her to never marry just so he had someone to wash his clothing and make his meals. As for Henry, there weren't many young Amish women who could meet the qualifications of land and money.

"What would happen," she began to ask in a slow,

deliberate manner, "if you wanted to marry someone who did not bring money or land to the marriage?"

"Ah." Henry took a long moment and then nodded his head as he turned to face her. "Then, Catherine, I would have a very difficult decision to make. A man must make his livelihood in order to support his family. Without the livelihood, what use is having the family?"

For a long while after that, they rode in silence. Catherine felt as if a pit had formed in her stomach. As the oldest daughter, she had neither money nor land. All of that would get passed onto one of her younger brothers. So why had Gid Tilman not only encouraged her friendship with Ellie but urged her to be in Henry's company, not once but twice now? With nothing to offer the family that could possibly meet Gid's approval, she was fooling herself to think that she could ever have any hope of marrying Henry.

It was almost another half an hour before they arrived at Newbury Acres. Most of the drive was through pleasant rolling farmland, but as they neared the Tilmans' home, she noticed that the geography began to change. There were thick patches of trees and more woodland. At one turn, she was delighted to see a male pheasant standing on a dead tree trunk on the side of the road. Henry slowed down the buggy so that she could see the fowl as it seemingly posed for her.

"We're almost there now," Henry said. "Our woods are renowned for their pheasants. This one must have stood guard," he added with a wink.

"Really? I don't think I've ever seen one before. He was magnificent, *ja*? Truly one of God's prettier creatures, even if they are not normally included in such discussions."

Henry laughed at her. "I never thought of it that way, but you're right!"

After a mile stretch of forest, she noticed small clearings with old farmhouses and barns. Many of the houses had clothes lines with sheets and towels or dresses and pants drying in the sun. But the properties were small and not one of them had enough land for crops, just paddocks for their horses.

"Is this Newbury Acres then?" she asked.

Henry nodded. "It is. Over the years, as the family acquired more and more land, people have come to call our farm Newbury Acres. In reality, however, the entire area is Newbury Acres. It can be confusing, for sure."

She agreed with Henry on that point.

They rounded another bend and came across a large clearing, this one with large, plush, green fields surrounded by a simple post and wire fence. Far in the distance, she saw acres and acres of corn, with tassels gleaming in the sun. When the buggy drove past a break in the fence, she saw a long, tree-lined driveway, paved, not graveled. At the very end, she could see the house. Even the thick patch of pine trees planted to hide the view from the road could not cover the enormous white stone farmhouse from sight.

Catherine caught her breath and, without realizing it, reached out to grab Henry's arm. "Is that...?" She couldn't finish the sentence.

But Henry could. He sighed as he said, "*Ja*, that's our home."

It was easy to pick out the original house: what would have been a simple two-and-a-half-story home with a stone foundation. Catherine could imagine there was a large loft on the top floor, the roofline creating a low ceiling with alcoves to tuck in beds for the younger children as well as two small square windows for curious eyes to peer outside instead of sleeping. Certainly, the second floor had four bedrooms for older children while the master bedroom was most likely on the first floor. That was typical for so many of the older Amish farmhouses.

But, apparently, *that* had not been large enough, for someone had added an even larger white clapboard house onto the northern side. If the one house could shelter upwards of twelve people, the new addition could do that as well. And then there was another addition, one that was more modern with a peaked roof and large windows. There was even a circular covered porch area on the end that overlooked the back fields. This house also looked as if ten or twelve people could live there.

"How…how many of you…?" Once again, she could not finish her sentence. She felt absurd asking the question in the first place. Clearly more than one family lived in that house.

So when Henry responded with a quiet "Four," her mouth fell agape and she stared at him, shocked. "Four? Just four? Why, that's…"

"… Ridiculous, *ja*?" he interrupted. "I agree, Catherine. The house is designed for three families. Three large families. There is even a small *grossdawdihaus* on the other side. You can't see it from here. Yet only four people occupy it."

"That's…outrageous." She could hide neither her surprise nor her contempt.

"And I agree. There's also an unused farmhouse on

the property he inherited when my mother's parents died."

Catherine turned and stared at him. "Unused? Why, that's so wasteful!"

The Amish were taught to use everything and waste nothing. Gid Tilman acted as if he were a kind man, providing jobs for so many people in the community— a community that he practically owned, she reminded herself. To hold onto so much land, more than he could use, and have so much housing that wasn't even occupied, was more than wasteful.

"Well, it's not completely unused," Henry said. "I work the fields over there and there are times when I stay there. It's just easier since I put in such long hours. Why, there are times when Ellie has no companions at all! *Daed* and Freddie sometimes travel for the wood shop business, meeting with distribution places in other Amish communities. But other than that, the houses sit here unoccupied."

"And the bishop or preachers haven't complained?"

Henry shook his head. "*Ja*, Catherine. But my *daed* hasn't listened. And what can the church do? If *Daed* was shunned, the people couldn't work and earn money to feed their families."

"Do you agree with this?" she asked, practically holding her breath as she awaited his answer.

He took his time, thinking of the right words before he responded. She could see that the question she asked was one that he had pondered before, and for that she was glad. If he had responded with a quick "yes" or "no," she would have been less tempted to believe him.

"Catherine, I would be much happier if I could live on my mother's childhood farm, raising a small herd of cows and farming my own land. I do not like being beholden to other men to take care of my land or herds. And I'm fairly certain that they feel the same way: not wanting to be tied so tightly to the Tilman family in order for their families to survive."

"And you've told your father this?"

Henry nodded his head. "*Ja*, Catherine, I have. And he has told me that I should keep my opinions to myself."

Catherine lowered her eyes. She should've thought twice before she had asked him that question. Poor Henry, she thought. Trapped in a life that was more ostentatious than any true Amish man would ever want. Yet, if he stood up to his father, he risked losing his livelihood. Even though he was young, losing his job was not a simple matter. And as a good Amish son, he was also expected to honor his father, even if he did not always agree with him.

Suddenly, she realized that the next two weeks at Newbury Acres might not be as much fun as she had anticipated. Clearly there was more to Gid Tilman than first met the eye, and this new insight into his character both intrigued and intimidated Catherine. And one burning question filled her mind: Why had Gid wanted her to come for a visit in the first place?

Chapter Seventeen

After they had arrived at the farm and gotten settled, Catherine and Ellie took an afternoon walk down a path that led through a patch of trees behind one of the barns. It was shaded and cool. Ellie had told her it was an old logging trail that her great-grandfather had cut when expanding the original farm. Now she used it for a walking path in the heat of the day.

Catherine was glad to be outdoors. She needed the fresh air and time alone with her friend.

From the moment she had stepped foot into the overly large farmhouse, Catherine had felt as if she were in another world. While the house was massive on the outside, the inside remained plain and simple. Each room was painted a pleasant shade of light grayish-blue with window shades just a touch darker, for contrast. The moldings around the doors, windows, and floor-boards were bright white, which made each room appear crisp and clean.

Only the kitchen floor was not hardwood. Instead, it was a plain speckled white linoleum: practical and easy to clean. But the rest of the house had hardwood floors, stained in a dark maple color. They shone as if they had just been refinished that very same week. While Catherine had only seen a few rooms of the house, such as the kitchen and the guest room where she would sleep, she could tell that everything was meticulously cared for. There was not a speck of dust or one thing out of place.

Apparently, the Tilmans occupied only the middle part of the house. She had learned this fact when Gid Tilman showed her around the house and property. Surprisingly, Gid had been waiting for her to arrive with Henry and immediately helped her down from the buggy. Then, with Ellie in tow, Gid took Catherine to tour the two large dairy barns as well as the horse and mule stable. He seemed quite impressed with himself when he walked her the quarter mile to the wood shop, which on Saturdays closed at two o'clock so that his workers could enjoy the afternoon with their families.

"Everything is so…" She sought for the appropriate word. "…so organized and well-thought-out."

If she didn't know any better, she would have thought that she saw Gid's chest puff out at the compliment.

"I suppose your *daed*'s farm runs as well?" Gid asked.

Catherine shook her head. "He has enough helpers, but they are not as efficient as here."

"What of the Andersons? Isn't their farm as nice as here?"

Catherine frowned. "The Andersons? Why, of course they have a lovely farm. But no farm in Fullerton would compare to the…" She hesitated as she sought the appropriate word, fearing that she might offend Gid by expressing her honest opinion. "…well, nothing in Fullerton compares to the grandeur of Newbury Acres."

Despite noticing that Gid seemed to take that as a compliment, which wasn't entirely her intention, she could not deny that everything under his control seemed to operate like clockwork. And despite her concern over the workers feeling beholden, she did not sense any tension or resentment when she walked through the different buildings. The only tension she ever seemed to feel regarding Gid Tilman came from his own children.

But it was the house proper that intrigued Catherine. It was so large and so underutilized that she couldn't imagine only four people living in it. Especially after she saw how large the kitchen and gathering room were. The large farmer's table appeared to be able to seat twelve people. The top was made of wormy maple, and even though it was so long and almost two inches thick, it appeared to be made from just one solid piece of wood. Catherine couldn't help but run her fingers along the edge as she walked past it.

When she came to the end, she wandered across the barren space toward the back windows that looked out on the eastern fields. She could imagine that the sun properly warmed up the room in the mornings. Next to the farthest window was a door. It was plain and simple, no fancy woodwork or moldings. She presumed it was a bathroom. She reached out her hand and had placed it on the knob when Gid stopped her with one word: "No!"

Startled, she turned around.

"I'm sorry," she said. "I thought this was the bathroom."

He shook his head and pointed to another door that she hadn't seen under the staircase. "That's the bathroom."

"Where does this door lead?" she asked, curious because of his reaction.

"That leads to the other side of the house. We do not go there."

That was all the explanation that she received from him. From the expression on his face, he wasn't encouraging any further questions from his guest. "I see," she said and dropped her hand.

"Perhaps, Ellie," Gid said as he redirected his attention to his daughter, "you and your friend might go for a nice walk. I'm sure the exercise would do you both good after the buggy ride. I have my own things to go over at the shop, but I'll expect supper at five o'clock precisely. We have church tomorrow and will need a good night's sleep." Without another word, he turned and left both women standing in the kitchen staring after him.

"Oh, dear," Catherine said. "I hope I didn't upset him."

Ellie shook her head and motioned toward the door. "*Kum*, Catherine. There's a *wunderbarr* walking trail and mayhaps we'll see Henry. He said he wanted to go inspect the corn crop after he changed his clothes."

Now that they were alone and walking down the trail, Catherine managed to ask Ellie why their family lived in the middle section of the house, rather than the newer one.

At first Ellie laughed, and then she sobered as she gave a little shrug of her shoulders. "We used to live in the newer section, but after *Maem* died, *Daed* moved us to the middle section and locked the adjoining door."

They came to a fork in the road and turned toward the left.

Catherine frowned. "Locked the adjoining door? Does that mean that you don't ever use that part of the house?"

Shaking her head, Ellie sighed. "*Nee*, and it's a shame. It would be much nicer to host worship service in the large gathering room. The windows open more and there's always a fresh breeze because of it being situated near the woods. But *Daed* refuses, and when it's our turn to host worship, we hold it in the oldest section of the house."

Once again, Catherine found herself pondering the conflicting stories she was learning about Gid. "He must have loved her very much to feel such heartache that he cannot return to the place where she cared for all of you."

This time, it was Ellie who frowned. She glanced over at Catherine and asked, "Is that what you think? That he chased us away from our home so that he wasn't tearful over her memory?" Then, softening her tone, Ellie said, "That must be your romantic heart speaking, Catherine. To certain people there are some things more important than love. My *daed* falls into that category, I suppose."

Catherine knew enough to ask no more questions. Despite wanting to know more about Ellie and Henry's *maem*, she knew that it was not proper to pry into other people's business, especially when their discomfort was increasingly clear. But she could not deny that her curiosity over this woman, the woman who had borne Henry Tilman, only increased with the air of secrecy that seemed to surround her short life.

"I don't suppose you would be able to show me that house," Catherine asked. "I would so like to see it."

Ellie stopped walking, her arms falling limp to her sides as she seemed to contemplate Catherine's request. For a long moment, Catherine feared that she had offended her friend and almost wished that she could take back her question. But when Ellie turned to look at her,

her eyes bright and full of hope, Catherine knew that no offense had been taken.

"*Ja*, Catherine," she said in a soft, even voice. "There is no reason why I should not. I know that *Daed* has kept everything as *Maem* left it, but he has never expressly forbid us from entering. Why, you are so right! I would like to see the *haus*. He has kept it the way *Maem* did. I just never thought to go there after he locked the door!"

Catherine felt her heart pounding as Ellie took her arm and turned her around, their feet headed back toward the massive farmhouse at the entrance to the path.

"*Ja*, this is right *gut*," Ellie continued as if she were speaking to Catherine, but in reality, she appeared to be reassuring herself. "It has been ten years since *Maem* passed."

Catherine's heart broke for her friend.

"I still miss her every day," Ellie continued.

"Were you here when she passed away then?" Catherine asked.

"*Nee*, I was not. *Daed* had sent me to Banthe to visit relatives. She had been ill for some time, but her death was very sudden. Unexpected."

Catching herself from gasping, Catherine wondered how her friend had dealt with such a blow at her young age. "I'm so sorry, Ellie," she whispered. "That's an empty space that cannot be filled."

Nodding her head, Ellie met her gaze. "My *daed* acts as though she never existed. But I miss my *muder*. I have no memento of her, nothing to hold onto. Although she taught me how to cook and bake and sew from a young age, I've had no one to teach me how to be a young woman." She glanced at the locked door. "And it's all in there," she mumbled. "Only ten steps from the very kitchen where I have been cooking and cleaning and serving her sons and husband!" Suddenly, something changed in her eyes. "Why shouldn't I be allowed to go there?"

With a slight hesitation, Catherine slowed her steps. The last thing she wanted was to get her friend in trouble with her father, especially on her very first day staying at Newbury Acres. "Ellie," she said. "If your *daed* is that upset about people seeing the newer section of the house…"

But Ellie cut her off. "*Nee*, Catherine," she said in a sharp tone that Catherine took no personal offense to hearing. "It's not about people seeing the newer section of the *haus*. It is more that he does not want anyone to remember us living in that section of the *haus*. My *daed* has all but banished any memory of our *maem*. For what reason? There is no way to truly answer that."

"Oh, help," Catherine muttered to herself.

"Oh, help, indeed!" Ellie replied sharply. "A child has the right to remember her *maem*. To push the children out of the *haus* and lock the door is a terrible thing. And I thank you for encouraging me to challenge him. I have the right to see her kitchen and her quilts. To understand how she organized the kitchen and her pantry! It isn't as if I've had any other maternal leadership since she passed away! How on earth can I pass on her recipes, Catherine, if I don't have access to what she had written down? My *daed* has done a grave disservice to me and my own future family by hindering me from learning all of these things."

By this time, they were approaching the house. Catherine felt grave remorse for having mentioned anything about their deceased mother at all. The last thing she wanted was to upset anyone in the Tilman family, although she wasn't certain who frightened her more: Henry or his father! Reluctantly, she followed Ellie into the front door of the middle house, knowing that she alone had caused this invasion of Gid Tilman's house.

"*Kum*, Catherine," Ellie beckoned as she went to the forbidden door. "I cannot thank you enough for having given me the courage to do what I have wanted to do for the past ten years!" She gave Catherine a nervous smile. "That is exactly why I wanted you to come here, you know. To give me courage where I normally lack it!"

Catherine finally found her voice. "Please, Ellie," she pleaded. "Don't do anything that could jeopardize either of our standings in the family. I'm so looking forward to being here."

"Hush now," Ellie said in a light tone. "You were curious about my *maem*, *ja*? Well then, it is high time to have your and everyone else's questions answered! Let no whispers of scandal stop us from doing what should have been done long ago!"

Scandal. It was the exact word that Catherine had been thinking. She recalled John Troyer's comments that one day about saving her from the Tilmans. And while she had grown to adore Ellie and thought more than highly of Henry, she was, indeed, beginning to feel that a scandal lurked under their roof. Clearly, Gid Tilman had not cared for his wife as much as Catherine would have assumed. From what she could gather, he had married her merely to expand his enormous estate, wanting her property since it adjoined his. Catherine could only wonder if he had courted his wife with false kindness.

Ellie hurried to the kitchen cabinet farthest away from the mysterious door. When she opened it, she began looking through several keys hanging from hooks on the inside. Finding what she was looking for, she took it down and pressed it into her palm. "Here! I have the key!" she said and walked back to the door. "There's a room in between this kitchen and the one from the other section. We used it for large gatherings and worship services." Ellie exchanged a look with Catherine as she unlocked the door and, after taking a deep breath, opened it.

The room was dark, the shades having been pulled down so that barely any light filtered through the windows.

"Oh, help," Ellie muttered. "I best get a flashlight."

She left Catherine standing there by the open door so that she could rummage under the kitchen sink for a small flashlight. "This should do."

But no sooner had she flicked it on and taken one step into the room when a deep voice called out from behind them.

"What are you doing, Ellie Tilman?"

Both young women froze. Catherine felt Ellie clutch her hand, squeezing it before turning to face her father. "I…I was showing Catherine the other section of the *haus*," she stammered. "I wanted to show her *Maem*'s quilts and fetch her recipes so we could…"

"Enough!" His voice boomed in the large room. "You know we do not go into that side of the house. And I will not have your *maem*'s things brought over."

Catherine lowered her eyes as she stepped back into the kitchen. She couldn't believe that Gid's feelings for his wife were so bitter that he couldn't bear to see her things. To deny even something as simple as recipes to her only daughter? Something terrible must have happened to her indeed.

Chapter Eighteen

Nothing further was said about Ellie's *maem* or Ellie's attempt to show Catherine her mother's things. However, Catherine noticed that Gid seemed to look at her in a new, different way. Often, she caught him studying her when he was in the room. Whether or not it was her imagination, she couldn't decide. But she tried to be on her best behavior and give him no reason to fault her further.

The following day, which happened to be a worship Sunday in Newbury Acres, Catherine stood next to Ellie as they greeted the other women. While Catherine found most everyone to be pleasant and interested in learning more about her, Catherine couldn't help feeling shy under their inquisitive attention. She clung to Ellie's side so that she could be properly introduced to the different women who wanted to learn more about her.

"They met you in Banthe," one woman said. "And you've come visiting already?"

Ellie gave the woman a gentle look. "Isn't that *wunderbarr*, Naomi? How fortunate I am that her family agreed. It's so pleasant having a friend at the farm."

Naomi raised an eyebrow and narrowed her gaze as she studied Catherine. "And what, exactly, does your *daed* do then?"

Catherine wasn't used to being the center of attention. Oh, how she wished the service would start! "He's a farmer. In Fullerton."

Another woman jumped into the conversation. "Fullerton? Why, that's a good hour drive by a hired van, *ja*?"

"Which is exactly why Catherine came to stay with us directly from Banthe, Millie," Ellie answered quickly.

Catherine noticed that Naomi and Millie exchanged a look, one that she couldn't quite decipher.

When the two women joined a group of other women to chat, Ellie leaned over and whispered, "They're the Holden sisters, and they live in town behind the quilting store. They own it and are quite up on all of their gossip of the comings and goings of people."

"So I sensed," Catherine replied.

"They're sisters by birth and they married the Holden brothers, who lost their farm fifteen years back."

Catherine gasped. "Oh, help!"

"*Daed* bought the land and leased the farms to their sons."

For a moment, Catherine didn't quite understand what Ellie had said. That made no sense to her. Why purchase the land only to lease it back?

As if she read Catherine's mind, she said in a low voice, "*Daed* gets the rental income as well as a percentage of Paul and Marvin's crop sales."

Startled, Catherine pulled back and looked at Ellie, almost as if her friend might laugh and tell her that she spoke in jest. But the seriousness on Ellie's face told

Catherine the truth. If Gid bought bankrupt farms like that, was he any better than a land baron? She knew about those from Jane Austen novels.

Her opinion of Gid, which wasn't very positive to begin with, suddenly sank a little bit lower.

That afternoon, when they returned to the farm, she was startled that Gid insisted they all sit together in the large kitchen. He read from the Bible while Henry, Ellie, and Catherine played a game of Scrabble, quietly talking amongst themselves and laughing about the different word combinations that they came up with. When Catherine won the first round, Henry quipped in a good-natured way that it must be all of her reading that gave her such an expansive vocabulary.

"I never knew that *qanat* was actually a word," Henry teased as they removed the tiles from the board in preparation for another round.

Ellie pointed to the dictionary. "It's in there."

"Ah! I don't argue that it's in here," Henry said, tapping his finger against the dictionary and smiling mischievously at the two women seated opposite him at the table. "But how did it get in there?" he asked, pointing to Catherine's head. "A tunnel from Persia? Only an avid reader would know such a word."

Catherine shrugged as she helped Henry to shuffle the tiles. "Or someone with a great memory of strange but valid words for Scrabble!"

Henry laughed at her and tossed a tile in her direction. She caught it and placed it back in the box lid where the other unused tiles waited to be selected.

From the other side of the room, Gid grumbled under his breath. The noise was irritating him.

"Perhaps we should take a walk?" Henry suggested,

glancing at his father and then back at Ellie and Catherine as he motioned toward the door with his head.

It took a moment for Catherine to catch on. "What? Oh! *Ja*, that's a fine idea!" She pointed at the score card. "Besides, I clearly was going to win anyway."

Henry raised an eyebrow. "I take that to mean a rematch is in order, Catherine Miller?" he teased.

"If you're going for a walk, get on with it then!" Gid growled. He raised his head from the Bible long enough to scowl at the three young adults. "And don't take too long. We have to milk the cows at four o'clock."

Once they escaped the kitchen, Catherine felt as if it were easier to breathe. There was something oppressive about being in the same room with Gid Tilman, and she much preferred to enjoy the company of his children out of earshot from him. All day, Henry had been quiet and somber, even before the worship service. And Catherine noticed him sitting with the preachers and bishop during the fellowship meal. It was almost as if he was one of the church leaders, even though he was not.

She was glad that Henry had suggested that they leave the house for a walk, even if she suspected it was because their father was getting annoyed at their laughter over the Scrabble game.

Slowly, the three of them walked down the lane toward the road. The cows grazed in the paddock behind the barn, and Catherine paused to look at them. Henry stopped walking and turned around to watch her. She could sense his eyes on her. "There's something about grazing cows," she said softly. "I missed seeing them while we were at the lake."

He moved closer to her and followed her gaze. For a moment, he didn't respond to her comment. Instead, he simply watched the herd as it slowly meandered in the field. They were black and white Holsteins, although there were a few pure black ones here and there. "I've always loved working with the cows," he said at last. "I much prefer farm work to shop work any day of the week. Even though my *bruder* makes more money and it's less work for him, I wouldn't change places with him for anything!"

Catherine turned her face toward him. "There is no price tag for happiness."

"Quite true." He continued staring into the field. "If only *Daed* thought that."

"What do you mean?"

Henry glanced at her. "My *daed* does not put happiness before profits. In fact, he insists that all of his children marry into families that will contribute to the growth and expansion of Newbury Acres as an ideal Amish community."

A gasp escaped her lips. "That's pride!"

"Indeed it is," Henry said with a sad sigh.

For a moment, she thought on his words. Was he trying to tell her something? Warn her that a future with him could not be possible? Prepare her for disappointment as far as their friendship went? But then why, she wondered, was I invited here at all? "And what if you find someone," she asked in a soft voice, "that does not 'contribute' to the growth and expansion of Newbury Acres, Henry?"

He gave her a sad smile. "Then, if that were the case, I would be faced with a rather difficult decision, I fear." He looked away from her gaze. Ellie had continued walking and now stood in a patch of wild daisies, plucking some from the ground to make a bouquet.

"Come, Catherine," Henry said, extending his hand for hers. For the briefest of moments, their hands entwined. "I'll race you to where Ellie is and we can see which one of us can collect the most flowers for the kitchen!" He tugged at her hand gently and she followed him, half running down the lane toward where Ellie was.

"Why, look at the two of you!" she laughed when they caught up with her. "Like school children running around in such heat." Even though she scolded them, she did not look genuinely concerned.

Once each one of them held a large bunch of flowers, they decided to head back to the house.

Gid looked up when they entered, eyeballing the flowers. He nodded his head in approval but returned his attention to his Scripture reading. "'The flowers appear on the earth; the time of singing has come, and the voice of the turtledove is heard in our land,'" he quoted. "Which reminds me that you should take the buggy to the singing tonight, Henry." He looked at Catherine as he spoke. "It would be better than walking since it's being held at the Esh family's home."

It was the first time she had heard about a singing that evening. While she wasn't partial to attending youth gatherings, she knew that she would enjoy a buggy ride with Henry.

Ellie collected their flowers and carried them to the sink. "I've a busy day tomorrow. Henry, you wouldn't mind taking Catherine alone, would you?"

He looked at Catherine and suppressed a smile. "I suppose. If you insist."

When Catherine's mouth opened, stunned into silence, he laughed at her.

"You keep teasing me," she exclaimed in a soft voice so that Gid didn't hear.

He lowered his voice as well. "And you keep falling for it."

She blushed.

"Do you enjoy singings?"

His question made her falter. She couldn't lie, but she didn't want to miss a buggy ride with him. "I…I do not, Henry, but I would be interested in seeing more of Newbury Acres. Perhaps we could do that instead?"

He nodded his head as he winked at her, lifting his finger to his lips as if indicating that it would be their secret.

By the time Catherine and Ellie prepared supper, it was almost six o'clock. It was late for eating supper but Henry had no help, besides Gid, to milk the cows on Sunday.

After supper, Henry excused himself to harness the horse and hitch it to his buggy. Catherine helped Ellie clean the dishes.

"You should go and get ready," Ellie suggested. "If you want to anyway. I can handle the dishes."

Catherine glanced down at her dress. She wore her light green dress and hadn't soiled it during their walk or dinner preparations. "I don't think I need to change. Besides, I wouldn't feel right leaving you with all of this work."

"Then go help Henry." She set a wet plate onto the dish rack. "I can handle this." She gave Catherine a pleasant smile. "Go and have some fun."

Since Ellie wouldn't take no for an answer, Catherine hurried outside, secretly pleased to have that extra time with Henry.

She peeked her head around the open door to the horse stable. She saw Henry in the stall with the horse. "Need any help?"

He peered over the horse's withers. "*Nee*, I've finished grooming him already."

He opened the stall door and led the horse outside. With swift hands, he quickly managed to harness the horse and led it to the doorway. She watched as he walked the horse in a circle and backed it between the two shafts of the open-topped buggy. Without being asked, she hurried over to help guide the one shaft into the tug stop. Then she attached the trace to the hook on the end of the whiffletree. Finally, she attached the brake strap and stood back as Henry walked around to her side.

"Oh." He looked surprised. "You work fast, don't you?"

"Easier with two, *ja*?"

"Indeed it is." He tossed the reins over the dashboard of the buggy and waited for Catherine to step on the mounting step. Then he climbed up beside her. "Ready?"

For the next hour, he drove her along some of the back roads of Newbury Acres, pointing out the school where he and his siblings had attended to eighth grade. He showed her where they shopped, at an Amish market which was next to a garden supply store, also Amish owned. To her surprise, she realized that there were almost no *Englischers* living in Newbury Acres.

"How is that possible?" she asked when Henry confirmed her observation.

He shrugged. "I suppose we've just managed to hold onto the land. Seventy years ago, there was nothing here. Our great-grandfather moved here with four other families. The land was cheap and they worked it. New families joined them when they married and couldn't afford land in the other communities. When land became unavailable for new families, that was when my father came up with the idea of the farming co-op. And any farmer who has land that tries to sell it, always sells to other Amish people."

"Even if it's a financial loss?"

He nodded his head. "*Ja*. They'd rather it stay within the community than risk having *Englischers* come in and develop the land."

She wondered why other communities didn't do the same thing. Even though she wasn't bothered by the *Englische* who lived in Fullerton, she knew that it would be much nicer to have fewer outsiders, who often built stores or restaurants which attracted tourists.

"It's nice here," she said when the silence between them grew.

"I agree." He turned the horse down a lane. "This is the road behind our farm," he said as he pointed out the window. Despite being wooded, a fence bordered the road.

"Are we going back already?" She couldn't hide the disappointment in her voice.

His mouth twitched when he glanced at her. "Not ready yet?"

She shook her head.

"Then I will show you my favorite place. Would you like that?"

He guided the horse down another road that was hidden by tall grass on the other side of the road. She listened to the horse's hooves pounding on the dry dirt that made the lane. She wondered how the horses fared during the rainy season that always accompanied April and October. Surely the roads were too muddy then to travel by buggy.

As the horse rounded another bend, she could see a small white farmhouse sitting almost in front of a red barn with a tall white silo. A windmill spun next to the house. To the east of the house was a large grassy field that seemed to go on for as far as she could see. To the west was a fenced paddock for the horses. The two-story house had a covered porch that wrapped around the side that faced the barn. In front of the house was a white picket fence that surrounded what she imagined was a garden that had not been planted that year.

"Who lives here?" she asked.

"You like it?"

How could she not like it? "It's a perfect setting. The house looks as if it's been loved through the years." She looked at him. "But you didn't answer my question. Who lives here?"

"No one."

His answer stunned her. "No one? But it's in perfect condition."

"*Danke* for noticing." His eyes twinkled.

It took her a moment to realize where he had taken her. "Is this your mother's childhood farm?"

He nodded. "It is indeed. We call it the Woods farm."

She returned her gaze toward the house. "I don't understand why no one lives here. With so many people wanting to farm…" It made no sense to her. Gid Tilman was so outspoken about the Amish staying close to their agricultural roots. Why didn't he rent it out? That would have been better than having it sit vacant.

As if he read her mind, Henry took a deep breath

and sighed. "Her parents did outlive her, Catherine. And when they passed last year, we talked about renting it. But I admit that I wasn't fond of that idea. One day I would like to live here."

She caught her breath. "But your *daed*'s farm…"

He shrugged. "I love the dairy and the cows. I'd have a small herd here. But my heart is in working the soil."

"Does your father know this?"

Once again, he nodded. "He does. Perhaps if Ellie married a man interested in farming, he would consent. Or if Freddie ever settled down and had sons…" He left the sentence unfinished. Neither scenario seemed likely to happen anytime soon. It was just one more way that Gid had managed to control his children, pressing his own ideals of happiness upon them.

"I'll pray that your dream comes true," she said softly.

For a long few minutes, they sat in the buggy staring at the house. While she would have liked to have seen the inside, she knew that it would be improper for her to ask. Henry would never consent to her entering the house alone, and it would be improper for the two of them to be alone in an unoccupied house. If anyone caught sight of them, her reputation would be ruined.

Finally, he looked up at the sky. "Sun's setting. I reckon we better head home. We've a lot of work to do tomorrow." He made a playful but sad face. "Vacation is over."

He stepped off the brake and slapped the reins against the horse's rump, urging it to start walking again. This time he drove back toward the lane that ran behind the Tilmans' farm. Disappointed that the ride was ending, she was grateful that it still took thirty minutes to travel the roads to their driveway.

"*Danke* for sharing that with me," she said when Henry stopped the buggy in front of the house.

He nodded.

Carefully she stepped through the door on her side of the buggy and stood away from the buggy, watching as Henry drove it toward the stable. Quietly, she entered the house, not surprised that the kitchen was empty. As Henry had said, their vacation was over. Gid had looked tired during the supper meal, and Ellie would have to get up early to make coffee and start preparing breakfast. At eight-thirty in the evening, it was bedtime on a farm. Even though the sun had not yet fully set, Catherine didn't mind that the day was ending. She settled into her bed, the kerosene lantern burning on her nightstand and her latest book clutched in her hand, ready to read. For her, it had been the perfect Sunday.

Chapter Nineteen

When morning came, Catherine found the house unusually quiet and Ellie already at work in the kitchen.

"Good morning," Catherine said as she walked down
the steps. "I can't believe it's almost seven-thirty! I
never sleep this late!"

Ellie turned from the sink and smiled at her friend as
she entered the kitchen. "Then you must've slept well!"

"I did," Catherine admitted. She noticed that Ellie
was already in the middle of making bread, the flour
on her black apron giving away her most recent chore.
"What might I help you with? I love to bake bread."

For the next two hours, the two women worked side-
by-side, talking and laughing as they kneaded the dough
and worked on making cheese from the fresh milk that
Henry had brought in from that morning's milking.
Catherine learned quickly from Ellie and found that
she liked cutting the curds and setting them into the
cheese press. It was a chore that she had never done before, and as she set the weights on the end of the press,
she knew that she had just discovered something new
that she enjoyed doing.

"What types of cheese do you make?" she asked Ellie.

"Oh, many different kinds, but my favorite's the Colby cheese. It is so creamy and moist. And it comes out in a perfect round." She motioned toward the cheese press. "I don't know if it's the press or the milk, but I often make twelve rounds a week, and they are always in demand from the local people, both the Amish and the *Englische*. It seems that I can't make enough to satisfy their demands."

Catherine glanced around the kitchen at the mess that they had made. "We should make more then," she said. "Two hands and lots of milk...we can press twice as many rounds, don't you think?"

So, the challenge was set.

At Ellie's urging, Catherine wandered out to the dairy barn to retrieve more fresh milk for another batch of curds. She lingered by the door, staring at the long aisles of Holstein cows. Some had already been turned out into the pasture while some still remained standing in the large holding pen. She knew that they had already been milked so she wasn't certain why they hadn't been turned out.

"Come to milk some cows then?"

Catherine quickly turned around and took a step backward, pressing her hand against her chest as she faced Henry. "You startled me!"

"Did I, now?" He leaned against the wall and smiled at her. "You're fun to startle, Catherine Miller."

Playfully, she scowled at him. "Please don't make a habit of it," she said. "My heart can't take too much startling!"

He laughed.

"Ellie sent me to fetch more milk," she said, changing the subject in the hopes that she could contain the blush that threatened to cover her cheeks.

"Oh? More?" He cocked his head and narrowed his eyes as he studied her.

"*Ja*, more. We're going to double her cheese production. She says everyone loves her cheese rounds so much that she has more demand than she can supply. I figured that two sets of hands can make double the cheese and, therefore, double the sales."

Henry didn't say anything for a long moment. Then he raised his hand to his bare chin and rubbed it as if in deep thought. Not once did his eyes leave hers. "You like making cheese then, Catherine?"

She shrugged. "I've only just learned how thanks to your sister. And she's going to teach me how to make macramé wall hangings and pot holders, too."

"All of these things are new to you?" he asked.

She nodded. "*Ja*. I like learning new things, though."

"What else do you like doing?"

She thought for a moment. He already knew that she loved to read books. What else did she enjoy doing? Suddenly, it came to her. "There *is* something I do like doing."

"Oh, *ja*?" His eyes lit up. "And what is that?"

"Being helpful. If I'm to be a good guest at your *haus*, I'd like to help your sister as much as I can."

He smiled at her, a soft and kind smile. She could see that his eyes softened and there was something curious about the way he stared at her. "That's very kind, Catherine. I know that she enjoys your company. Such a shame that you don't live closer."

She glanced away rather than respond to his comment. It was true that she lived too far away from Newbury Acres to visit on a regular basis. It would take a driver almost an hour to return her to Fullerton. But Catherine certainly wanted to enjoy her budding friendship with Ellie while she was staying under the Tilmans' roof. And, of course, spending any extra time in Henry's company was definitely a benefit, too.

"Well, here's the problem with her requesting more milk," Henry said, still rubbing his chin. "The milk's already been picked up for the day."

Catherine looked up, disappointed to learn that there was no milk to be had.

Henry, however, held up his hand to stop her. "Now don't look so crestfallen," he said lightly. "Several of these girls haven't been milked yet. We use them to feed the veal calves who need to be fed throughout the day. So, what do you say to helping me milk them? We can do it together and have the freshest milk possible, right from your own hand."

To Catherine, that sounded like a fine idea. She nodded her head and eagerly followed Henry as he went to retrieve a milking stool and a clean bucket from the back room.

While she knew how to milk cows, she hadn't done it by hand since she had been a little girl. On her father's farm, they used mechanical milkers, all powered by a propane generator. Milking by hand, however, always seemed like such a peaceful way to collect the milk. Using the milking machines was far too impersonal, a process rather than a connection with nature.

Henry set the stool down beside one of the cows and instructed her to take a seat.

"Now, place the bucket under her udders," he said in a soft but authoritative voice. "Then sanitize her teats with this." He handed her a plastic container with a green cup on top. "Just place the cup under each teat and then dip the teat into the liquid. That's it! You got it, Catherine."

She did as she was told, reacting to his voice as well as his encouragements to how well she listened to him. She thought that she could sit there and listen to him for hours. If Henry Tilman talked to all of his workers in the same manner, they must enjoy working for him.

"Okay, now grab one of her teats and roll your hand down the length of it."

Catherine did as he told her but nothing came out. She tried again to no avail. "Oh, help and bother!" she fussed. "What am I doing wrong?"

Henry laughed. "Nothing, Catherine. It just takes some time to get used to it. Here, let me help." He leaned over her shoulder and reached down to cover her hand with his as he gently helped her properly grasp the teat and press her fingers into the sides as she rolled her hand down. This time, a steady stream of milk came out and hit the side of the metal bucket. The noise sounded like rain on tin. Delighted, Catherine immediately did it again, not paying too much attention to the way that Henry still lingered over her shoulder.

"I'm doing it! I'm doing it!"

Once again, Henry laughed. "*Ja*, that you are! And doing a good job at it, might I add. Now, keep working on that one, and if you are feeling adventuresome, you can use your right hand to work on another one. True milkers can do two teats at once."

Never one to step away from a challenge, Catherine did as he told her, and within a few minutes, she had managed to get two streams of milk going into the bucket at nearly the same time. She would tug at the one teat and then pull at the other. She began to sense a musical rhythm to how she was milking, and in her mind, she could hear the song of milking cows. It was a beautiful tune.

Still, Henry never left her side. He lingered by her shoulder, his one arm pressed against hers. When she stopped listening to the music of the milk, she could hear the sound of his heart in her left ear. The pulsing beat made another song, one that she hoped was beating extra fast simply because he was near her. But she knew better than to ask. It was safer—and more proper—to simply make up her own romantic story in her head. If Henry fancied her, she wasn't entirely certain. But she wanted to believe that he did so, the sound of his heart beating only adding to her yearning for him to stay near her side.

By the time she finished milking the cow, the bucket was brimming with fresh, pure, white milk.

Henry straightened up and took a step backward, clearing his throat. When he spoke, his voice sounded husky and thick. Strange indeed for a man who never seemed at a loss for words.

"Well then, that's a job well done," he managed to say, a throaty tone to his voice. "Now, let's move the stool and I'll carry the bucket to the house for you, Catherine."

She knew full well that she could carry that bucket without his assistance. After all, her father raised cows, and while the boys helped him in the barn, Catherine certainly helped, too, especially when James was traveling for his work.

Regardless, she let Henry carry the pail. She liked that he took charge, helping her in a protective kind of way. Back at her father's farm, her brother James often did the same, taking on the burden of the harder chores even though he knew that Catherine and even his younger brothers were more than capable. To Catherine, that was an indication that her brother would be a good husband one day. Now that she saw the same signs of chivalry in Henry, she suspected that he, too, would treat his own wife with gracious understanding and solicitousness.

In silence they walked side-by-side back to the house.

Ellie already had three large pots ready. She looked up from where she sat at the table, reading the newspaper, and smiled when they walked in. "That didn't take long," she said with a smirk on her face.

After setting the bucket onto the counter, Henry wiped his hand on his pants. "The milk had already been picked up, so we had to do it by hand, sister," he explained. "But Catherine's a real expert at hand milking," he teased gently. "I reckon she could hand milk all those cows faster than my machines."

"What. Ever!" Catherine said in jest, but she knew that her cheeks had turned pink from his compliment.

Ellie laughed and Henry winked at Catherine before he slipped through the door to finish his other chores.

"He's in an awfully good mood," Catherine commented as she watched Ellie pour the milk into the large pan.

"He always is when *Daed* isn't around."

Catherine had wondered about that very thing. Both Henry and Ellie were much more relaxed without Gid Tilman in the house. Truth be told, so was she. "Where is your *daed*?"

"At the wood shop, I'm sure. He won't be home until supper."

That was a relief to Catherine. She wouldn't have to deal with Gid during the day if he worked at the shop.

Together, they worked at bringing the fresh milk to eighty-two degrees before adding the mesophilic starter. Then they set the three pots into water baths to provide indirect heat during the ripening period. While Ellie monitored the temperature of the baths, Catherine made dough for baking bread. By the time Ellie added the rennet to the ripened milk, Catherine's dough had already risen once and she was kneading it for a second time.

"It's much more fun to work with company," Ellie commented joyfully.

Catherine shaped four loaves and set them into the waiting pans before covering them with a clean cloth. "I can't imagine not having all of my sisters in the house," she said as she moved to the sink to wash her hands.

"You're fortunate to have sisters."

The way that Ellie said it made Catherine regret that she had made such a comment.

"But one day I will have two sisters," Ellie added cheerfully. She leaned over one of the pots. "Hmm. I think the curds are ready to be cut. Look here."

Catherine walked over and glanced over Ellie's shoulder. The milk had solidified into a large, watery dough. Gently, Ellie poked at the top and it sprang back.

"Want to see how I cut them and then you can try it yourself?" Ellie asked. She took a long knife and began to slice through the coagulated mass in the pot. "It's important that you cut it diagonally. See? Like this." Carefully, she slid the knife into the large curds, pulling it toward her. As the curds separated, water rose along the cut line. She made several perforations in one direction before she started cutting across the lines, making a checkerboard-like pattern.

"Easy, right? Now you try."

Catherine took the knife and did the same to the second pot.

"Perfect! Do the third one, too, *ja*?"

As Catherine cut the curds of the third pot, Henry walked into the house. He stopped when he saw Catherine and Ellie at the counter. He chuckled and walked over to them, peering over their heads to see what they were doing. Catherine jumped and the knife slipped. "Oh, help!" Concerned that she might have ruined the curds, she looked at Ellie. "Did I mess it up?"

"*Nee*, it's fine. Just finish cutting them. We'll let them cook a little longer and stir them a bit. Just gentle, though." Ellie turned toward her brother. "How is your day going?"

"Right *gut*, I reckon." He took off his hat and wiped his forehead. "Getting hot out there. Thought I'd grab a cool drink before I hitch up the team to drag the back pasture before dinner. I noticed that no one did that while we were gone."

Ellie made a sound of disapproval in her throat. "That's what happens when people work on land that isn't theirs," she explained. "They don't notice such things as clearing the manure from the pasture."

As Catherine finished cutting the curds, she wondered about Ellie's reaction. It was the first indication that Ellie disapproved of her father's model of farming. If the tenants didn't properly care for the land, why would Gid lease it to them? Despite being curious, Catherine knew better than to ask the question. It wasn't any of her business. Still, she sensed that there was an undercurrent of tension in the house that went far deeper than Gid's gruff manner.

After grabbing a glass, Henry poured some chilled water into it and drank it all in one long gulp. He smacked his lips and sighed. "Nothing like chilled water to freshen you up after working in this heat." He set the glass into the sink before adding, "Well, chilled water and meadow tea. Hint, hint." He winked at his sister.

"Why don't you walk Catherine out to the garden and she can collect some tea leaves? I missed our meadow tea while we were in Banthe," Ellie said.

"Only if Catherine makes it," her brother teased playfully. "I want to see if she can match your recipe." He turned to face Catherine. "Ellie is renowned for her meadow tea."

"Oh, I don't know about that. I sure wouldn't want to compete with her," Catherine said. "I'd be sad to think that I might steal that title from her."

He laughed and Ellie frowned. "Another challenge? I reckon we shall have to make two batches then."

Outside, Henry led Catherine to the side of the house. Not far from the edge of the porch was a large raised garden. It was an impressive garden, large enough for even the biggest Amish family, never mind a family of four. There were multiple sections, each planted with rows and rows of plants with nary a weed to be seen. In one section, Catherine saw four long rows of tomatoes, and ten rows of corn grew along the back. In the middle of the garden were sections of beans, beets, carrots, celery, zucchini, and cucumbers. And, of course, there were a few vines of watermelons as well.

"And not one single weed," Catherine observed. "Who takes care of all this?"

"Ellie. It's one of her favorite things. Gardening."

"But when would she have weeded? She was away for well over a week."

He shrugged and held his hands up as if he didn't have the answer. "The mystery of Ellie. Her well-guarded secret: How does she do everything so well and with no help?"

Catherine let her eyes rove over the garden, feeling a bit of envy at the thought that she had never created such a magnificent garden. Just as quick, though, she shook her head as if to chase away the thought. Envy was a sin. Instead, Catherine decided that she needed to learn everything she could from Ellie during her stay at Newbury Acres. "Cheese, macramé, and a gorgeous, weed-free garden. Why, she *is* remarkable, indeed."

"Just don't tell her that. She's as modest as she is remarkable," he said as he leaned against the fence that surrounded the garden. "I'd hate for that to change."

He waited until she cut her mint and then he walked her back to the house.

"I'll be anxious to see which one of you wins the mint tea test!" he announced as she opened the kitchen door.

"Me, too!" she replied. "I suspect I know the answer." She motioned toward the kitchen with her head.

He laughed and started walking backward toward the stable. "Two hours," he called out. "That should give you enough time to give it your best shot, ladies."

"I might need it." But she was laughing when she turned away from him. If the morning was any indication of the rest of her stay with the Tilmans, she was going to enjoy herself more than she had anticipated.

Chapter Twenty

At Newbury Acres, Catherine quickly found an easy routine to follow.

During the day, Catherine helped Ellie with the household chores and cooking, which, given that only four people were in the house, didn't occupy too much of their time. After dinner, Ellie would take her into an empty room upstairs and show her how to weave yarn on the loom, knotting it in certain places, to make beautiful wall hangings. Then, they would spend the rest of the afternoon walking on the different trails through the property, usually ending up in the back fields where Henry worked.

The first time she saw Henry seated on a baler that was pulled by six mules, Catherine had to pause to give herself time to reconcile the two images that she had of him: the relaxed vacationer from Banthe and the hard worker at Newbury Acres. If she had grown fond of Henry in Banthe, now that she saw him in his personal environment, at both home and work, Catherine realized that she admired him even more.

And what wasn't there to admire?

Like Ellie, Henry had a magical way of doing a

dozen different things at the same time and completing all of them without one complaint. Without doubt, Catherine had never met a harder working man. And yet, he never appeared overly tired or weary. And he was not one to complain about the amount of work. In fact, he was *always* pleasant, even in the heat of the summer sun, which caused beads of sweat to soak through his shirt. On most days, when he saw them approaching, he would greet them with a big smile and a happy wave, immediately stopping whatever he was doing so that he could spend a few moments visiting with them.

By Friday, he must have anticipated their arrival, for he already had the mules resting under the shade of some nearby trees when his sister and Catherine emerged from the walking trail.

"Is that a picnic basket I see you hiding there?" he said, overexaggerating the question as he stared at the basket so obviously hooked over Catherine's arm. "My, my! I hope it contains some wonderful treats! And some of Catherine's award-winning meadow tea? All of this hard work sure does make a man hungry! But wait, mayhaps you brought this to share it with someone else?"

Ellie gave him a playful push on his arm. "Whether or not it's hard work that makes you hungry, I'm not certain, Henry! You've always been one with a right *gut* appetite."

He helped spread an old quilt on the grass, and the three of them sat down to enjoy the fried chicken, corn, and biscuits that were neatly packed inside of the basket. And, of course, Catherine's "award"-winning tea from the tea-making contest.

"I'm glad that you're here, Catherine," Henry said after he finished his meal. He was stretched out on the quilt with one knee bent as he leaned his head against his hand. "You're doing a world of good for Ellie. So often she's alone here. Or with only me for company, which doesn't say too much…"

Catherine clucked her tongue. "I'm sure your company suits her just fine, Henry Tilman."

He gave a soft chuckle. "She might argue with that. Anyway, on Monday, I must go to the other property to cut and bale hay for a few days. There are several pastures that need their third cutting for the season. It's just easier to stay there. At least with you here, I can take comfort knowing Ellie isn't alone."

"While I'm happy to be here, she certainly wouldn't be alone. Your *Daed*'s here," Catherine said quickly, hoping to mask her disappointment. The thought of Henry not being at the farm made her heart sink.

Henry raised his eyebrows and stared up at the blue sky. "*Daed* will return to Banthe tomorrow."

"Your *daed* returns to Banthe so soon?" Catherine's mouth opened as if to say something, but then she thought better of it.

"He'll spend a week or so there and return with Freddie next Saturday." Absentmindedly, Henry plucked at a blade of grass and held it between his thumbs. "He likes to attend worship there when it's our off-Sunday here." He blew into the grass, which made a loud and silly trumpet noise, causing the two women to giggle.

Frankly, with the exception of Henry's absence and Freddie's eventual return, nothing could please Catherine more! While Gid did not force his presence upon the Tilmans' guest, she could sense it when he was around. There was something heavy and oppressive about him that made it hard for her to breathe properly when he returned from the wood shop, although in an entirely different way than how Henry often made her catch her breath.

When she realized that Henry was staring at her, Catherine cleared her throat, hoping that her expression did not give away her thoughts. "I'm sure that Ellie and I will be the champion cheese makers by the time of your return. We'll probably have a whole inventory of macramé to sell to the tourists as well! And perhaps she might learn a few tricks about my meadow tea."

He laughed at her good humor and even Ellie smiled.

"I'm sure the stores in Farmington will be thrilled with the extra pieces of macramé." Ellie brushed some grass from her skirt.

"Farmington?"

"*Ja*, you know, where the Andersons are from," Ellie replied to Catherine. "They probably have seen my pieces at the store. The owner says that he can hardly keep them on the shelves."

At the mention of the Andersons, Ellie frowned. "They aren't from Farmington," she corrected. "They're from Fullerton. My town."

"Oh?" Ellie looked confused. "I'm sure my *daed* said they were from Farmington."

Catherine shook her head. "*Nee*, not Farmington, although I believe they have relatives that live there." She tried to remember what she could about the Andersons and their extended family. What had her father told her a while back? "One of them has a rather large farm, I recall *Daed* telling me once. Well, anyway, we certainly can keep that store busy, don't you think?"

"We'll have our work cut out for us next week, that's for sure and certain," Ellie replied.

"But, in the meantime, we shall have a lovely Saturday afternoon and Sunday, won't we?" Henry directed the question to his sister. "Perhaps some fishing on Saturday? And, if we are successful, a fish fry that evening?"

To Catherine, nothing sounded more exciting than spending a lazy afternoon at the large pond toward the back of their property. She had never gone fishing before, but she knew that she would enjoy it, especially if it meant more time with Henry. After all, for the past few days since she had been at Newbury Acres, she had barely seen Henry at all, except at meal times and when she and Ellie walked to the back fields where he worked in the afternoon.

"Fishing!" Ellie exclaimed, wrinkling her nose. "Ugh! You can count me out!"

Immediately Catherine fought the urge to express her disappointment. If Ellie did not go fishing, she surely could not. After all, she was Ellie's guest, not Henry's. And it wouldn't be proper for her to go fishing alone with a man she hardly knew.

"Such a shame," Henry said, making an exaggerated sorrowful face. "I was so looking forward to fresh fish for supper one night."

Catherine mirrored the sentiment, more for the act of fishing than the act of eating, but she remained silent on the topic. Instead, she stared off in the direction of the trees that separated the fields in the back of the property from the ones near the farmhouse.

"What. Ever!" Ellie said teasingly. "I dare say you don't need my permission to go fishing. Nor my presence, either."

"It's no fun to go fishing alone, dear *schwester*."

Ellie stood up and stretched. "Then don't go alone, Henry. Perhaps Catherine likes fishing more than I do and would still accompany you. You certainly do not need me to tag along. You know how fish and worms make me squeamish." She headed toward a patch of wildflowers, which she began to pluck, collecting them into a pretty bouquet.

Henry shifted his weight on the quilt, turning toward Catherine. His dark eyes sought hers as he tilted his head, raising one eyebrow at her questioningly. "Well, Catherine, what say you? Are you a fisherman?"

"I don't know about that," she started to reply, but noticing that his expression started to change to disappointment, she quickly added, "Fisherwoman, *mayhaps*."

He smiled broadly. "Oh, *ja*? Fisherwoman, eh? Well, can this fisherwoman stand to be with a certain fisherman for hours on end with a pole in hand, hoping for a bite or two on our lines?"

In her mind, she shouted, "Yes! Yes!" But propriety forced her to respond with more reserve. "Only if this fisherman will show a certain fisherwoman *how* to fish. If so, she would gladly accompany you!"

He slapped his hand against his bent knee as he sat up. "It's a deal!" Stretching out his hand, he waited for her to shake it. When she did, he held onto her hand for a few seconds longer than necessary. "I shall think of little else between now and then," he said in a soft voice. Then, speaking louder, he called out, "Did you hear that, Ellie? Fresh fish we shall have on Saturday after all!"

As he walked toward his sister, Catherine stared after him. Had he truly just whispered those words of affection to her? Or had she misheard him? She tried to calm her beating heart, hoping deep down that it was the former and not the latter.

When he joined his sister, they bent their heads toward each other and spoke. Catherine couldn't hear what they said, but she saw Ellie toss her head back and laugh. Henry grinned, looking quite pleased with himself. He glanced over his shoulder at Catherine, and when he saw that she was watching him, he winked at her and then returned his attention to Ellie.

Catherine began to repack their basket, sad that the picnic was over but excited for the following day's activities. While she had noticed that Ellie often found a reason to leave Henry alone with her, it was usually only for a short period of time. But tomorrow... Catherine smiled to herself. Tomorrow she would have Henry all to herself for over three hours. She couldn't imagine any better way to spend a Saturday afternoon.

"We should head back now," Ellie said as she rejoined Catherine. "Henry will need to start the afternoon milking soon."

"Such a shame that he will be away most of next week," Catherine lamented.

"It is rather taxing on him, working the two farms." Ellie shook her head. "Such a shame that no one lives there. I still don't know why *Daed* doesn't rent it out or even better sell it to a nice young couple. It makes no sense to me."

Catherine bit her tongue.

"It's such a pretty place. You'll have to be certain to see it."

Henry walked over, a stick in his hand. He swung it absentmindedly at the grass. "See what?"

"Our *maem*'s place. The Woods farm."

"Ah, the Woods farm." He looked at Catherine and winked. "You liked it well enough, *ja*?"

Ellie's eyes widened as she realized that her brother had already taken Catherine to it.

"We just drove by it," Catherine was quick to point out. "Last Sunday."

"I see," she responded, a secretive smile forming on her lips.

"We never left the buggy," Catherine offered quickly. She certainly didn't want Ellie thinking that anything improper had occurred between her and Henry.

With a knowing smile, Ellie nodded. "No other thought crossed my mind," she said in a gentle tone.

Henry walked away toward a clearing that led to the pathway back to the farm.

"Perhaps this week we might walk over to surprise Henry. Mayhaps Wednesday. Then we could ride home with him in the buggy," Ellie whispered.

Catherine nodded. "That would be fun. The outside of the house is charming. I can't imagine what the inside is like." She paused before asking the one question that was on her mind. "But if it's so close, why does he stay there?"

"Despite it being so close, it takes over thirty minutes to drive to it. Even though that's not a lot of time, it seemed enough of a reason to convince our *daed* that Henry should stay there when he's cutting the hay." She lowered her voice. "Frankly, I think Henry fancies the place and likes spending time there. Makes him feel closer to our *maem*, I suspect."

Lowering her eyes at the mention of their mother, Catherine felt sadness in her heart. She simply could not imagine not having her mother to talk to every day. Just thinking about it made her feel more than a little homesick. After all, it had been almost a month since she had been home. She wondered what her family was doing at that very moment. Most likely, the younger children were outside playing while James and Richard helped their father with the last afternoon chores.

At they began to walk home, Henry stayed ahead of them, his mood having changed from jovial to more reflective and somber. Catherine and Ellie walked side-by-side, talking about what they would do in the morning before the big fishing excursion. Once Catherine noticed Henry glance back in her direction, but she couldn't read the expression on his face. Her self-confidence began to fade. She wondered what he was thinking, and when he didn't even smile, whether he was still thinking of their fishing trip with the same enthusiasm as when he extended the invitation to her.

Ellie seemed to read her thoughts. "Don't fret, Catherine. He always gets a little sullen and reflective whenever the Woods farm is brought up. I told you. He fancies the place. I reckon that's why *Daed* never sold or rented it."

Still, there was something else lingering beneath the surface, and Catherine couldn't stop worrying that it had something to do with her. The sporadic furtive glances he cast in her direction during their walk back to the house only added to her anxiety. She wasn't used to this side of Henry and she felt panicky. When they finally returned to the farm and Henry wandered off to the dairy barn, her nerves were frayed and she excused herself to go upstairs and lie down for half an hour. Like Henry, she too needed some quiet time and space to reflect.

Chapter Twenty-One

The edge of the water lapped against the large rock where Henry and Catherine stood, fishing poles in hand and a cooler of bait by their bare feet. The sun hid behind a cloud, keeping the heat at bay. In the distance, there was a boat with two young Amish boys who sat back-to-back with their own fishing poles, lines in the water as they waited for a nibble on their hooks.

Earlier that morning, rather than take his horse and buggy, Gid had left with a hired driver to return to Banthe. It was only a twenty-minute drive, and he hadn't wanted two horse and buggies there. As soon as he had departed, Catherine felt rejuvenated, almost as if her vacation with the Tilmans had started anew. She sensed the change in Ellie and Henry almost immediately. Ellie spent more time at her regular chores, not worried about ensuring that dinner was ready exactly at noon. She also sang as she embroidered, something Catherine had not heard her do while Gid was around.

As for Henry, he invited Catherine to help him with the cows, a task she readily accepted. She never would have done that if Gid was lurking around the farm. Even though he did not always come home for the noon meal, he would pop into the house at odd times as if checking on what his two children were doing. And his appearance was always followed with some complaint about something they were—or were not—doing to his satisfaction. Without Gid at home, Henry seemed even more relaxed and cheerful than he usually was.

Shortly after one o'clock, Henry had indicated that they should walk to the pond. He would need to return at four-thirty to oversee the evening milking. Now, thirty minutes later, they were almost alone at the pond with the song of nature to entertain them as Henry tried to teach her how to fish.

"What type of fish again?" Catherine asked, feeling awkward for the first time in Henry's presence. While she didn't consider their fishing together a date—he had invited his sister to join them—she did feel that something was shifting in their friendship. She had never courted anyone, and she wondered if this might be a precursor to such a relationship. The thought made her hopeful.

"Bass. It's stocked with large-mouthed bass and crappies," he said.

"And those boys over there. Who are they?"

He fiddled with his pole, tying a new hook on the end of the line. "They're the sons of two of our workers. Nice boys. They help with the haying at my *maem*'s old farm. At least during the summer."

"Will they be helping you on Monday then?"

He nodded but did not reply, his attention focused on what he was doing.

She watched as he worked, amazed at how he managed to knot the thin line around the hook. When he finished, he reached for the cooler and opened it, revealing several Styrofoam cups of dirt. He dug through the dirt with his finger and pulled out a large worm. It wiggled and she made a face.

"You don't like that, eh?"

She shook her head. "Mayhaps you can do that part. Putting the worm on the hook."

"*Kum* now, Catherine. It's just a little worm. To be a real fisherman, you need to learn how to bait your hook." But he pushed the hook through the worm and wrapped it around twice. "See? That's not so bad, *ja*?"

"Whatever," she said, still making a face, and he laughed.

He handed her the pole and then placed his hands on her shoulders, gently turning her around so that she faced the water. "Now, it's really easy, Catherine," he said, his hands still touching her. "You release the lock on the reel…" He moved one hand to show her how. "Be sure to keep your thumb here…"

"Like this?"

She sensed that he nodded.

"*Ja*, that's right. And then you are going to pull the rod backward…" This time, one of his hands covered hers as he tilted the top of the rod so that it was behind her shoulder. "And you are going to fling it forward and release your thumb so that the line can sail into the water at a distance."

With his help, she did as he instructed. The reel made a whizzing sound as the hook was flung out and into the pond.

"Perfect!" He took a step backward so that he wasn't standing so close to her.

She glanced at him. "Now what?"

"What do you mean now what?"

She shrugged her shoulders. "Now what do I do?"

He raised his hand and removed his hat, wiping his forehead with the back of his arm. The sun had emerged from behind the clouds and was beating down upon them. "Well…uh…you wait."

"I wait," she repeated.

"*Ja*, you wait for a fish to take your bait."

"I see." She turned her head to look back at the pond, trying to see where her line met the water. "And how will I know if that happens?"

He began to prepare his own rod. "You'll feel a tug on your pole and, when that happens, you jerk it backwards, just once, before you reel in the line." She heard him digging for another worm, the bottom of the cup making a scratching noise against the rock. "But I'm here, Catherine. I can help you with that, if the fish is so big that it pulls you into the water. Don't worry," he added with a bright smile at her concerned expression.

After he had cast his own line in the other direction, a silence fell over them. She waited a few minutes before she sat down, dangling her legs over the side of the rock. He did the same. Despite their rods being pointed in different directions, they sat side-by-side, close enough so that their hips almost touched. For a moment, Catherine almost moved away but thought that he might be offended or take it the wrong way.

The birds chirped from the trees behind them. Occasionally, something would jump from the water, sending ripples toward where they sat. In the distance, they heard a loud bang, most likely the backfiring of a car on a nearby road. Other than that, it was quiet and peaceful sitting on that rock with the reflection of the sun bouncing off the top of the water.

"Wish I had brought sunglasses," she said out loud, more to herself than to Henry.

"Here." He reached into his pocket and pulled out a dark black pair. "Use mine."

She hesitated to take them.

"It's okay. I wasn't using them anyway."

Reluctantly, she accepted the sunglasses and slipped them on. For a moment, everything looked too dark as she let her eyes adjust. "It's nice out here," she commented. "Just sitting here and being. Just being. I don't think we do much of that. At least I don't."

Henry tilted his head as he looked at her. "Why is that?"

"At home, there's always something to do. Between the younger *kinner* and the chores, there isn't a lot of time to just sit back and listen to God's orchestra."

"God's orchestra?" he asked, a soft smile on his lips.

"*Ja*, that's right. His orchestra. The birds. The leaves. The water. Even those crickets. Do you hear them, Henry?"

She watched as he looked over his shoulder toward the woods behind him. When he turned back around, he stared into her face, his eyes studying her for a long moment. "I do," he admitted at last. "And it is, indeed, a beautiful song." He turned back toward the pond. "I'm rather glad that I'm listening to it with you."

For another long while they sat in silence, watching and waiting for something to happen with their fishing poles. If she had previously felt uncomfortable being alone in his company, now she began to relax. She could imagine an author writing this very scene into a romance book, and in her mind, she began to formulate the words as if she were crafting it herself. She described the bright green leaves that hung from the trees, the dark water with light ripples, the blue sky with a scattering of clouds. And then she tried to describe Henry.

A tall and handsome man sat on the rock, his fishing rod in hand, as he waited for a fish to take the bait. His dark hair hung in loose curls that were tucked behind his ears. He wore a white short-sleeved shirt that was perfectly pressed, almost as if it were for Sunday worship. The young woman seated beside him glanced furtively in his direction. She had never been fishing before and prayed that she was doing everything correctly. The last thing she wanted was to disappoint her companion.

He realized that she was watching him and turned to face her. When their eyes met, a bird began singing from a nearby tree. It was as if the bird sang the song just for the two of them.

"Catherine?"

Startled out of her daydream, she blinked and looked at him in surprise. She wondered how long he had been watching her. Embarrassed, she felt her cheeks turning pink. "*Ja?*"

He pointed toward her pole. "You have a bite."

"A…bite? Already?"

He tried not to laugh at the expression on her face. "On your hook. If you want to catch the first fish of the day, I suggest you start reeling it in."

"Oh!" Quickly, she jumped to her feet, the pole still in her hands. As she steadied herself, she clutched the rod and tried to turn the reel at the same time. Her fingers fumbled as she felt the pole being tugged away from her. "Henry!" She looked at him, pleading for him to help her. She was frightened that in the struggle with the fish she might lose both the fish and the pole. "It's pulling!"

"Of course, it's pulling! It's not happy, I'm sure. Would you be if you were caught?" Chuckling, he stood up to help her. Once again, he stood behind her and reached around her shoulders so that he could help steady the rod while she tried to turn the reel, slowly collecting the line. The tip of the rod bent over and she feared that it would break. Henry, however, remained calm and focused, apparently not worried about the fishing pole. "Slow and steady," he said softly, his breath against her ear. "Easy does it."

She shivered, a tingling sensation flooding her body at his nearness, and she thought she heard him give a soft laugh.

As he helped her by keeping the rod steady and encouraging her to stay calm, she reeled in the line and, with it, one of the largest fish she had ever seen. It wiggled and twisted as Henry reached for the end of the line and swung the fish onto the land.

"Not bad for a fisherwoman who has never fished before," he said good-naturedly. "That's a ten pounder if I ever saw one."

"Is that good?"

He laughed as he stepped on the fish and pulled the hook from its mouth. "*Ja*, I'd say so. You keep pulling these in and you'll be eating fish all week!"

She watched as he tossed the fish into the cooler and hooked another worm onto her line. "That was easy," she said.

He gave her a sideways glance. "Easy enough for you to say. Now it's my turn."

For the next two hours, they alternated between sitting on the rock waiting for a fish to take the bait and standing up to reel in their catch. For Catherine, it was the best two hours that she could remember. Besides the excitement of catching the fish, she was able to enjoy spending time with the person who was rapidly becoming more and more dear to her. If she could replicate those two hours every day for the rest of her life, she knew that she would never find better happiness.

Chapter Twenty-Two

The next day, immediately after breakfast, Henry left to visit with some of his friends, declaring that he would be back in time for the afternoon chores. Since there were no worship services for the Newbury Acres Amish community that week, Catherine and Ellie spent a leisurely morning after breakfast. It was *verboten* to knit, embroider, or quilt on Sunday, and they certainly could not cook. So they decided to pack a light lunch of day-old bread and jam with some freshly cut fruit and snacks so that they could take a walk to the very pond where Catherine had gone fishing the previous day.

This time, however, they sat at a small picnic table on the other side of the pond. It was shaded from the sun, which was directly overhead by the time they arrived.

"Did you enjoy yourself yesterday?" Ellie asked her as she unpacked the food onto the table.

Catherine caught herself gazing across the pond to the other side where she had sat with Henry for so long. "I did, Ellie. It was so peaceful and quiet. And the fishing was *wunderbarr*!"

"I know that Henry enjoyed it. He told me as much before he left after supper last night."

Catherine wasn't certain how to interpret that comment. Was Ellie trying to tell her something about Henry's affections for her? Or was she just being kind and friendly? Rather than question her friend further, Catherine decided to change the subject. "Isn't it extra work for Henry to manage the two farms?"

"You mean the Woods farm? My *maem*'s family farm?" Ellie plucked a ripe cherry from the container and plopped it into her mouth. "Oh, *nee*! I dare say that he much prefers the farming over there to the work here."

That was surprising to Catherine. She was under the impression that Henry spent very little time at the Woods farmhouse. "Is that so? Why do you think?"

Ellie gave a slight shrug of her shoulders. "Probably because he is free to do as he pleases over there. Our *daed* rarely goes over to inspect anything. He leaves all of the responsibility to Henry." She reached for another cherry but hesitated before she ate it. "It's not a large farm, Catherine. Only fifty acres or so. And the house is just a typical old farmhouse. I never quite understood why *Daed* was so determined to acquire it."

Catherine frowned. "I thought he acquired it because he married your *maem*?"

"*Ja*, that's true." Ellie gave her a thoughtful look. "You have a right *gut* memory, Catherine."

"So, did he love her or the property?"

Ellie waved her hand absentmindedly at Catherine. "Oh, who knows? And is it really important? After all, that's long before any of us were around and it truly doesn't matter anymore, does it?"

But Catherine wasn't so easily convinced. If the three

Tilman children had been raised in an environment that was founded in opportunity for advancement and not love, what could be expected of their futures? How would they model their own marriages: after their *daed*'s forceful demands or their *maem*'s furtive dreams?

"Tell me about your parents, Catherine," Ellie said, turning the conversation away from her own family and back to the Millers.

"My family? Why, they are just ordinary farmers!"

"No one is ordinary," Ellie countered. "Have they always lived in Fullerton?"

Catherine began to recount her family's history, what little she knew of it. She talked about how her parents met and how they had moved into the family farm shortly after marriage. It was the only home that Catherine knew and the only one that she could use as a measurement for others.

"So how do we measure up?" Ellie asked, her eyes wide with curiosity.

The question took Catherine by surprise. How could she answer that? "I didn't mean it that way," she offered as an explanation. "I don't compare us to other families."

Ellie raised an eyebrow.

"I mean that we are just farmers, Ellie. Your family farms, too, but your family is different. It's…" How could she explain what she was thinking? The last thing she wanted to do was to say the wrong thing and offend her friend. "Most Amish families work together. Your family has different businesses and the family is more divided, with Freddie working at the wood shop and Henry at the farm. And you have help from others.

Your *daed*'s farm is a community project and that's a good thing, I suppose."

"It is," Ellie admitted. "These people don't have the means to buy their own farms in Newbury Acres. *Daed* is committed to keeping the people working among each other and away from the *Englische*." She reached for her napkin and wiped her lips. "Tourists bring worldliness, and that, in turn, brings problems."

Catherine wasn't certain how to respond to that. She knew that there were issues in Fullerton with some of the young adults experimenting with technology and even alcohol during their *rumschpringe*, the period of time before they joined the church. But problems were few and far between. Many times, she had overheard her parents talking about the much worldlier youth from Holmes County, Ohio, where many youth did not join the Amish church, opting to join the less conservative Mennonite churches instead. But the youth in her community tended to stay Amish.

Ellie looked up at the sun. "Oh, help! It must be close to two o'clock. I promised to take some cheese over to our neighbor, Mary Fischer. She's having family this week. Perhaps you would like to come along?"

Catherine shook her head. "*Nee*, if you don't mind, I'd like to read a little and perhaps write a letter to my parents."

Standing up, Ellie began packing up their things. "I probably won't be home until suppertime. It's a good twenty-minute walk, and she'll certainly want me to stay to visit."

By the time they returned to the house and Ellie left, it was almost three o'clock. Catherine offered to clean up from their picnic so that Ellie would not be delayed.

In the quiet of the house, Catherine hummed to herself as she washed their plates and utensils. As she shut off the faucet, her hand lingered on the knob and she raised her eyes to stare out the window.

Without Gid, somehow the farm felt more alive. Catherine couldn't help but wonder if his wife had felt the same oppressiveness from her husband or if she had made the home more cheerful. She imagined that it was the latter. She couldn't imagine any woman being able to live under Gid Tilman's strict rules.

And that was the moment she realized that, with no one else home, she would be able to sneak over to the other side of the house at last. As much as she tried to chase that thought away, it quickly returned, every time in a more overwhelming way.

For a few long moments, she argued with herself. She went back and forth, trying to decide whether or not she should take advantage of being alone to explore the forbidden rooms. On the one hand, she knew that Gid did not want her to see these rooms. Yet she countered that argument when she reminded herself that Ellie had been more than willing to take her there.

Finally, she made up her mind and walked over to the cabinet where she had seen Ellie fetch the key. With a trembling hand, she opened the door and reached inside, taking the key from the cupboard and holding it in her hand. For a moment, she hesitated and reconsidered. Then she glanced at the clock. It was not even three-fifteen. Catherine knew that she would have enough time to go explore the forbidden side of the house undetected. But her conscience pricked at her. Did she dare do the one thing that Gid Tilman had so vehemently prohibited? Even if he didn't know, she would know, and the guilt might be easily seen in her face when she saw him again, especially if she discovered the truth about his deceased wife. And what was the truth that she was looking for? What, exactly, did she think that she might discover?

She held the key in her hand and shut her eyes. What was their mother like? Was she like Freddie and Gid, who focused on their own personal gain rather than the comfort of others? Or was she more like Ellie and Henry, compassionate and caring? And had Gid loved her, or had he only married her for her land?

Determined to learn the truth, Catherine hurried to the door and fit the key in the lock. She was almost surprised when it opened easily.

Pushing the door open, she stood there for a moment and contemplated turning back. But her curiosity got the best of her and she stepped through the doorway into the forbidden section of the house.

To her amazement, she walked right into the large gathering room and kitchen. Someone had opened the shades and, unlike the previous day, today the room was now bright and airy, giving her a feeling as if she stood outdoors, not in a house. The sun shone through the windows, the rays exposing little specks of dust that floated through the air. Catherine walked toward the staircase, her footsteps sounding extra loud in the quiet of the empty house. She noticed the bookshelf along the back wall beneath the windows and peeked at the titles. Devotionals. Bibles. *Martyr's Mirror*. Nothing out of the ordinary. It could have been a bookshelf in her own family's house.

She tried to step lightly as she climbed the staircase. The handrail felt smooth beneath her fingers, as if someone had just cleaned it with a good wood polish. In fact, as she glanced back at the room, she realized that everything appeared neat and tidy, not a speck of dust gathered on the counters or table. If no one was permitted in this section of the house, who cleaned it? She couldn't imagine Gid doing it, but clearly someone was taking care of the rooms.

At the top of the stairs, she noticed that the door to one of the bedrooms was open. She approached that room first. To her amazement, it appeared as if someone had been staying there. The bed was made, a pretty quilt spread on the bed. She reached out her hand and touched it. The quilt had been made by hand and with perfect little stitches. She wondered if it had been a wedding quilt, made to celebrate their mother's marriage to Gid Tilman. The pillow still had a dent in it as if someone had slept there just recently. And on the nightstand was a kerosene lantern with a smoky hurricane. Beside it was a Bible. She recognized it as Gid's and caught her breath. Did Gid still sleep in the room that he had shared with his wife?

"What are you doing in my *daed*'s bedroom?"

Catherine spun around and gasped when she saw Henry standing in the doorway. "Henry! You are back so soon!"

He studied her with a somber expression. "My visit was shorter than expected." He took a step into the room and stood before her. There was an expression of curiosity on his face as he faced her. "And how did you manage to find your way here, if I might ask?"

She glanced at the quilt. "I…well…I wanted to see her quilts."

"I see." He arched his eyebrow. "Has Ellie spoken much about our *maem*?"

"*Ja*," she said and then shook her head. "Not so much, I suppose."

"Uh huh." He considered her answer with a cool expression.

"Ellie was going to show me the other day," Catherine suddenly gushed.

"And?"

"Your *daed* stopped us."

He made a noise in his throat. "So, you thought you could come see them yourself since no one was home?"

It sounded so much worse when he said those words. Embarrassed, she lowered her eyes. "I'm so sorry."

He pressed his lips together and shook his head. "I'm surprised at you. Truly I am."

"I just wanted to see…" But she couldn't finish the sentence. Her quest into the forbidden section of the house now seemed frivolous. All that she had learned was that Gid stayed in this section of the house and kept it pristine, perhaps in honor of his deceased wife. Had she truly thought that she might uncover some family secret? "I wanted to learn more about your mother. No one speaks of her, yet I know that Ellie misses her so. And your *daed* refused to let her come here and see her quilts and find her recipes and there was so much secrecy so I…I thought…"

"You thought what?"

Once again, she lowered her eyes. "I thought that he hadn't been very fond of her," she said in a soft voice.

Henry seemed to contemplate this and nodded his head. "I see," he said once again. There was a long, drawn-out moment of awkward silence between them.

When Catherine finally looked up at him, she saw that he appeared to be observing her with a new eye. His expression, usually so tender and kind, was void of any emotion. So she was surprised when he reached out for her hand. "Come, Catherine. Let me introduce you to my mother. She was much more than a pretty house."

Startled by his gesture, she accepted his hand.

"She loved to quilt," he said and pointed to the bed. "You already know that. This was her last quilt that she made the winter before she took ill."

"It's…it's lovely."

He gave a soft smile as if the memory of his mother quilting pleased him. "She always quilted in the winter. She'd sit by the windows downstairs and spend hours each evening quilting. She had patience, that was for sure and certain. Come into the other room and see some of her other quilts." He led her out of the bedroom and toward a door that was shut. When he opened the door, he stepped aside so that Catherine could enter first.

Inside the room, there was a quilting frame leaning against the wall. On a folding table, there were three quilts neatly folded. Catherine walked toward them and rested her hand on the top one. "What are these?"

"There is one for each of her children. For their weddings." Henry leaned against the doorframe and crossed his arms over his chest. "She knew that she was dying, Catherine, and she made certain to have everything in order. She knew that she would not live to see her children get married, so she made these the winter before she died."

She lifted the top one and stared at the second quilt. "They are beautiful."

"I agree with you," Henry said. "And so was she."

Catherine looked at him.

"I've been told grief takes many forms, Catherine," Henry continued slowly, his gaze on the quilts, but his thoughts elsewhere. "Perhaps once he lost my mother, my *daed* realized how he had neglected her when she was alive. Maybe caring for her things is his way of making it up to her. Perhaps he does not forbid us from being in this section of the house in order to forget her but because he wants to keep her memory alive for himself. Selfish? Perhaps. But it may be his strange way of making amends."

She followed his gaze toward the quilts, saddened at the thought of so much love being shut away, lost to the children who most needed it.

"So your father…did he love her?"

"In his own way, maybe he did. Just not in a way that you and I would recognize." A spasm of grief and anger crossed his face before he said abruptly, "Now, if you have satisfied your curiosity, I think it is best that we leave the past alone." He spoke in a terse tone as he moved from the doorway so that she could exit the room. "And return to the other side of the house where you belong."

In silence, she walked down the stairs and followed Henry through the kitchen and gathering room. When she passed through the door that she had unlocked, she kept her back to Henry, listening as he shut the door and locked it. He did not return the key to the cabinet but slid it into his pocket.

He did not speak to her as he left the house. She watched through the window as he marched toward the dairy barn. Only when he disappeared did she sink onto the sofa and cover her face with her hands, allowing the tears to fall. She knew that she had disappointed him, and in doing so, she had disappointed herself as well.

Chapter Twenty-Three

"There's a letter for you," Henry said as he walked into the kitchen.

Both Ellie and Catherine looked up, presuming that he was addressing the other one. When Catherine realized that he was speaking to her, the first time since the previous day, she wiped her wet hands on her apron and hurried across the floor toward Henry. "Has the mailman come already?" she asked, glancing at the clock on the wall near the staircase. It was eleven-thirty. Henry would have dinner at noon and then depart for the Woods farm immediately afterward.

He didn't respond as he handed her the letter.

"*Danke*," Catherine said, hoping that he might meet her gaze and smile. Ever since he found her in his mother's room yesterday, he had been quiet and reflective. Several times she had caught him observing her with an unreadable expression on his face. Despite his kind handling of her invasion into his mother's part of the house, she knew that he had been disappointed with her behavior. And that disappointment had certainly washed away any hope on her part that he had grown fond of her in the same way she felt of him.

Thankfully, Ellie seemed oblivious to the shadow that had fallen across her relationship with Henry. Catherine had thought long and hard about whether to confess her trespass to her friend, and decided not to. Why distress Ellie and spoil the remaining time they had together? Henry knew what she had done, and that was burden enough to bear. As for Gid: she knew confessing to him would be impossible, even if in some strange way it might be a relief to her conscience.

Sighing, she sat down at the table and opened the envelope. "It's from James," she explained as she began to read. Her eyes scanned the words on the page, and as she realized their import, she covered her mouth with her hand. "Oh, no!"

"What is it?" Ellie asked. She joined Catherine at the table, taking the seat next to her.

"I don't even want to say! It's so awful!" She continued reading and gasped. "Oh, I shall never want a letter again!"

Henry approached the table. "Is everything alright?"

"No. Not at all!" Catherine kept reading the letter and gasped. "Poor James!" She set down the letter and looked at Ellie first. "His engagement to Ida Mae is no more." Then she looked at Henry. "It appears that she is engaged to another man."

"Another man?"

Slowly she nodded. "I'm almost not believing it, but I know James would never lie."

Ellie and Henry remained quiet, and she knew they dared not ask for more information, realizing that the matter required the utmost tact.

"I must ask a favor of you," she said at last, knowing that what she would say would hint at the news. "If, during my stay, your *bruder* is to return to Newbury Acres, please let me know ahead of time so that I might return to my family early."

Ellie raised an eyebrow and Henry frowned. "Freddie?"

Catherine hesitated. "Something dreadful has happened that would make it very uncomfortable for me to be in the same *haus* as him."

The muscles in Henry's jaw tightened. "I suspect Ida Mae has left your *bruder* for ours," he said in a firm, angry voice.

Catherine hadn't wanted to tell them, but she knew that they must learn the entire story. "And it's even worse, because it appears she is engaged to Freddie."

Henry winced and Ellie caught her breath.

"It's highly unlikely that Freddie would become engaged," Henry said at last. "I'm sure you have been misinformed."

She glanced down at the letter and scanned the back of the first page. "He says it quite clearly right here. While James was back in Fullerton, Ida Mae was seen courting Freddie on a daily basis. James returned to Banthe and learned of…" She paused, looking for the right word to use. "… An indiscretion of some type, although he doesn't say how he learned of it."

"Indiscretion?" Henry repeated the word as if it tasted foul.

Ellie leaned forward as if to read the letter herself. "Are you certain of that?"

Catherine gave her the letter and pointed to the line that mentioned the engagement. "Such inconstancy!"

she said more to herself than to Ellie or Henry. "And how is this possible? They barely know each other."

Ellie read the letter, and when she came to the end, she sighed and handed it back to Catherine. "I still find it hard to believe."

"Our *daed* will never permit our *bruder* to marry such a senseless woman!"

Startled at his harsh words, Catherine returned her attention to Henry. "But it's already been announced!"

Henry shook his head. "Prepare yourself, Ellie, for your new sister-in-law! Inconstant, indiscreet, and foolish!"

Stunned, Catherine stared at him. She had never heard him speak poorly about anyone, even John Troyer. She wondered if his anger stemmed from his own feelings about her.

"Perhaps she is simply young, naïve, and impetuous. I would welcome a sister-in-law with those traits." Ellie glanced at Catherine. "But I agree that the circumstances do not reflect well upon her character."

The severity of the situation hit Catherine, and she suddenly found herself blinking back tears. "How could she do something like that to James? He loved her. Of that I'm sure." She couldn't imagine how James felt. He had only been gone two weeks! How could Ida Mae replace him so quickly?

"Freddie has a way of charming the young ladies," Ellie said in a soft voice.

But Catherine found it hard to believe that anyone would be attracted to Freddie Tilman. While he might be considered handsome, she had seen through him right away. In her opinion, his character was far too flawed and marred any external appeal he might have. "He's…he's done this before?" she asked naively.

Ellie nodded slowly but deliberately. "I'm just surprised that he would settle for such an easy target."

"Oh," she said under her breath.

Henry stepped forward and knelt before Catherine. He covered her folded hands with his and stared up at her. "I'm sure this is shocking to you." He spoke in a gentle voice. "While it appears that Ida Mae has mistreated your *bruder*, Catherine, I can assure you that she will pay a high price for her choice. I know for a fact that my *bruder* is not capable of being the kind and attentive husband that I'm sure your brother would have been."

Catherine swallowed. While she was angry with Ida Mae for hurting her brother, she also felt sorry for her. No woman went into marriage expecting to be mistreated, and Ida Mae was likely due for a rude awakening.

"What's done is done, I'm sure." Henry gave Catherine's hands a soft squeeze before standing up, but she was so miserable she could hardly take in the sympathetic gesture.

"Poor, poor James," Catherine whispered, still dismayed at how her brother might be feeling. In the letter he had said nothing more than the bare facts of the situation, but she could read between the lines. She knew he was hurting.

"Better to find out now than later, though," Ellie said. "What man would want such an unfaithful woman?"

Catherine bit her lower lip and glanced at Henry. She felt a tightening in her chest as she remembered how she had deceived them all by going against Gid Tilman's wishes. If she had hoped that he might have affections for her, surely she had destroyed that, just as Ida Mae had destroyed her chances with James. Surely James would never take her back now that she had publicly humiliated him! Although, Catherine thought, it was too late for such hope anyway if Ida Mae preferred to marry Freddie.

Just then the full ramifications of the news settled in. Ida Mae and Freddie: married. Poor Ellie and Henry, to have to live with such a sister-in-law! Quickly Catherine turned from being the consoled to being the consoler, saying, "Perhaps she will be better behaved in your family. She might be more consistent anyway, if she truly loves him."

Regardless of Catherine's kind words, Henry's mood did not improve. "She'll be consistent, for certain, unless a wealthier man with a finer business comes along!"

Catherine gasped. "You think she did this out of greed?"

"Undoubtedly!" he snapped. He paced the floor, shaking his head. "And she has not only hurt James, but she has hurt you. You thought her a good friend, even with her flaws. Now I'm certain you feel as abandoned as your *bruder*. While I pity your *bruder* for his loss, I am equally aware of your own."

While touched—and relieved—by his concern, for it showed that he did still care for her, Catherine felt compelled to correct him. "Henry, I'm hurt by her actions, but I'll not waste a moment more grieving the loss of such a so-called friend."

Henry stopped pacing and looked at her for a moment. Something changed in his countenance. Without any warning, he suddenly walked over to the counter and reached for his hat. "I believe I will take my leave sooner," he said as he slipped the hat on his head. "I've lost my appetite and prefer to be on my own for the moment."

He walked out the door, Catherine staring after him. Surely, he was reflecting on more than just Ida Mae and Freddie. Undoubtedly, he was thinking about his disappointment from the previous day. Catherine sighed and folded the letter.

"I think," she began in a soft voice, "that I'll take some time in my room, Ellie, if you don't mind. I'm not very hungry anymore."

Ellie patted Catherine's shoulder. "Of course, I understand. I think we've all lost our appetites after such distressing news."

Quietly, Catherine climbed the staircase and retreated to her room. She lay down on the bed and let her tears fall. Whether she cried for James's loss or her own, Catherine wasn't certain. All she knew was that there was a pain in her chest and that it came from deep within her heart.

Chapter Twenty-Four

After receiving James's letter, she had been in a sour mood. Her disappointment at Ida Mae was countered only by her sympathies for James's broken heart. She had appreciated Henry's kindness to her during her distress, but this morning he had departed for the Woods farm without even saying good-bye. She suspected that he was still upset with her for having gone to the other side of the house, and thinking of the incident still brought a deep pit of guilt to her stomach. Apparently, he had kept the discovery of her invasion of privacy to himself, for Ellie appeared as good-natured and kind as always. That made Catherine feel even more guilty about her decision to break Gid's rule.

And her guilt made her realize that she was in no position to judge anyone, even if she wanted to. "Let him who is without sin among you be the first to throw a stone," Jesus had said. Well, Catherine certainly did not consider herself as being without sin, that was for sure and certain.

And then, not even the next day, when a young boy stood at the door with the mail, to Catherine's surprise, he marched right up to her and held out a small white envelope.

"Another letter?" Catherine wiped her hands on her apron and reached out to take the envelope from the boy who had fetched the mail and brought it to the house. She forced a smile of appreciation at him, too aware that he was most likely living in one of the Tilmans' properties and charged, by Gid himself, with the daily task of bringing the mail to the house. The more she learned, the more Catherine was aware that Gid seemed to have his fingers in a lot of pots in Newbury Acres.

Holding the envelope, she moved to the table. "This one is from Banthe," Catherine said as she sat down. "I imagine it's from Ida Mae." Her voice was flat and emotionless. Unlike when she had received the letter from James on Monday, she was not excited as she held the unopened letter in her hand. She already suspected what it would say, and therefore, she dreaded opening it.

Ellie joined her at the table. "You should read it before making judgments over the contents, Catherine," she said in a compassionate tone. "It might not be as bad as you believe."

Somehow, in the mood that Catherine was in, she highly doubted that.

Now, with a heavy heart, Catherine slid her finger under the back flap and opened the envelope, slipping out several sheets of folded pink paper covered in small handwriting. "Oh, dear," she mumbled at the length of the missive. She turned over several sheets, disheartened to realize that Ida Mae had written on the front and back of each sheet. When she finished scanning it, she looked at Ellie and raised her eyebrows. "Four pages? Both sides?"

"Seems she has a lot to say," Ellie commented dryly.

Taking a deep breath, Catherine began to read the letter. Her eyes studied the first few lines and then she squinted, pausing to reread them. *Dear Catherine*, it began. *Banthe has become such a bore without you here. The tourist season has ended and we have once again returned to the quiet seasonal town that is largely forgotten throughout the remainder of the year. But the children must return to school, and Banthe becomes nothing more than a pleasant memory for those who visit, leaving the year-round residents to wonder at their folly while vacationing here.*

Catherine paused and shook her head. Had Ida Mae truly begun her letter in such a way as if nothing out of the ordinary—or extraordinary!—had happened? Had she actually referred to the actions of others as folly when she, herself, was guilty of so much more? She returned her attention to the letter. *I fear that there has been a misunderstanding between me and James. I am writing to beg of you to speak to him on my behalf. You know that he is the only man I have ever, and will ever, love.* The more Catherine continued reading, the deeper the frown became on her face. By the time she turned over the first page, she began to read faster, skipping entire lines as she merely glanced through each of the remaining pages. Disgusted, she let the letter fall to the table and leaned back in the chair.

"What did she write?" Ellie asked.

"It's off!" she declared. "Everything! Her engagement with James, her relationship with Freddie—done!"

Ellie gasped. "Are you sure?"

"She starts off the letter as if nothing has happened at all!" Catherine shook her head in disbelief. "She talks of

the summer season ending with the vacationers returning to their homes as school starts soon." She looked up.
"School! She talks of children and school!"

Ellie clicked her tongue in disapproval.

"She speaks of the folly of the tourists!"

"Their folly? Oh, dear…" Ellie's voice trailed off
and she shook her head. "Perhaps she is in denial of
her own foolishness?"

"I don't think so. She has asked me to speak to James
about a 'misunderstanding' between them." Catherine
scowled. "She actually called it that. A 'misunderstanding.' Can you imagine? She broke off her engagement
to my *bruder* for another man! I fail to see any 'misunderstanding' about that."

"Will you?"

Catherine tilted her head. "Will I what?"

"Speak to James for her?"

The idea horrified Catherine. "Absolutely not! While
I will forgive her for what she has done, that does not
mean I will forget! And I would not want to have my
bruder suffer any more under her idea of what a 'misunderstanding' truly is! If she were baptized, she'd
most certainly be shunned for what she did with…"
Her voice trailed off as she remembered that the other
person who gave such offense was none other than Ellie's older brother.

"Well, at least Freddie is safe from Ida Mae Troyer,"
Ellie said in a tone that dripped with sarcasm. "I'm not
surprised."

"I am!" Catherine exclaimed. "She claims that James
is the only man that she loved. Yet she threw it away
for your *bruder*." She reached forward and pushed the

letter farther away from her. "I wish I had never met that Ida Mae Troyer!"

Ellie remained silent as she stood up and gave Catherine some space to deal with the emotional upheaval.

Her anger subsided as she reached for the letter and read it once more, this time with a calmer countenance. She remembered all of their talks about reputations and Ida Mae waving off Catherine's concerns. Now Ida Mae was reaping what she had sown. She had lost more than her reputation and her fiancé; she had also lost a friend.

Still, Catherine couldn't wrap her head around Ida Mae having left James in the first place. While Henry suspected that Ida Mae's actions stemmed from greed and wanting to further herself, Catherine had a hard time accepting that. There was only one other person she had ever met who thought like that: Gid Tilman. And that made her wonder about Freddie's personality. What little she had known about him prior to this situation had not impressed her. Now he had fallen even further than she had thought possible.

She would have to work extra hard at forgiving him for what he had done. And it would surely take time.

"One thing I don't understand," Catherine said at last, "is why your *bruder* would have made such a fuss over Ida Mae and even led her to believe they were to marry. What they may or may not have done in privacy is their own business, but publicly he all but acknowledged her as his girl. And then he simply withdrew his affections? What is to be gained from that?"

Ellie took a deep breath. "Freddie's always had his vanities, just like Ida Mae. He is very similar in character to our *daed*, Catherine, and they are both very accustomed to having their way. It doesn't matter who might get hurt in the process."

Catherine remembered her conversation with Henry on the first evening she was at Newbury Acres. Hadn't he said as much regarding his father and how he wished him to marry well in order to contribute to expanding the farm?

"Although usually he doesn't make his conquests so public," Ellie quipped.

Conquest? Although she had already learned that this was not the first time Freddie had toyed with the affections of a young woman, Catherine caught her breath as she realized the full extent of Ida Mae's humiliation. "Oh, dear! Perhaps I will lighten my bitterness toward Ida Mae."

Ellie gave her a sad smile. "She will recover from this, I'm sure. And be all the more wiser with her future choices. Surely, she was looking for a way to a better life and thought she would become Freddie's wife, living here at Newbury Acres. Even if Freddie had wished to settle down—and he does not—*Daed* would never have allowed such a connection."

Catherine felt the color drain from her cheeks. If Gid Tilman would not permit Freddie to marry just anyone, certainly he would not permit Henry to consider marrying her!

Ellie seemed to notice Catherine's silence. "But, Catherine," Ellie said as she leaned forward and covered Catherine's hand with her own. "Please don't think that any of Freddie's moral flaws are exhibited in our other *bruder*, Henry. He is as different as could be from Freddie."

"I...I know that," she managed to say, still feeling a sinking feeling in her stomach.

Ellie patted her hand. "Good. And, with any luck, our dear Henry will return to us by supper time tomorrow!" She stood up and returned to the kitchen counter to continue her work. "The days are so long when he goes to the other farm." She glanced over her shoulder at Catherine. "And that is why I'm so fortunate you came to stay here, Catherine. How lonely I would've been with no company to keep!"

Catherine took a moment to refold the letter and stick it back in the envelope. She knew that she should write a response to Ida Mae, but she wouldn't. Not yet anyway. She couldn't bring herself to let Ida Mae know in words how she really felt. Her silence would speak loud enough, she suspected.

Chapter Twenty-Five

Her room was completely dark when she awoke to the sound of a man yelling for Ellie. At first, she thought she was dreaming, but by the third time the voice called out her friend's name, Catherine sat up in bed and waited. She couldn't tell what time it was, certainly after midnight. With a yawn, she swung her legs over the side of the bed and stood up, pausing to rub at her eyes. She shuffled over to the window and peered outside. To her surprise, she saw a car waiting near the barn, the headlights pointed away from the house and toward the road.

What on earth! She reached for her robe. Wrapping it around herself, she walked to her nightstand and searched for matches to light the kerosene lantern. Surely something was wrong. No one came calling in the middle of the night when things were going well. She only hoped that nothing had happened to Henry. Even though their relationship had seemed strained after she was discovered in his mother's room, Catherine still held her feelings for him close to her heart and prayed for his forgiveness.

"Ellie!" It was Gid! He bellowed one more time before Catherine heard the bedroom door from down the hall open. The soft bare footsteps on the hardwood floor were certainly Ellie's. "Get down here right now!"

Catherine pressed her ear against the door, too afraid to open the door but too curious to retreat. She could hear nothing but the muffled sound of voices from the bottom of the staircase. Ellie's voice seemed to plead with her father while Gid's loud, boisterous voice came and went in waves. All that Catherine could catch was "driver," "away," and "deceit."

Oh, help, Catherine thought and turned her back to the door so that she could lean against it. Certainly, Gid had learned about Freddie and Ida Mae. Perhaps they had reconciled after Ida Mae had written that letter. Perhaps they had run off, simply hired a driver and disappeared from Banthe. Such a scandal would infuriate any parent, although most Amish families would not react as vocally as Gid Tilman was reacting right now. But Catherine could understand that he would be angry: he had such high hopes for Freddie running the woodshop business. And she could only imagine that anyone who went against Gid's wishes would encounter his wrath.

Whatever! She thought bitterly as she remembered how Ida Mae had used her and deceived James. It might serve Ida Mae right to get a taste of her own medicine.

There was a soft knock at her door. Catherine startled and pushed herself away from the door. She took a moment to compose herself and opened the door slowly, not surprised to see Ellie standing there. Her hair hung over her shoulder in a long braid, and she wore a simple white nightgown.

"Ellie! What is going on? Is everything all right?"

she asked her friend. From the pale look on Ellie's cheeks, Catherine suddenly wondered if she had been mistaken about Freddie and Ida Mae being the source of Gid's late-night outburst. Before she could stop herself, she blurted out, "Please, Ellie! Tell me now that it has nothing to do with Henry, right?"

Ellie avoided looking at Catherine.

"Oh!" Catherine sank down onto a chair and began to tremble.

Ellie noticed and quickly stepped forward and knelt before her. She reached for Catherine's hands and held them tightly in her own. "*Nee*, Catherine. I'm sorry. Henry is fine, if that's what you mean."

Shutting her eyes, Catherine looked up toward the ceiling and said a quick prayer of gratitude to God. If anything happened to Henry, especially with him still feeling so disappointed in her behavior the previous weekend, she wouldn't be able to handle her emotions.

When she opened her eyes, she noticed that Ellie was still staring at her, an expression of sorrow engraved on her face. "Then what is it, Ellie? What's wrong?"

"Nothing is wrong, Catherine," she answered slowly. "But my *daed* has returned from Banthe with instruction that you are to return home."

Inwardly, Catherine groaned while on the outside, her shoulders slumped and she sank farther into the hard ladderback chair. Gid had learned that she disobeyed his wishes about no one going to the other side of the house. Since Henry was the only one who knew about it, he must have confided in his father. "He knows," she whispered.

Upon hearing Catherine's words, Ellie blinked, but she did not speak.

"I will pack first thing in the morning."

But Ellie placed a hand over hers and shook her head. "*Nee*, Catherine. Not in the morning."

"Then when?"

Pressing her lips together, Ellie hesitated before she said, "Now."

"Now? It's the middle of the night!"

Ellie did not respond but held Catherine's gaze.

Now the waiting car made sense. Gid must have learned about what happened and, in his rage, hired a driver to bring him back from Banthe and then take Catherine on to Fullerton.

"Have…have I offended your *daed*?" Catherine asked in a soft, frightened voice. Certainly, she understood that he might be upset with her, but to send her packing in the middle of the night? What kind of man would do such a thing?

"I'm so sorry, Catherine," Ellie whispered, standing up and backing away from her. "I…I want you to know that I don't agree with *Daed*, but he will hear no argument otherwise. He's…enraged."

"I…I deserve to be sent away," she whispered. "I knew Henry was upset with me. Surely he spoke to your father."

Ellie remained silent.

Catherine fought the tears that threatened to fall down her cheeks. "Henry must have told him what I did." She couldn't finish the sentence.

"*Nee*, Catherine," Ellie said. "I know my *daed*'s reasons and…and I'm embarrassed for him. I feel shame for my *daed*, turning you out in the middle of the night."

Fighting the urge to cry, Catherine nodded. She couldn't speak for fear of losing her self-control. She understood that Gid would be so upset with her for having disobeyed his insistence that no one visit the newer section of the house. However, to throw her out in the middle of the night? He had invited her to stay at the house, and she had never once questioned that he would take care of her as a proper guest. Now, she was to pack in the dark and leave as if she were the worst of sinners? The penalty did not fit the crime, and without another moment of control, she felt a tear slide down her cheek.

"Please tell Henry I'm so very sorry," she whispered.

"It's not your fault, Catherine."

She shook her head, another tear spilling from her eye. "*Nee*, it is. I...I should have been more forthcoming instead of being discovered in such a manner. Please, Ellie, tell that to Henry and..." She raised her head and, through tear-stained eyes, met her friend's gaze. "... Please do not hate me, Ellie. You are the very best of friends. Perhaps one day we can move past this and be friends once more?"

Ellie gave her a soft, understanding smile. "Of course, Catherine. But for now, it is best that you start packing. May I help you with something?"

While Catherine changed out of her nightgown, Ellie folded her other clothes and placed them in her suitcase. The silence in the room was deafening, and it was all that Catherine could do to keep her hands from shaking as she finished pinning her dress. After such a wonderful trip to Banthe with the Andersons and to Newbury Acres with Ellie and Henry, she would return home disgraced for disobeying Gid Tilman. How would she explain this to her mother?

"Let me carry this downstairs," Ellie said in a soft voice. She lifted the suitcase off the bed and started to walk to the door. Before she opened it, she paused. Without looking at Catherine, Ellie stared at the doorknob. "I cannot express how sorry I am that your visit has ended in such a rude, ungracious way," she said. Then, she reached out and opened the door, quietly passing through the doorway and hurrying to the stairs with the suitcase.

Downstairs, a small kerosene lantern burned in the kitchen, the flame casting a soft glow around the counter where it sat. Catherine glanced at it and was startled to see Gid standing in the shadows, his arms crossed over his chest and a scowl planted upon his face. She paused for a long moment and stared at him. She wished she had the courage to say something to him, to apologize for having gone into the other side of the house. But she couldn't muster the nerve to open her mouth.

If only she could take back that one day...

"*Kum*, Catherine," Ellie said, reaching out to touch her arm. Catherine thought she saw Ellie glance in her father's direction, a furtive look as if pleading with him to change his mind. "The driver is waiting for you. I will walk you out."

But Catherine shook her head. "*Nee*, Ellie. I will go on my own." She reached down and took the suitcase from her friend. "*Danke* for everything."

To her surprise, Ellie leaned over and embraced her. It was a warm gesture that lingered far too long for Gid's pleasure. He cleared his throat in a gruff manner that indicated it was time for Ellie to step away from Catherine.

"Here's some money to pay the driver," Ellie said, slipping some bills into Catherine's hand.

Catherine pushed the money back at Ellie. "*Nee*, I have my own money." She had barely touched any of the money that her parents had given her. But even if she was completely broke, she wasn't going to accept any charity from Ellie or any other Tilman. Not when she was being sent away like a shunned member of the church.

"Then I guess this is good-bye," Ellie said. It looked as if she might cry when she whispered, "Good-bye, Catherine."

"Good-bye, Ellie," Catherine whispered, averting her eyes once again from where Gid stood, glaring at her. She felt a fresh surge of anger. What type of man threw a young woman out of the house in the middle of the night? And for what reason? Just because she had dared to explore the other side of the house? She shook her head, amazed at this turn of events. When she had been so happy for so long, she now only felt misery tinged with anger at the man who was punishing her with banishment.

Finally, she lifted the suitcase off the ground and turned around, her back toward both Ellie and Gid. She walked to the door, which was already open, and stepped outside. She let her eyes adjust to the darkness before she climbed down the porch steps and headed across the yard toward the awaiting car. Its headlights lit up the lane, and Catherine could see that the driver had dozed off while waiting for her.

She opened the door and pushed her suitcase on the seat before climbing in beside it.

"You all set then?" the man said.

She nodded, and then realizing that he couldn't see her, she managed to say, "*Ja*, all set."

The driver pulled the gear shift down, and the car began to move forward. "Fullerton, right?"

"*Ja*, Fullerton."

"Haven't been that way in a long while," the driver said as he navigated the car down the lane and toward the main road. "And certainly not at this hour. I hope everything is all right with your family."

Catherine blinked and stared into the rearview mirror to catch the man watching her. "My family?" she asked.

"Isn't that why you had to leave so late at night?"

Catherine turned her head so that he couldn't see her expression. With a heavy sigh, she merely said, "My family's fine."

The driver sensed that she didn't feel like talking and asked no more questions of her. For the next hour, the car moved down the dark roads, away from Newbury Acres and toward Fullerton. Catherine stared out the window, watching nothing as she tried to imagine how she would explain her unexpected return to her parents.

Chapter Twenty-Six

"What is the meaning of this?" Ruth asked when Catherine showed up at the breakfast table.

She stood at the foot of the stairs in bare feet and her brown work dress, looking forlorn. Her hand rested on the banister as she tried to gain enough fortitude to take that final step and tell her mother that she had been sent away from Newbury Acres in disgrace.

"I've come home, *Maem*," she said in a soft voice. Reluctant to disturb the sleeping household, she'd told the driver to drop her at the end of the road so that she could quietly creep into the house without alerting anyone. She hadn't wanted to answer any questions. Not yet. She was tired and embarrassed as well as upset. She couldn't fathom what had made Gid so angry that he would throw her, a young woman, out of the house in the middle of the night.

But now, with her mother standing before her, Catherine knew that she couldn't hide from explaining what, exactly, had happened.

Ruth put her hand on her hip. "God gave me two eyes, Catherine. I can see that you've returned home."

Ruth's brows creased as she frowned. "The question, however, is why? You weren't scheduled to come back till Saturday!"

Catherine looked down at the floor.

"Oh, dear," Ruth mumbled to herself and hurried across the floor toward her daughter. "What happened, Catherine? *Kum*." She reached for her hand and gently tugged so that Catherine had no choice but to follow her mother toward the sitting area. "You best talk now before the *kinner* awaken and descend upon you. Then you'll never get a word in edgewise! And they'll be certain to have lots of questions."

Sitting in the chair next to her mother, Catherine folded her hands on her lap and stared at them, her shoulders slouched forward and her heart heavy. "They asked me to leave," she said in a soft voice. "It was all my fault, *Maem*. But their father turned me out in the middle of the night."

Her mother's back stiffened. "What could you have possibly done that could warrant such abuse?"

Once again, Catherine felt conflicted. She didn't agree with Gid Tilman's rash decision to expel her from the house in the middle of the night. Yet, in her heart, she knew that she had broken his rule, no matter how silly a rule she thought it was.

"I...I disobeyed Gid Tilman's wishes," she admitted at last.

"It must have been a very big wish to send you home so unexpected." Ruth reached out her hand and gently caressed Catherine's back.

She tried to find the words to explain to her mother. "I went into a part of the house that he had closed off and forbidden to me. But I was curious about what was so important to him that needed to be kept secret. Oh, I shouldn't have done it!" She wrung her hands on her lap. "I realize that now." She covered her face with her hands. "I shall never see them again. I'm so ashamed."

Her mother sat beside her while she wept, consoling her as best she could.

"*Maem*, I love them, Ellie and Henry, I mean," Catherine whispered at last. "And I have ruined any chance of retaining their friendship."

"Just friendship?" her mother prodded gently.

Catherine broke into fresh sobs. "And more. With Henry, I disappointed him, too. I saw his face and sensed his withdrawal, and we had been so happy! If only I hadn't let my curiosity get the best of me! I just needed to know whether or not their *daed* loved their mother, or did he mistreat her like he does so many others. He is so forbidding, *Maem*, so stern, you can't imagine. But oh! Why did I go into those forbidden rooms?" A sob escaped her throat and she let her tears fall. "I will never read another romance novel again."

Her mother cleared her throat. "I'm sure that God's purpose will be seen soon enough." She paused for a few seconds as if thinking about something. "Still, I wonder whether we should have learned more about the Tilman family before accepting their invitation. Clearly, they are strange people. Although Wilma spoke highly of them…"

Catherine shook her head. "*Nee*, *Maem*. It wasn't their fault, but mine. I should have listened to their *daed*'s rules and not been so nosey."

"Well, except for the ending, the rest of your trip sounded like you enjoyed yourself," Ruth said. "Wilma told us all about Banthe, and of course, we heard about that woman…" She made a sour face. "Poor James, he was rather distraught over his girl's change of heart. I don't understand why young people are so quick to announce their engagement! In our day, we kept things much more secret so that people's reputations could be protected should one of the parties back out."

Catherine bit her lower lip to keep from blurting out the truth, how Ida Mae had chased Freddie Tilman. She didn't know how much information James had shared with his parents, and she knew better than to speak out of turn about anyone else.

The sound of footsteps filtered down the staircase. The younger children were awake. Within minutes, their bare feet thumped on the steps as they ran downstairs to the kitchen.

"*Wie gehts*?" her brother David cried out as he jumped the last three stairs and landed on the floor. "Catherine's home! Catherine's home!" he shouted and ran over to give her a big hug. He was followed by the youngest, George, and the youngest two sisters, Elizabeth and Harriet. The four of them hugged her, wrapping their arms around her waist and shoulders as they fought for her attention.

"My goodness!" she said, forcing her voice to sound much more cheerful than she felt. "Such a greeting! I shall have to go away more often if this is how I'm received when I return!" She looked up at the sound of another set of feet walking down the stairs: her sister Sarah. "Why, hello, Sarah!"

Sarah grumbled at her and walked straight to the coffee pot.

Catherine caught her mother's eyes and smiled when her mother made a face.

"Well then, Catherine," her mother said. "Best get started with breakfast, *ja*?"

But Catherine could hardly move. The younger children hung on her, clinging to her arms and waist as if they would never let her go. She laughed as she tried to extract herself from their grip.

"What was it like, Catherine?" nine-year-old Elizabeth asked. "The lake! Was it everything you thought it would be?"

Catherine gave her one last hug before extracting herself. "Oh, *ja*, it was beautiful. We went walking almost every day, and the little town was close enough to walk to, too. One day we went berry picking and I made lots of pies and jam with Wilma."

"Did you go fishing, too?" David asked as he leaned against the back of her chair.

"Not at the lake," she said slowly.

"Then where?"

She glanced at her mother, but she was already busy preparing breakfast. To Catherine's relief, her sister Sarah was helping her. "At Newbury Acres," she stated, returning her attention to the children. "I went fishing at Newbury Acres."

"Did you catch anything?"

Catherine laughed at her brother. His eyes were almost larger than his head, he was so excited. "*Ja*, I sure did. I caught a largemouth bass and a crappie."

Young George's eyes grew large. "You just said a bad word," he whispered.

"It's a type of fish, silly," Catherine said and hugged him. Oh, it felt good to be at home. Even though she missed Henry and Ellie, she hadn't realized how much she had missed her own family.

"Who'd'ya go fishing with?" David asked.

Catherine glanced at him and wondered how to respond. "I…well…I went fishing with Henry Tilman. I stayed at their farm at Newbury Acres."

"Was it a nice farm?" Elizabeth asked.

"It was, *ja*." Catherine smoothed down George's hair, which had ruffled after she had hugged him. "They have a great big *haus* that is actually three large houses together. But they only live in one part, just the four of them."

"Aw, man! I bet they don't have to share rooms!" George said and kicked at the floor with his bare toes.

"No, that they do not."

"And this Henry?" Elizabeth asked. "Was he a…?"

When her sister didn't finish the question, Catherine lowered her eyes, but she couldn't stop the color from flooding to her cheeks. "He was the kindest of men, a truly righteous Christian and all that he should be."

Harriet leaned against her leg and stared up at her face. "Are you in love with him?"

Quickly Catherine hurried to her feet and forced herself to disentangle herself from her siblings. "Don't be silly," she scolded them. "Of course not." But when she felt her pulse quicken and her palms become sweaty, she knew that she had not spoken the truth.

A wave of panic washed over her as she realized that she would never see Henry Tilman again. He had been upset at her intrusion into their private lives, and as a result, informed his father, who had immediately returned to Newbury Acres to send her away. Whatever love she felt for Henry was certainly in vain, for he would never return her sentiments.

"Leave your *schwester* be now," their mother said

sharply as she carried a mug of hot coffee over to Catherine. "She's just gotten home and will have plenty of time to answer your questions about her trip. For now, perhaps you four could go see if *Daed*, James, and Richard need any help in the dairy."

Taking the coffee, Catherine gave her mother a look of gratitude as the younger four children scurried outside, David leading Elizabeth and Harriet while poor little George trailed behind trying to keep up.

"*Danke, Maem*," she whispered so that Sarah could not hear.

"You sit a while, or busy yourself with unpacking. Sarah will help me this morning." She turned toward her other daughter. "She's become quite useful in the kitchen since you left, if I do say so myself."

Sarah made a face and rolled her eyes, but there was a look of accomplishment about her. Catherine took another seat, cradling the mug of coffee between her hands, and watched as her sister moved about the kitchen with a confidence that had never existed before. Has so much changed in such a short period of time? she wondered. Have I, too, changed? The thought lingered in her mind long after her coffee cooled and the children returned from the barn in time to enjoy their breakfast.

Chapter Twenty-Seven

"I'm so sorry about what happened," Catherine said to her brother James. She was working in the garden and James had come out to keep her company. He sat in the grass while Catherine weeded between the rows of tomato plants. With the children still asking her questions and bothering her about Henry, Catherine had breathed a sigh of relief when her mother sent her to work outside.

James held a stick in his hand and was peeling away the bark with his thumb nail. He looked thinner than when she had last seen him in Banthe and certainly less happy. "I don't understand what happened," he said as he broke the stick in half and tossed part of it into the grass. "I thought she loved me." He looked up at Catherine. "Truly I did."

She tugged at a weed that was growing up one of the plants. "I did, too, James." She tossed the weed into the plastic bucket by her side.

"But she apparently loved herself more."

Catherine gave him a serious look. "Herself? Or money?"

James frowned. "Is that what you think this was about? Money?"

She shrugged her shoulders. "She told me about your letter, the one you had a driver send to her. She seemed rather disappointed that you weren't going to inherit the farm and that she'd be living in a *grossdawdihaus* until you could afford your own farm."

He winced at her words. "For that reason, she left me for another man?"

"A man with more property and money than we could ever imagine." She leaned back on her heels and stared around her. Her eyes took in the barn and the pastures, the house and the silo. While it wasn't anything like the Tilmans' farm, it was home to her. "I don't see why people feel that they need so much. What we have is just perfect. Sometimes even having just enough is too much. It still leaves people wanting more."

She thought of Gid Tilman with his five hundred acres and still wanting more. Yet, for all of his desire to accumulate more, he was not a happy man. He might have the best of intentions in creating the farming co-op, but he was not well-respected by his children nor his community. Even his bishop refused to stand up to him, afraid to reprimand Gid about his pride and his focus on his possessions. No matter how much he had, Gid Tilman was a man for whom enough was never enough. He spent his life figuring out ways to keep on building and little to no time on living. What kind of a life is that? she wondered.

James leaned back and stared up at the sky. "I heard that she was engaged to Freddie Tilman."

"So you said in your letter."

"I heard that they were engaged, not from her lips or hand but from others when I returned to Banthe."

Catherine raised an eyebrow. She hadn't known that James had returned there. Of course, it made sense that he would want to go see his fiancée. "You returned to Banthe?" she asked. "What happened?"

"I didn't want to write it in a letter," he said solemnly. As he began to explain, Catherine understood his discretion. "But I arrived with John, and Ida Mae was nowhere to be found. No one knew where she was, Catherine. So John and I drove around looking for her. I began to panic, worrying about something awful. It's all those mystery books that she read, I fear. I began to think someone had harmed her or..." He let his voice trail away and covered his eyes with the back of his arm. "Never once did I think that she would harm herself. Not in the way that I found her."

"Found her?" Catherine blinked her eyes in shock. "James, you must tell me what happened."

"She was leaving the Tilmans' cottage in Banthe, Catherine. It was almost dark and she came traipsing out the door, not even wearing her prayer *kapp*, and her hair..." He shook his head. "Her hair was a mess. I knew that Freddie Tilman was there on his own, that you were at Newbury Acres with the rest of the family. She had no business being alone in that man's cottage!"

Immediately, Catherine thought back to the late Sunday drive she had taken with Henry. Oh, how she had wanted to see inside the Woods farmhouse. But even there, with little to no risk of being discovered, Catherine had known that even making such a request could damage her reputation. What would Henry have thought of her? She could only imagine. Yet his older brother seemed to have no problem consorting with a woman who would enter the house unchaperoned.

"Perhaps there was an explanation?" she asked, although her voice gave away her own doubt.

James sat up and stared at her. "I had heard enough of the rumors, Catherine. Whatever she did or did not do in that house, she never should have been there in the first place. Regardless, her own reputation is ruined, and no other reputable man would consider courting her now. She's ruined herself, exactly like you said, for wanting more than just enough."

Catherine felt as if her heart would break all over again for her brother. Just one look at the dark circles under his eyes told her that he had lost many nights' sleep over this situation. And she didn't blame him. She, too, had not slept since she had left Newbury Acres. Instead, she tossed and turned, fretting over the fact that she would never see Henry again and had most likely lost what could have been a lifelong friend in Ellie.

"I'm so sorry, James," she said once again. "If there are any words of wisdom I can offer it is that you are better for knowing of her moral flaws now, rather than later."

He gave a soft laugh. "Moral flaws?"

"Poor judgment?"

He laughed again. "I'll say. She immediately told everyone that she was engaged to Freddie, not me. Not even two days later, I received a letter from John, begging me to reconsider my proposal. Apparently that Freddie Tilman just up and left Banthe with nary a word to her. Ida Mae locked herself in her bedroom and cried for two days, her folly exposed along with her true character. And yet, when she wiped away her tears, she actually believed that I would take her back!"

Folly. There was that word again. Ida Mae had used it to describe the tourists, instead of herself. Perhaps Ellie had been correct when she stated that Ida Mae was in denial. How else could anyone explain her foolishness? Her lack of common sense was shocking, especially since Catherine knew that she came from a good family. Just like the proverb: "Such is the way of an adulterous woman; she eats and wipes her mouth, and says, 'I have done no wickedness.'" Catherine thought back to the letter that Ida Mae had sent to her, asking if she might try to help James reconcile with her. But she held back this bit of information from James. There was no sense furthering his emotional distress over the situation.

"I'm glad that you rejected John's attentions," James said. "At first I felt sorry for him, for he seemed to think there was something there, when I could see that you obviously didn't care for him. I thought his boastful ways were amusing when it was just the two of us, but when he boasted of you!" He sighed and shook his head. "Be careful where you place your heart," James concluded as he stood up and reached down for his sister's hand. He helped her to her feet. "A broken heart is not easily mended."

Catherine faced him, wondering at his warning. Had he heard about her feelings for Henry? If only he knew that Henry Tilman had not wronged her, but she had wronged him. It dawned on her that Henry's heart must have been broken by her deception. When he had left for Woods farm, he must have realized the extent of his own hurt and contacted his father. Certainly, Gid Tilman was already aggrieved over his older son's mischief in Banthe. The last thing Gid wanted was more problems. That must have fed his fury on the evening he returned so suddenly.

"You will love again," Catherine said to her brother. "A woman who is worthy and kind, who loves you for you and not what you can do for her."

He sighed. "I do hope so, although I dare say that it will be a long time before I venture to trust another so easily."

"You know what the Bible says: 'He heals the broken in heart, and binds up their wounds.'" She tried to smile at him as she folded the quilt. "I suppose we both just need to remember that God knows what we need and trust in that."

James reached out for the folded quilt. "Sometimes I wish his lessons were a little less painful," he mused. Then, returning her soft smile, he turned to walk with her back to the house, both of them reflecting on what had happened and how they had grown because of it.

Chapter Twenty-Eight

Catherine lay under the shade of a large oak tree in the backyard. She had spread an old quilt on the ground and lay upon it, her head resting on her arm as she stared up through the expansion of limbs filled with dark green leaves. Many years ago, she had enjoyed this very spot, not for the tranquility and solitude that it afforded her, but because there was a large limb with a swing attached to it. When she was little, she had swung on it for hours on end. But one day, during a terrible storm, the limb had fallen, taking the swing down and ruining the prospects for any other children to enjoy the tree in the same way that Catherine had.

Today, however, she enjoyed the tree simply because it gave her shade from the sun so that she could gather her thoughts.

They had attended worship that morning, but Catherine could hardly pay attention to the preachers, even when her father stood up and gave the second sermon. Her mind transported her back to Newbury Acres. Surely Henry had returned by now, perhaps even with Freddie, although she didn't care two shakes for that

Tilman. She could envision the two brothers sitting side-by-side at worship, the younger one paying attention and the older one eyeballing the unmarried women who sat on the other side of the room. She shuddered at the thought.

After the service, Catherine imagined them enjoying fellowship with the rest of their community before walking home to their large, empty farmhouse. They would spend the rest of the afternoon in silence, although she imagined that Freddie would slip out and not be seen again until the following morning. But certainly, Ellie and Henry would sit in the kitchen, perhaps playing a game of Scrabble or just reading a devotional. It would be a quiet day for them—of that she was certain.

Her morning had passed in much the same way as she imagined that the Tilmans' had. But in the afternoon, the children were allowed to play outside. James and Richard had put the harness on the horse and hitched it to the open-top buggy. While they had invited her to go riding, she had declined, preferring to escape to the large oak tree so that she could spend some time alone. The last thing she wanted was to go out with the other youths, plastering a fake smile on her face while her heart broke inside of her.

In the distance, she could hear the sound of her younger siblings. They were laughing inside the hay barn. She wondered if they were swinging on the rope swing that James had put up after the storm took away the tree limb. Catherine had never played in the hay barn, too loyal to the old wooden swing of her own youth. Plus, she didn't like the big spiders that sometimes hid in the loose straw. Still, she was glad that

David, Elizabeth, Harriet, and George had something fun to do on a sleepy Sunday afternoon.

"Catherine!"

She shut her eyes and groaned.

"Catherine! Catherine!" the shrill voice screamed out.

"I'm over here, Harriet!" she called back.

Her youngest sister ran around the side of the house, straw in her hair and her eyes wide open.

"What is it?" Catherine asked.

"There's a man. A man on a horse coming down the lane!"

Sitting up, Catherine caught her breath. Why was Harriet telling her this, and not her parents? Didn't Harriet recognize the man? Was it possible that the visitor was for her?

She got to her feet and quickly brushed any stray dirt or grass from her dress. Then she walked after Harriet, who ran back to the driveway in the front of the house. Catching up to her sister, Catherine peered down the driveway and, shocked, recognized their visitor. "Henry Tilman!" she said far too loudly before she regained her composure.

"Oooh, the handsome Tilman boy who taught you how to fish?"

Catherine glared at her sister and, through gritted teeth, shushed her. "Go on, Harriet. Let *Maem* know we've a visitor!"

Harriet did as she was told but, she made a big show of glancing back in Henry's direction as she ran toward the house.

As he approached the gate, Henry stopped the horse and swung his right leg over so that he could dismount.

Immediately, the horse dipped its head and began to graze, clearly winded from such a long journey.

Alarmed, Catherine imagined only the worst news could have brought him to Fullerton. "What on earth are you doing here? Is everything alright? Has something happened to Ellie? Are you okay?"

He removed his black hat and held it in both hands before him. "I suppose I should ask you that very question, Catherine." His eyes bore into her and she blushed at the intensity. "Truly. Are you well?"

Still astonished that Henry stood before her, she merely nodded.

He rolled the hat in his hands, appearing a bit uneasy which was not the Henry Tilman that she remembered. After a brief silence, he left the horse's side and took a long step toward her. "I...I came to apologize, Catherine." His words rushed out.

"*Nee*! It is I who should apologize!" she gushed. "I...I should never have gone into the other side of the house. I knew your *daed* forbid it, and I was so wrong to let my imagination run so wild."

"Catherine..."

But she continued. "You were so angry...and rightfully so."

He took a step forward. "It's true that I was disappointed, Catherine. I will not say otherwise. But that was easily forgotten. It certainly wasn't something that I would let fester."

She blinked her eyes. "So, you aren't angry with me anymore?"

He gave a soft laugh and shook his head. "Would I be standing here if I were, Catherine?" He didn't wait for her to answer. "*Nee*, it is I who should find out if *you* are angry with me."

Stunned, she gave him an incredulous look. "Angry with you? Why would I be angry with *you*?"

"Well, you *were* mistreated quite badly," he whispered in a voice that dripped with shame. "I had to come to you. To see if you and your family could possibly forgive me for my *daed*'s irrational decision, never mind his reasons behind it, that sent you rudely away in the middle of the night with no explanation."

Catherine glanced over his shoulder and noticed that David, Elizabeth, and even young George were staring at them from the doorway to the hay barn. David grinned at her and Elizabeth smiled from ear-to-ear. "I…" She looked back at Henry, who was staring at her with an expression of desperation. "I'm sure I don't understand, Henry."

"Catherine!"

Inwardly she groaned as her mother called out for her. "Over here, *Maem*!"

"Who's here?"

It took Ruth only a few seconds to descend the porch stairs and round the side of the house where Henry and Catherine stood. She stopped short when she saw them standing before each other.

Henry extended his hand toward her. "Henry Tilman," he said.

"Oh!" Ruth gasped. Catherine wasn't certain how to read her mother's reaction.

"I've come to check on Catherine's well-being," he explained. "I meant to come sooner but was prohibited from doing so."

Catherine was certain she understood what *that* meant.

Henry shuffled his hat from one hand to the other. "I do not expect that I am welcome here after…"

"Nonsense," Ruth said quickly. "My Catherine has done nothing but speak highly of both you and your *schwester.*"

"But my *daed…*"

Ruth pressed her lips together and grimaced. "Let us not speak of the past, shall we? Any friend of Catherine's is welcome in our home."

Relieved, Henry nodded his head in appreciation of her kind words.

"I'll let the two of you finish visiting and then, perhaps, you would stay to have supper with us?"

He glanced at Catherine as if seeking her approval. When she made no reaction, either for or against his staying, he returned his attention to Ruth. "I'd be delighted, but only if Catherine says she feels the same."

This time, Catherine felt the heat rise to her cheeks. His arrival in Fullerton was beyond unexpected. Just days ago, she had wept to her mother that her chances with Henry were ruined. Yet now he stood before her. And at such an effort! Being that it was Sunday, he could not hire a driver, so he had resorted to riding his horse. She could hardly imagine such a journey. It had taken her almost an hour by car late Wednesday night when she had returned. Even though the distance was not so great, the roads were winding and not always in the best of shape. She wondered if he had taken some short cuts through people's farms.

When she realized that he was waiting for her response, she quickly said, "Of course you must stay. You've ridden a far way, Henry."

She saw him wince as if he had expected a different answer, or perhaps he had expected she would be much more enthusiastic. But she was too dumbfounded to formulate her words properly.

"I'll add a plate for dinner while you two visit a while," Ruth said pleasantly. "I'm sure you have some things to discuss."

Catherine pressed her lips together and averted her eyes. But Henry stared only at her, waiting for her mother to return to the house.

"Shall we walk a little?" he asked, and when she looked up, he glanced over his shoulder in the direction of the barn. Her younger brothers and sisters were staring, mouths hanging agape as they far too obviously eavesdropped. "I would like to speak to you in private, if that is alright with you."

They walked around the back of the house, and Catherine gestured to the oak tree she had been sitting beneath prior to his unexpected arrival.

"I'm surprised to see you here, Henry," she said as she sat down.

He tilted his head. "I'm surprised to hear you say that. I'd have come sooner, but *Daed* insisted I was needed at the farm and would not let me go till today."

She blinked. "But...but you were so angry with me."

"Angry?" For a long, drawn-out second, he seemed to contemplate her words. "Why would you think I was angry?"

Her heart began to race and her lips felt dry. "I...I presumed because I disobeyed your *daed*'s orders about not going in the other side of the *haus*. Isn't that why I was sent away?"

Henry took a deep breath and exhaled slowly. "Catherine, you were sent away for completely different reasons."

Her breath stopped and she pressed her lips together. If his appearance in Fullerton was unexpected, his announcement was even more so. "I cannot possibly imagine how, then, I may have offended your *daed*."

He nodded his head, as if to indicate that he understood her bewilderment. "It's not something that you did, but something that you weren't. You see, my *daed* knew the name Anderson as being associated with a childless couple who own a large farm in Farmington. He mistakenly presumed *your* Andersons were one and the same. Because you were vacationing with them and he knew they had no children, he thought that *you* were a potential heir to their property."

Catherine's mouth fell open and she stared at Henry, a shocked expression on her face.

Henry shut his eyes and held up his hand before him. "I know. It's a horrid presumption."

"Where would he have gotten such an idea?" she cried out.

"Apparently, your friend's *bruder*, John, caught my *daed*'s ear after worship service that one Sunday in Banthe."

"John Troyer?" How on earth was John Troyer involved in any of this? She could hardly believe what Henry had just told her. "What could John possibly have to say to your *daed*? And about me?"

This time, Henry shrugged. "I only know that my *daed* asked him if he knew who you were. We were standing together—you, me, and Ellie—talking, and he spotted us. Remember?"

She nodded, vaguely remembering seeing Gid speaking with John. Clearly, she should have paid more attention to that unusual exchange.

"John said you were very close to the Andersons and that they had taken you under their care."

Catherine gasped. Why on earth would John Troyer have made such a statement? "I was only under their care while in Banthe!"

Henry pursed his lips. "There's more, Catherine. John said he intended to marry you so that he could inherit everything that the Andersons have." He leveled his gaze at her. Henry had told her about his father's feelings in regard to his sons and daughter marrying well. And now Catherine realized what had truly happened.

"Your *daed*...he thought you'd marry me and acquire the Andersons' farm? The ones from Farmington?"

Henry nodded his head. "*Daed*'s sole focus in life is to acquire more land. He claims it's for the good of the community, that with his extra wealth he's just making sure to preserve the land for Amish families to farm, but I fear that he has just found a way to rationalize his own greed."

Was that why Gid had invited her to visit? Had he hoped that Henry would court her, and that through their marriage Gid would gain more land? Clearly, when Gid realized that he had the wrong information, starting with the wrong Andersons, he had no further use for her and, therefore, sent her away in the middle of the night.

"The only reason," Henry said gently, "that you were

banished from Newbury Acres was not for what you did, Catherine, but for what you were not."

"Wealthy." She whispered the word and stared down at the quilt.

"Exactly." Henry took a deep breath. "I want you to know that I knew nothing about his decision to turn you out of the house. When I returned and learned of the situation, I told my *daed* that his actions were unforgivable!"

Catherine bit her lip.

Suddenly, Henry stood up and began pacing, his hands behind his back as he continued talking. "The entire situation made me realize that, in many ways, there was truth to the suspicions that led you into that forbidden side of the house." His eyes shifted toward her, but when she met his gaze, he looked away nervously. "It's true, Catherine, that my *daed* did not treat our *maem* like a husband should treat a wife. And while the mystery you sought through that locked door is no more than a man who cherishes property over love, there will always be a mystery as to why she consented to marry him in the first place."

"Henry, you don't have to explain…"

He interrupted her. "I do, Catherine. I do have to explain. Perhaps that was why I was so surprised when I saw you standing in that room. You knew something that all of us have denied. What you thought was anger was nothing more than my own inner turmoil. I realized that our *maem* did not have the loving husband she deserved. Realizing this made me see that I never wanted to be like my father." He stopped pacing and stood tall, staring into the distance. "And when I returned from the other farm and found that you had been banished, just tossed from the house as part of my *daed*'s ongoing quest for…" He paused and caught his breath. "For whatever it is he seeks…well, Catherine…" He turned to look at her as she sat on the quilt, watching him with intense attention.

"Oh, bother!" he mumbled to himself and hurried over to kneel beside her. "Catherine, I came here today to check on your welfare. That is true. But I came to tell you that I've stood up to my *daed*. I told him that what he did to you was unacceptable, and I do not intend to choose my marriage partner based on *his* selfish desires for land and money. What I want is to fulfill God's plan for a true, loving marriage with a friend and partner."

When he paused, Catherine swallowed. She felt as if she were imagining his words, perhaps misinterpreting them. She had never thought she'd see him again and now, here he was, kneeling before her, his hands fumbling with his hat and struggling to speak.

"What are you saying, Henry?" she asked in a soft whisper.

"Catherine, I believe that friend and partner is you."

"Oh!"

He dropped the hat and took ahold of her hands. Cautiously, he leaned toward her. Her eyes widened and she stared into his face as he gave her a nervous smile.

"Catherine Miller, I'm asking you to be my wife. I don't know where we will reside, whether in Newbury Acres, Woods farm, or somewhere else. But if you can see fit to honor me with your affection, I promise you that, even if my father disowns me for my decision, I want to be with you, and I will work hard to cherish and care for you and all of our children." He clutched her hands, pulling them gently toward his chest so that she was forced to kneel with him. "Catherine Miller, will you marry me?"

With tears streaming down her cheeks, she nodded her head. "Oh, Henry! I…I…" She laughed and pulled one of her hands free to cover her mouth. "Yes! Yes, I will marry you!"

He reached out for her and pulled her into his arms, her cheek damp with tears of joy pressed against his shoulder. "I was so afraid that I had lost you," he said. "My dear Catherine. I never want to feel that way again. I never want to feel lost or have you far from my side."

"And I you."

He pulled back and placed his hands on her cheeks. His eyes searched her face, brightening as he did so. Then, he leaned forward to gently, if not a bit hesitantly, brush his lips against hers. "I love you, Catherine Miller," he whispered. "Of that you will never have to doubt!"

She laughed through her tears.

Reaching out his hand, he used his thumbs to wipe away her tears. "May these be the only tears you ever shed during our lifetime together. I want only to bring you joy and happiness." Slowly, he lowered his head and once again brushed his lips gently against hers. "You will live your romance novel, my Catherine. I promise you that."

Epilogue

Catherine stood at the kitchen sink, monitoring the temperature of the curds. She didn't hear the door open and Henry's soft footsteps as he tiptoed across the floor, a bouquet of wildflowers in his hand. He waited until he was almost directly behind her before he slid his hand around her, the flowers magically appearing before her.

She jumped, her hand dropping the thermometer. But as soon as she realized it was Henry and the flowers were a surprise gift, she reached out for them and turned around, her expanding waist gently brushing against his stomach. "What beautiful flowers!" she said as she buried her nose into them. "Where did you get them?"

"The back field near the wood line." He let his hands fall onto her arms, gently holding her. "The first of many more this spring, I imagine."

Lifting her eyes to peer at him over the flowers, she saw the smile on his face. "Why are you smiling like that?" she asked suspiciously.

"I just enjoy walking through that door and seeing you here, working in the same kitchen my *maem* grew up in."

Catherine tried not to smile at his joy. Ever since they'd moved to Woods farm, shortly after their wedding in October when Gid finally relented to sign it over to his son, not one day had gone by that he had not tried to fulfill his promise. Her life was exactly like one of those romance novels that she used to read. Every day he would greet her with kisses and help her whenever she needed him. She often went to the barn to help him with the afternoon milking so that they could spend more time together. And every time he went to town to purchase something, he always came back with a new book for her to read.

"Well, I reckon that's a good sign," she teased. "To enjoy walking through the door and seeing your wife. I'd be sorely disappointed if you did *not* enjoy doing that."

He laughed and leaned down to kiss her forehead. As he did so, he let his hand drift to her stomach. "How is he?"

"She's fine," Catherine replied quickly.

Henry raised an eyebrow and gave her a playful scowl. Releasing her from his hold, he walked over to the refrigerator and pulled out a pitcher of chilled water. Without being asked, she handed him a clean glass from the drying rack.

"Are you ready for tonight?"

She looked around the kitchen. Everything was clean and orderly. The table was set for four, and she already had the Scrabble board on the top of the bookshelf. "*Ja*, I believe so. It'll be nice to spend a leisurely evening with Ellie and James."

"We haven't seen much of them since our wedding," Henry admitted.

Catherine found herself leaning against the counter, a wistful gaze on her face. "Who would have thought," she wondered out loud, "that everything would have turned out so perfect?"

At their wedding in October, Catherine and Henry had paired up Ellie and James at the dining table. Little did they realize that sparks would fly. Her calm maturity attracted him, and his ambitious and hard-working nature attracted her. By the time February rolled around, it was clear that James and Ellie were courting. Catherine suspected that they would announce their intentions to marry in the spring. The irony was not lost on Catherine that James would end up living on the very farm and with the very family that Ida Mae had hoped to marry into.

With two of his three children apparently settled down, Gid seemed to release a little more control over them, especially since Ellie was courting a man who appeared willing and able to take over the farm. That even made him accept Catherine with more open arms, although she still felt uncomfortable in his presence.

As far as Freddie was concerned, she rarely saw him. But she had learned to forgive him all of his past transgressions. After all, he had saved James from an ill-suited marriage, which had enabled him to find love with Ellie. It had turned out for the best. Just as Catherine had said to her brother, God had healed his broken heart and bound his wounds by showing him a far better woman to cherish.

Henry walked up behind her and wrapped his arms around her, his hands resting comfortably upon her stomach. "It is perfect, isn't it?"

She leaned her head back and shut her eyes, a smile

still playing on her lips. "As perfect as anyone could have written. In fact, our story could be a great romance," she said softly, "if only someone would write it."

"And who would read such a story?" he teased.

"Everyone!"

He gave her a gentle hug. "I like the idea of keeping it to ourselves. Our own little romance novel." He kissed the top of her head but made no move to separate from her. Catherine didn't mind. She was in no hurry to return to her chores, preferring to spend as much time in the arms of the only man she would ever consider to be her hero: her husband.

She did not have to write this romance novel. She was living it.

* * * * *

SPECIAL EXCERPT FROM

Love Inspired

*Paralyzed veteran Eve Vincent is happy with the
life she's built for herself at Mercy Ranch—until her
ex-fiancé shows up with a baby. Their best friends died
and named Eve and Ethan Forester as guardians.
But can they put their differences aside and build a
future together?*

Read on for a sneak preview of
Her Oklahoma Rancher *by Brenda Minton,*
available June 2019 from Love Inspired!

"I'm sorry, Eve, but I had to do something to make you see how important this is. We can't just walk away from her. It might not be what we signed on for and I feel like I'm the last person who should be raising this little girl, but James and Hanna trusted us."

"But there is no *us*," she said with a lift of her chin, but he could see pain reflected in her dark eyes.

The pain he saw didn't bother him as much as what he didn't see in her eyes, in her expression. He didn't see the person he used to know, the woman he'd planned to marry.

He had noticed the same yesterday, and he guessed that was why he'd left Tori with her. He'd been sitting there looking at a woman he used to think he knew better than he knew himself, and he hadn't recognized her.

"There is no *us*, but we still exist, you and me, and Tori needs us." He said it softly because the little girl in his arms seemed to be drifting off, even with the occasional sob.

"There has to be another option. I obviously can't do this. Last night was proof."

"Last night meant nothing. You've always managed, Eve. You're strong and capable."

"Before, Ethan. I was that person before. This is me now, and I can't."

"I guess you have changed. I've never heard you say you can't do anything."

He sat down on a nearby chair. Isaac had left. The woman named Sierra had also disappeared. They were alone. When had they last been alone? The night he proposed? It had been the night she left for Afghanistan. He'd taken her to dinner in San Antonio and they'd walked along the riverfront surrounded by people, music and twinkling lights.

He'd dropped to one knee there in front of strangers passing by, seeing the sights. Dozens had stopped to watch as she cried and said yes. Later they'd made the drive to the airport, his ring glistening on her finger, planning a wedding that would never happen.

"Ethan?" Her voice was soft, quiet, questioning.

He glanced down at the little girl in his arms.

"What other option is there, Eve? Should we turn her over to the state, let her take her chances with whoever they choose? Should we find some distant relative? What do you recommend?"

He leaned back in the chair and studied her face, her expression. She was everything familiar. His childhood friend. The person he'd loved. *Had* loved. Past tense. The woman he'd wanted to spend his life with had been someone else, someone who never backed down. She looked as tough, as stubborn as ever, but there was something fragile in her expression.

Something in her expression made him recheck his feelings. He'd been bucked off horses, trampled by a bull, broken his arm jumping dirt bikes. She'd been his only broken heart. He didn't want another one.

Don't miss
Her Oklahoma Rancher *by Brenda Minton,*
available June 2019 wherever
Love Inspired® books and ebooks are sold.

www.LoveInspired.com

LIEXP0619

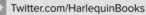

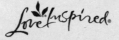

Love Inspired®

Inspirational Romance to
Warm Your Heart and Soul

Join our social communities to connect
with other readers who share your love!

Sign up for the Love Inspired newsletter
at **www.LoveInspired.com** to be the
first to find out about upcoming titles,
special promotions and exclusive content.

CONNECT WITH US AT:

Facebook.com/groups/HarlequinConnection

 Facebook.com/LoveInspiredBooks

Twitter.com/LoveInspiredBks

LISOCIAL2018

Earn points on your purchase of new Harlequin books from participating retailers.

Turn your points into **FREE BOOKS** of your choice!

Join for FREE today at
www.HarlequinMyRewards.com.

Harlequin My Rewards is a free program (no fees) without any commitments or obligations.

MYR18